# COURAGE
# JOHNATHAN

### HEATHER NADINE LENZ

# COURAGE JOHNATHAN

HEATHER NADINE LENZ

Published in the United States by Plum Tree Press

Conceived, created, and designed by Heather Nadine Lenz and Plum Tree Publishing.

Published in the United States by Plum Tree Publishing.

ISBN: 978-0-9980129-6-4

This novel is a work of fiction. The names, characters, and incidents in it are the work of the author's imagination. Any resemblance to actual persons, living or dead, events or localities is entirely coincide

TO HOLLY, NATHAN, NICK

### Jennifer Ibiam for Readers' Favorite

"Courage Johnathan by Heather Nadine Lenz is a beautiful book that speaks to everyone. Sometimes in our lives, we face hard decisions, leading us to weigh our options. Do we go along with settling for the greater good or choose ourselves? Can we live with the consequences? This book explored themes like deceit, selfishness, resilience, manipulation, and more. Heather did a fantastic job with the plot and development of the story. I loved the witty and sarcastic nature of John's character. The book was also laced with humor that I laughed so much."

### Edith Wairimu for Readers' Favorite

"Courage Johnathan follows Johnathan and Caroline's tumultuous relationship and marriage. It includes important lessons about courage and authenticity. Despite his initial hesitation to make changes in his life and his later financial strain, Johnathan works to build a decent life for himself and his new family. The novel contains many interesting turns. From the onset, Caroline and Johnathan's relationship encounters many challenges. Both are flawed characters which makes their story convincing. I liked that the supporting characters are also well developed. Some surprises occur in the end as Johnathan learns dark secrets about his family and a close friend of the family."

### Lesley Jones for Readers' Favorite

"In Courage Johnathan by Heather Nadine Lenz, Johnathan believes his decision to marry Caroline is a huge mistake. Will Johnathan be able to make peace with the past and forgive those who have abused his trust? Courage Johnathan by Heather Nadine Lenz is an endearing story that just flows so beautifully. The characters are very realistic and their personality traits reminded me of people I have met. I absolutely adored Caroline, she was extremely level-headed and her outlook on life was inspirational. She never passed judgment on anyone's bad behavior and was always full of golden pearls of wisdom."

**Christian Sia for Readers' Favorite**

"Courage Johnathan by Heather Nadine Lenz is an explosive contemporary romance with well-developed characters and a plot that is tightly written and twisty. When his family makes it clear that he either chooses between his fiancée and his trust fund and business, Jonathan is faced with the biggest challenge of his life. Luxury and wealth are the fruits of hard work and he deserves every bit of it. But continuing with his marriage to the woman who made it feel like electricity when he embraced her the first time they met also means living without that wealth. He knows well that, "Money can't buy love and love can't make money." It is the moment to choose between Caroline, the woman from California, or the trust fund and business. How will he choose?"

**Pikasho Deka or Readers' Favorite**

"A heartwarming tale of love, sacrifice, and finding one's self-worth, Courage Johnathan is riveting to read from start to finish. Johnathan and Caroline seem well fleshed-out and that makes them easy to relate to. Having read Heather Nadine Lenz's previous book Courage Caroline, I appreciated the character of Johnathan Arrozzini getting further explored and delving deep into his complicated relationship with his family. I also enjoyed the character of Mark, who shines in every single scene he is in. The narrative flowed in an organic fashion that made it smooth to read and the dialogue felt crisp and concise. I thoroughly enjoyed Courage Johnathan, and I would recommend it to readers who crave well-written slice-of-life romance stories."

# CHAPTER 1

"I haven't exactly told my fiancée that I am planning on calling off our engagement. And sure, perhaps I've waited a bit longer than I should have. I know the wedding is tomorrow, but look, it's not like she is paying for any of it, and she didn't even invest much time in the planning."

Johnathan took a sip of his drink and set it back down on the smooth marble bar and looked at the bartender. The bartender looked back, without commenting, while continuing to clean a row of martini glasses.

"Which I'm telling you, I find weird. I mean, don't all girls fantasize about their wedding day and all the planning that they get to do? She just happily turned it all over to the wedding planner with a shortlist of requests. My fiancée has become the chilliest person I know. If something goes wrong the day of the wedding, she'll probably shrug her shoulders and answer, "okay," like she does all the damn time when difficulties arise lately."

"I'm listening," said the bartender.

"To be honest, her going on along with anything and everything is getting on my nerves. But that's not why I want to call off the wedding. My family has made it clear that it is either my fiancée or my trust fund and business. I've decided on the money and business."

Johnathan finished the gin and tonic and motioned to the bartender to refill his class.

"Listen, I can hear you judging me from here; I know your type. You look at me in my thousand-dollar athleisure clothes, see me working on my laptop while drinking champagne by the pool, and then you think you have me pegged. Greedy. Arrogant. Self-entitled. Superficial. Demanding. Sure, I've had those words hurled at me before. Yeah, I've heard it.

Why does a huge, seething mass of people seem to think money is evil or something, or that I should feel guilty for having so much while others have so little? I, unlike the desperate masses, love money. I love money. Did you hear me? I don't feel bad about it; in fact, I'll shout it from my penthouse rooftop if you want. Wait. What were we talking about?"

Johnathan accepted his new drink and shook his head. Here he was, a multimillionaire with, in theory at least, a phone full of a long list of friends and colleagues, and the only person he could confide in was a bartender?

"You want to choose the money," said the bartender and pushed his white hair back from his forehead.

"Oh yeah, so what if I'm choosing money over love? They say money can't buy love? Well, I say, 'love can't buy money.' It's not just about the money, anyway. Stop focusing on the millions I'll keep by calling off the wedding. I also said I am choosing my business over her. Did you not hear that part?"

Johnathan stood up and stretched and then leaned against the bar.

"Listen, I built this business up with my brother from the ground up. And I don't care what you haters have to say about it because I know how hard we worked. Sure, we had access to investment capital and come from money. So what? We worked twelve to sixteen-hour days. Yes, we failed a few startups and lost a boatload of dollars before we got it right. Our current business is a multi-million-dollar success story now.

I wake up in the morning, and I can't wait to go into the office? What small percentage of the humans humming along on this planet can say that? Architecture is my purpose and my calling. When I am in the flow of designing a new building, all time and space fall away.

Yes, you're right; I didn't relish all the client meetings and other icing that goes with the job. I mean, that was a fraction of my time. Most of my time I'm working, I'm living in the zone. Yeah, that's what I call it. So look, I was happy before Caroline showed up, maybe a little lonely, or whatever, but comfortable. I had gorgeous girls to select from to take out to events and parties around New York, and we went on luxury holidays and doing things like relaxing on yachts and going skiing in the alps.

Then this sexy woman, fat by my usual standards, ends up sitting at the same table as my family at my sister's going away party. I mean, what is that? I couldn't believe it when my parents agreed to let her sit with us."

Johnathan paused and lowered his voice.

"Do not repeat that bit about her being fat to anyone, yeah? That slipped out. Where was I? I mean, generally, my parents wouldn't tolerate having a stranger share a table with us. Maybe they were feeling more magnanimous or something due to my sister leaving for a year on her trip around the world.

Or it could be they were relieved at the arrival of a distraction. I mean, my family's great, but they can get at each other's throats. It's not like my parents are thrilled with my sister's life choices. Wow, when Mat decided to throw away the job that Dad had worked so hard to get her, I thought he would lose it right then and there.

I love how Matt told Caroline at dinner that winning the lottery was why she could afford to quit her job and go on her world tour. That was hilarious. As if she couldn't afford to travel the world for the rest of her life if she chose to do so. It isn't as if her finances limit her. Speaking of which, it just goes to show that life isn't fair. Of all the people who could win the lottery, my sister, who is awash in money, won more.

Forget my sister. I was talking about Caroline. So I was sitting

3

there, and somehow we began this joke, Caroline I, that we were dating. Oh man, it was so great to see the looks on my family's faces. Seriously. I had never dated a lady like Caroline; she is so far from my usual type. Gorgeous ballerina-type women with either trust funds, social status, or modeling careers were who I dated all the way up until I met Caroline."

Johnathan nodded and paused as if considering.

"I'll admit a bunch of ladies I dated were actresses or models trying to make it big in New York, but you get the idea. Now let me get back to my point I've been trying to tell you. It was so great to see the smug looks on my family's faces begin to falter when they started to question if they knew me as well as they thought they did. Caroline was a fantastic actress at that first dinner. Wow, she made it believable that we were together, but maybe that is because we clicked from the moment we met. It was all this great game at that first dinner, and then we changed seats.

The minute I put my arm around Caroline, it was like a jolt of electricity passed through my body. Yeah, like electricity. Except instead of being all charged up and agitated, I got all calm and mellow; I was laughing so much and so easily, you'd think someone had given me a special brownie and drugged me. I didn't want the dinner to end. I mean, when she was laughing, I looked over at her and just thought, man, is she beautiful. There was like a light beaming out of her, or something, pulling me towards her. She threw her head back, laughing, completely alive, and I thought, this is the woman with whom I'm supposed to spend my life. I know. I know. It's cheesy, right?"

Johnathan laughed and ran a hand through his hair and then drank down half of his drink on one go.

"Yes, it was like love at first sight and all that. My family was convinced that it was a passing infatuation, and perhaps it did feel good to shock my family for once. Then I met Caroline again. I had the exact same sensation and, like, inner-knowing. Caroline is the one. This random woman from California is supposed to be my wife.

So, okay, I'll admit, I thought it would be easy after that. I mean, I'd decided she was for me, and then it would be just a matter of splashing out with some lavish presents. I put her up in a luxury apartment for her stay in New York, bought her designer dresses and shoes, took her out to a premier event and a high-society party.

All that, and did we spend the night together? Yes, twice, and nothing happened. I mean, can you believe it? All that effort, and this body, I mean look at me, and nothing happened. And yet, I still kept chasing after the woman.

So, the deal is, there was this other dude, attractive guy, I'll even admit he's more charismatic than I am, and that's saying something. The guy is fun. Like, I could imagine us being great friends if we had met under different circumstances. The two of them had all this history together, and Caroline was into him until his ex-showed up and announced he had a baby because he hadn't known he'd gotten his ex-girlfriend pregnant. I know, right?

A man's worst nightmare. Okay, you speak for yourself, but if an ex-girlfriend showed up pregnant on my door, I would not be happy. Unless that is, she had broken up with me, and I was still in love with her, which was apparently the true story between them, which Caroline didn't know. Of course, he told Caroline that he and his ex-girlfriend had wanted different lifestyles and grew apart.

So this dude, Jolan, he made things a bit tough.

He was still in love with his ex-girlfriend, but he had fallen a bit in love with Caroline too, and he was like, oh-shit, what do I do now? So the situation put some heat into the mix. I needed to act, or I knew Caroline would be taken.

It's clear who won, right? I mean, look at me, is there a question who Caroline ended up choosing?

I was just about to propose to Caroline in the Met when she got a call about her Gram. I rushed her back to California to be with her dying Gram, and then that was the end of our relationship for a while. Really, between you and me, I thought, out of sight, out of mind.

It didn't turn out that way. I could not get that woman out of my mind. It was like she had some mysterious gravitational force pulling me back to her with a brilliant-cut diamond ring in my pocket.

If I had known she was going to shout 'no' at me and run away when I popped the question, then I wouldn't have shelled out so much money for the ring. I'm telling you that women are crazy, I'm nearing forty, and I still don't have them figured out. We're sitting there cuddling, watching the sun turn the water a soft shade of pink as it set over the ocean, and the next minute I know, she's kicking sand up into my face as she ran away.

No, I hadn't even asked her to marry me yet. I'd just told her I loved her.

Of course, I followed her, and then we got into this massive fight. I was shocked by it all, as she's generally so chill.

She went to bed, but I couldn't sleep afterward. I headed back down to the beach and walked along the moonlit waves, and called my brother. I've always called my brother when I hit a wall. Anyway, we talked it through, and he told me it was for the best to end things the next day with Caroline and head back home.

I fell asleep on the sofa a few hours before sunrise. Caroline's alarm went off upstairs at the crack of dawn. She'd told me about the yoga class. She thought I was gone when she walked downstairs and out the front door, and I didn't call out to her. I was so torn. I mean, on the one hand, I agreed with my brother. Caroline isn't from our world. Maybe he was right, and I was going through some midlife crisis. His theory to this day is that I already had the fast, flashy cars and women, so I went the other way by choosing a fat yogi. What? Don't look at me like that. If he says that in front of her, I'll punch him.

Can I get back to my story? When I walked into the yoga

studio, I planned on ending things on a nice note, you know, take her to brunch, kiss her good-bye, and head to the airport, only at the end of the class that's not what happened.

At the end of class, Caroline looked into my eyes and smiled. She has this way of looking into your eyes that's strange. It's like she sees down deep into your soul. Do you get me? Like she's seeing me. When I hug her, the world kind of softens at the edges, my head stops humming, and everything gets real still.

I don't remember with clarity what took hold of me to pull that ring out of my pocket and put it on her finger. One minute, I was standing in the yoga studio, planning to break things off, and then next, I was down on one knee. On the way back to Caroline's place to shower and change, I was on this incredible high, the kind you get at the end of a triathlon race where you come in the first place.

I didn't expect my family to react to the news the way they did. I was so excited about my future with Caroline that I couldn't help but call my brother Daniel with the news. He was not happy. He kept saying over and over again, 'it's not a good time to marry anyone.' I mean, what the hell does that even mean?

The following six days with Caroline were magnificent. I mean, I won't forget those days for the rest of my life. Then I had to go back to New York, and work kept me tied up there for the rest of the summer.

I knew the parents wouldn't gel with the idea of my moving to California right away. The notion that they would threaten to cut me off and that my own brother would try to oust me from our company if I married Caroline was shocking.

Caroline didn't help. Whenever I called to tell her how difficult the situation was with my family, how horrible the problem, and that I didn't know what the solution would be, she got quiet. 'You need to know what you want to do. There is no wrong answer here,' she kept telling me. I mean, that doesn't make a man feel great, you know? Here, pretty girls were flirting with me left and right in New York, and I knew tons that would have happily become Mrs. Johnathan, and my fiancée was ambivalent. I mean, if she was in love with me, then why wouldn't she move to New York to be with me? She refuses to leave California when she has nothing tying her there at all. No family. Just a few friends."

Johnathan settled into silence, gesturing for the barkeeper to refill his drink. He looked exhausted from his lengthy monologue. Johnathan sat down, leaned back in his chair at the bar, looked out at the palm trees, and let out a big breath of air.

"So, tell me, have any advice, old man?" Johnathan swiveled to reface the white-haired bartender.

The bartender gazed around the empty bar and then back at Johnathan. "You want her to want you for sure. She wants you to want her, for certain. I love money too. Money's beautiful. Is she the soul mate? Yes or no? Answer."

"It's not that easy. Weren't you listening to my story?" asked Johnathan.

"Is she your soul mate? Yes or no? Close your eyes and answer. Yes or no?"

Johnathan groaned. "Yes."

"Sure?"

"Yes."

Johnathan opened his mouth to say something, but the bartender spoke faster. "Why is she the soul mate? Why this woman and not the ballerinas? It doesn't matter," the bartender shrugged, waving a hand at Johnathan to keep him from interjecting. The lines around the bartender's eyes deeply creased as he broke into a smile.

"So much agitation. In your mind, you pushed this way, pushed that way. Letting the people into the head, including old you." The bartender paused and chuckled, tapping the side of his head, and looked at Johnathan. "You can decide now: I don't play any of your games anymore. Get quiet, listen, hear what to do on the wind. Maybe it's not an easy choice, maybe not a fun choice and makes no one happy, not even you. But it's the best choice; it's what the universe wants. Or a new idea. A new path to coming into full love and alignment, not only with this woman but also with who you will be together."

Johnathan blinked after a moment as if he had been in a trance. "Man, you are a wise old dude. Thanks," he said, as he stepped down from the chair and laid a few hundred-dollar bills on the counter on his way out.

Johnathan took off his shoes and walked along the beach, looking out at the turquoise of the water. Caroline had been acting so weird the entire trip in Bali. She hadn't even let him stay in the same hotel room as her. What was that nonsense? He hadn't told that information to the bartender; he was too humiliated. I mean, they were about to get married, and she refused to share a hotel room with him. What was going on? Was Caroline getting cold feet?

# CHAPTER 2

Johnathan woke up even earlier than necessary the following day to be the first one on the platform set up on the beach for yoga. He wanted to talk to Caroline before the other retreat guests showed up.

Caroline was busy rolling out yoga mats when he arrived, the sun just beginning to rise. She looked exhausted and pale with her hair pulled up in a messy bun. He stood there, trying to decide what to say, wanting to ask her why she had avoided him and why she was sleeping in a separate room but didn't know where to start. So all he said was,

"Caroline?"

Caroline walked over and, without a word, slipped her arms around his waist and pressed her cheek to his heart. Caroline melted into Johnathan's embrace as he wrapped his arms around her.

They stood there like that, watching the sun coming up over the ocean, and for the first time since arriving in Bali, Johnathan's thoughts stopped. A few minutes later, people started showing up, bleary-eyed and yawning or smiling and jovial. Caroline slipped out of his arms with a final squeeze.

Adam led the first hour of class, taking them through a sweat-inducing power yoga flow. It irritated the hell out of Johnathan that Adam made it look so easy. Johnathan had sweat dripping from his forehead into his eyes, and the old dude hadn't even been out of breath. The ninth time Adam told him to breathe through his nose, he'd wanted to hit him.

Afterward, Caroline led the meditation. Caroline guided them to place their hands, palm, up in front of their hearts, like a platter.

"Inhale, feel a warmth, visualize a light expanding in the heart center and feel the love flow out onto your hands, exhale, and the warmth of the love flows up from the hands, over the head, and through your entire body like a shower. Inhale loving energy, a light coming out from the heart onto the hands. Exhale, feel the loving energy, see the light, wash up, over, and through your entire body."

Johnathan didn't react, as in previous days when Adam led the meditation, with agitation or resistance. He didn't know if it was because the woman he loved was instructing it or if he just liked the visualization. Whatever it was, when she hit the gong to end the meditation, he didn't want it to stop. He'd felt so calm and blissed out.

"Where's Caroline?" called out Daniel as he strolled out the front doors of the hotel with Matilda, Brad, Alison, and Allen.

"She's not feeling well," said Johnathan with a shrug. "Caroline needs some time to relax before the big day."

"Again?" asked Daniel.

"She told me she was looking forward to our waterfall day tour," Matilda said as their private car arrived.

"Caroline has the right idea," declared Alison. "Now, if you will excuse me, I will find my way to the spa. Frankly, I don't know how you children convinced me to go with you the past two days."

"Come on, Mum, you're getting to be fun. Don't go ruining it now." Daniel threw an arm around Alison's shoulder and gave her his most charming smile.

Johnathan and Matilda exchanged glances. They knew their mother could never tell Daniel no when he smiled at her like that. Matilda rolled her eyes and shrugged. As kids, if they had ever wanted something, they had bribed Daniel to ask their mother on their behalf.

Johnathan shrugged and slid into the van. He had been excusing Caroline's absences on their adventure and sightseeing tours. Early each morning at six-thirty, Caroline did lead the yoga retreat guests for their daily hour-long yoga class, followed by the half-hour meditation.

Johnathan had tried to sneak out and skip the meditation the first morning. Adam, the co-leader of the retreat, had stopped him in his tracks, telling him the whole point of moving the body was to be able to sit still in meditation afterward.

Man, that guy had triggered Johnathan, and he hadn't been sure why. Okay, sure, he didn't like to be told he was wrong. When he tried to lay down for the meditation, Adam had made him sit up with crossed legs on a stupid pillow with a straight spine.

Johnathan had been listening to a deep guided meditation laying on his bed each morning for years, and then along comes this old yoga dude, with the tattoos on his arm and the stomach more defined than even his own, telling him it wasn't real meditation.

Johnathan had relented to sitting up with a tall spine for the meditation instead of lying down on his back like he wanted to because Caroline had been glaring at him to stop disagreeing.

Why? Johnathan still felt he was in the right. Laying down was far more relaxing.

Johnathan hadn't been thrilled to do the weird breathing for five minutes either with closing alternate nostrils. He had been tempted to get up and leave when Adam told them to focus their mind on some crazy Sanskrit mantra for the twenty minutes of silent meditation.

Ananda Hum? It sounded like Harry Potter casting some sort of weird spell, but Johnathan had decided he may as well give it a try after he had peaked his eyes open and saw the rest of his family sitting calmly. Everyone in the family was there, that is, but Daniel. Daniel had disappeared towards the end of the power yoga session, per usual.

At the end of the first-morning meditation, Johnathan had thought the entire exercise a pointless waste of time. Luckily, after the ninety minutes of yoga in the morning, the rest of the day was free for the yoga retreat guests to enjoy how they chose until the optional evening yin class and sunset meditation.

While most of the yoga retreat guests had chosen to relax by the pool, in the spa, or on the beach during the day, Johnathan's family had ventured out of the resort each day. Johnathan wasn't upset that the white water rafting tour they'd chose had prevented them from attending the first yin evening yoga session.

Johnathan wished he could disappear with his brother each morning and skip the seated meditation. The meditation went on for twenty torturous minutes. Instead of relaxed and happy afterward, he had felt agitated and irritable.

Luckily Johnathan's spirits had lifted each morning when they had climbed into the private tour car right after the morning yoga session. The family had decided on a day tour of some secluded beaches that culminated with a visit to the Uluwatu Temple the first day. Johnathan and his sister had been delighted by all the crazy little monkeys hopping around the place and enjoyed relentlessly teasing Daniel that he jumped a foot whenever one came near him.

While Johnathan's dad Allen and brother Daniel had been fascinated by the Hindu temple, Johnathan had thought it was too touristy and crowded. Instead, he had gone walking along the paths and had been blown away by the breathtaking views of the ocean from up high on the cliffs. The entire time Johnathan walked, he had wondered why Caroline had been avoiding him. He had returned for the sunset dance performance and laughed until he cried watching Daniel chase after a monkey that had stolen his designer sunglasses.

The morning meditation bliss vanished four minutes after being in the private tour car with his family. Johnathan had woken up excited for today, despite the bickering and fighting that had occurred between Matilda, Daniel, and his parents the previous two days. Daniel had chosen the white water rafting, Matilda the beach and temple touring, and now, at last, they were going to spend the day on what he wanted to do, which was to see some waterfalls.

No waterfalls, Johnathan decided, were worth listening to Matilda crying on her boyfriend's shoulder, his dad grinding his teeth next to him, or Daniel clicking the buckle on his backpack open and closed over and over again. Only Alison was quiet, sitting primly with her hands twisting in her lap.

"Can you give it a rest, Mat?" Johnathan asked. "The crying is getting on my nerves."

Matilda didn't answer. Johnathan turned around in his seat. Matilda's head was still buried in Brad's shoulder. Brad let out a big sigh and looked at the back of Allen and Alison's heads.

"Mat decided she's had enough of the New York lifestyle. We'd decided to move to New Zealand and buy this eco-neutral house near the beach and woods with its own self-sustaining organic garden. She was going to pursue her dream of painting full time, and we thought it would be the perfect place to start a family," explained Brad.

"What about your investment fund?" Allen turned in his seat.

"I can manage the investment fund from anywhere in the world. It's worked just fine the past few months, even with all the traveling. I get up at five each morning and work a couple of hours before we do some sightseeing, isn't that right lovely?"

"I'm not sure your clients are going to stay with you if you've moved permanently to New Zealand," said Allen with his eyes still looking out the front windshield of the car. "Indulging in a world tour is one thing. A permanent move? Quite another."

Matilda sat up and wiped the tears off her face with her fingertips. She ran her hands through her hair. "Dad's made it clear that if I move to New Zealand, then I forfeit the rights to my trust fund."

Johnathan shook his head. "You don't say? Amazing how often he likes to play that same card."

"I have enough money to buy the property on my own, Mat. You don't need that money. Go back to being excited about the move," insisted Brad.

"Dear, lovely Brad. It amazes me how little you know our daughter. She would love it for a few months in New Zealand, then get completely bored, miss her New York city friends, parties, art museums, job, charity work, and designer clothes; she would miss it all. And she would be stuck in the middle of nowhere alone." Alison held up a hand before Brad could protest. "Not that you aren't wonderful company, Brad, but a woman needs more than a man to keep her happy. She needs her friends. And her family, of course."

Matilda glared at her mother. "You haven't called me once since I left on my world tour. You haven't even answered my texts or anyone else for that matter," she added in a small voice. "I don't think they would notice if I were gone for good."

"Mat, tell them to keep their money. You can't let them control you like this," said Brad while wrapping his arms around her.

"Heavens, is that what all this is about today? Has no one been pining for you since you left on your outrageous extended holiday? They're busy, Matilda. Not that you would understand, would you? Most of your friends have babies and toddlers at home. I'm sure they will all be thrilled to hear all about your trip at your coming home party," soothed Alison.

Johnathan wanted to come to his sister's aide but had to admit he couldn't see her being happy in the middle of the New Zealand countryside in an eco-house. Not unless it was next to a country club and a landing strip so she could hop over to Sydney regularly for shopping trips.

"Oh, thank God," muttered Daniel as the car came to a stop.

"Well? I don't see anything," said Alison as she climbed out of the car. "Where's the waterfall?"

The tour guide paid their entry and led them through the archway and down a series of steps to a vast pebbly area at the bottom of the cascading waterfall. Johnathan found a place to sit down and wait as Matilda insisted Brad take a dozen photos of her in front of the cascading water from different angles.

The area was relatively empty of other tourists so early in the morning, and the guide encouraged them to change into their suits and swim in the waterfall basin. Alison was the only one who refused. Johnathan was the first to jump into the water.

The power of the water swirling around him made him laugh out loud in exhilaration. It was one thing to look at the waterfall from the shore. The experience of feeling the power of all that water from the fall was completely different. Gliding around in the water had the same effect on the rest of the group. At last, Alison couldn't bear being left out and rushed to change so she could plunge into the water.

Ten minutes later, the guide told them it was time to go. Daniel tried to persuade him to let them stay longer, but the guide insisted they needed to be at the next waterfall by nine forty-five. Everyone in the family had a smile on their face as they climbed the trail back up the other side of the waterfall. Allen bought them all coconut water from a stand, and then they all piled back into the private car.

Johnathan leaned back in his seat and let out a sigh of contentment. Alison announced that she hadn't been excited about this day's tour visiting the falls but that she was happy for once to have been overruled.

"I do love you, Johnathan. Please remember that this week," said Alison as she reached out and squeezed Johnathan's shoulder. Johnathan reached up and patted his Mom's hand in surprise. Johnathan couldn't help feeling anxious about what had brought on his Mom's strange announcement; Alison wasn't the most affectionate mother. An awkward pause followed, and Johnathan was the first one out of the car to follow the guide to the Tukad Cepung Waterfall.

"We have about a fifteen-minute walk down," announced the guide.

Johnathan followed the guide down the stairs while admiring the lush green vegetation and bamboo. Eventually, they reached a small river. The guide motioned for them to wade into the river behind him and a cave. When they came into the opening, the waterfall cascading from the opening overhead down into the cave came into view. The rays of early morning light slanted down through the green fringed opening overhead, reflecting in the glistening water cascade and projecting a rainbow. It was ethereal to wade forward into the sun-filled cavern and gaze up at the waterfall.

Johnathan closed his eyes, listening to the soothing sound of the waterfall and feeling the water swirling around his ankles.

Matilda pushed Johnathan aside. "I want a photo, stand back," demanded Mat, and motioned to Brad to take a photo as she reached her arms up toward the light streaming down into the cave from overhead.

Alison took a series of photos of Brad and Matilda together next, and Johnathan felt a pang of jealousy. He wanted to be the one standing near the waterfall, holding Caroline in his arms. He followed the guide away from the waterfall, back into the cave, and up a stair to the top of rocks to another place where light streamed down from overhead again. Johnathan stood staring in awe at the sun shining down through the leaves overhead, lighting up the rock walls and space with magical golden light rays.

After just a few minutes, the guide urged them to return to the car, announcing it was time for lunch. Reluctantly Johnathan left the sun-filled waterfall cave. The family hiked the steps back up to the car in silence.

Johnathan took in the panorama views of rice fields at the Tegalalang Rice Terrace as they ate lunch on the patio. The verdant views were beautiful, but his mind was still on the waterfalls.

Johnathan watched the tourists wander as Matilda played on the infinity swing. Brad faithfully took photos of Matilda with her every glide forward out over the rice fields. At last, Johnathan gave in to Matilda's pleas to take a try on one of the swings himself.

"You know I hate heights, Mat," Johnathan grumbled as he sat down on the swing.

"Don't be ridiculous. It's not dangerous. And you go on ski lifts all the time. What's the difference?"

Matilda gave the swing a big push, and Johnathan soared forward over the terraced rice paddies and palm trees below him. His belly jumped up into his throat, and his heart hammered harder than during the white water rafting trip. He did not like the sensation of air under his feet with only two ropes supporting him. At least a ski lift is made of solid metal, he thought.

"Okay, enough, Mat," he called out.

"No way. Not yet." Matilda pushed his back even harder, and he went flying forward.

"Mat, let me off."

Matilda burst into giggles and pushed him yet again.

"Relax, brother, and enjoy the damn swing."

Johnathan forced himself to breathe. After a few swings back and forth, his heartbeat began to calm, and Matilda stopped pushing him. Johnathan jumped off the swing and called out to Alison.

"Your turn, Mom."

"Yes, Mom, you can wear the skirt I bought, and we'll take a photo of you soaring out over the rice fields" Mat began to untie the skirt.

"Good heavens no," Alison breathed out. "I'm dizzy at the mere thought of it."

"You bought a skirt just to take a photo in it?" Daniel rolled his eyes. "You're something else; you know that?"

18

Matilda pulled the skirt around Alison's waist and tied it tight. "Fine. Sit on the swing and hold on and we'll take a photo like that," insisted Matilda.

Alison perched on the swing and grabbed the ropes rightly. Daniel snuck up behind her and gave her a gentle push. Alison's scream rang out and echoed through the rice paddies. Brad clicked Alison's photo from the back, the long pink dress blown out behind her as she sailed forward over the lush green below.

"That was dangerous, Daniel. What if she hadn't been properly holding on? She would have flown off the damn swing," Allen grumbled. He reached out a hand and slowed the swing.

Alison turned to look over her shoulder, taking a big breath. "Well, I have to admit. That was exhilarating." She reached down and clicked the safety belt around her waist. "Now push me again, Daniel. Harder this time. And Brad, you make sure you get a good photo of this."

The guide walked forward, explaining that it was time to go to the two-tiered waterfall for another swim. Everyone returned to the car.

Alison turned in her seat to face Matilda, Brad, and Johnathan on the ride back to the hotel. "I've missed you all so much. And I must say, I think this may be one of the best days of my entire life, experiencing all of this with you children. Jumping into waterfalls, splashing through caves, feeling my heart race as I soar out above palm trees and rice paddies. I would never venture out to do those things without you. It has truly been a magical day. Thank you. All of you."

"The day has been pretty great," admitted Johnathan with a grin. "I don't know what got into you today, Mom. You even snuck up behind Dad and pushed him into the water at that last waterfall."

Alison burst into giggles at looked over at Allen, who sat shirtless next to her.

"You better watch your back, woman. Payback will be sweet," laughed Allen.

"You wouldn't dare," declared Alison and then turned to her daughter. "I'm happy to be with you, Matilda. I've missed you."

Matilda reached out and squeezed Alison's hand. "I've missed you too, Mom."

Alison smiled and let out a sigh. "I'm thrilled you've changed your mind about the permanent move. I would miss you too much if you lived so far away. What a tragedy it would be to live so far from my grand babies. Now a little holiday home in New Zealand to escape to, why I think that is a perfect idea."

Johnathan glanced over at Daniel, who was staring out the car window. It wasn't like Daniel to be so quiet all day. What had gotten into his brother? Daniel had been acting strange, so they'd arrived in Bali.

Matilda was the only one thrilled to return to the resort in time for the sunset yoga session. Everyone else was ready for a shower and dinner, but Matilda wouldn't take no for an answer.

"The evening session is gentle and completely on the floor. Being too tired isn't an excuse. Come on guys, we've missed the sunset yin yoga session every day this week," pleaded Matilda.

"I suppose it would be something to remember, doing yoga with all of you while watching the sunset," mused Alison. "Count me in, Mat. We have enough time for a quick swim beforehand."

"Count me in too," agreed Allen. "It will be part of the perfect end to a perfect day together."

Johnathan let out a sigh. "All right. I'll come."

Daniel threw his hands up and shook his head. "I have a work call I have to take. My hands are tied. Pray for me, will you?"

"Meditation isn't the same as prayer," Brad started to explain.

"Whatever," Daniel answered as they got out of the car. "See you all later."

Sunset, Johnathan decided, fading into twilight was his favorite time of day. He loved the feel of the day gliding to a close, the light soft, the sun pulling its light away to the horizon, painting the sky in pinks and purples as the moon reappeared. Johnathan's breath deepened and slowed as he folded forward over his legs in the final pose.

After the closing meditation, Johnathan declined to join his family for cocktails, as did Caroline. He walked her to her room, pleading with her to spend some time with him, to tell him what was wrong, asking her over and over again why she was avoiding him.

Caroline insisted she hadn't been feeling well all week and was going to shower and fall into bed.

Dejected, Johnathan spent the rest of the evening working alone in his room on the design for the project they were to build in China's Huaxi Village. As always, he entered a state of flow while working that took him out of his thoughts as well as all sense of space or time. A little over two hours later, exhaustion kicked in, and he fell into a deep sleep as soon as his head hit the pillow.

The minute Johnathan opened his eyes, the questions about his future and if he should be marrying Caroline began terrorizing him. He rolled out of bed and headed to the beach for yoga. When he arrived, he was over ten minutes late. As quietly as he could, he snuck onto an open mat at the back of the platform.

Johnathan let out a sigh of relief when Adam announced that instead of seated meditation, they would be indulging in a guided yogic sleep. Relaxing down on his back, he placed his hands behind his head and allowed his body to relax. Adam came over and brought Johnathan's arms out away from his head and extended them down by his sides. Despite Adam's instructions to stay awake while listening to his voice, Johnathan was fast asleep within minutes.

Adam gently shook Johnathan awake. Johnathan sat bolt upright, looking around him. Everyone else was gone. He glanced at his watch. He had been asleep for over an hour.

"How long have the others been gone? Why didn't you wake

me?"

Adam shrugged, "If you could sleep that deeply on a hard platform, then I figured you needed the rest. I took some time to meditate on the sound of the waves."

Johnathan stretched and bounded up onto his feet. "Thanks, man. I feel amazing. I think you're right. I needed that."

Adam smiled and jumped down onto the sand. "Try to make it to the sunset yoga for a change, yeah?"

Johnathan grinned and nodded as Adam headed back up to the hotel. Johnathan jumped down onto the sand and walked out toward the waves.

The truth was that he had arrived in Bali convinced and pumped up to marry Caroline. Now, a few days later, and he wasn't so sure.

Johnathan had been confident that Caroline had been eagerly counting down the days to their wedding in Bali with as much excitement as he had. Sure, she was teaching at her first yoga retreat, but they had, in theory, tons of downtime to spend alone together.

Jonathan shook his head. He had expected this trip to be an even more blissful experience than their time in California as a newly engaged couple. Instead, Caroline was sleeping in a separate room and disappeared every afternoon back into her bungalow without him.

Johnathan kicked off his sandals and sat down under a palm tree, looking out at the waves. The money was one thing. Starting over from scratch was another. Daniel still wouldn't budge when he tried to persuade him about opening a California office or letting him work from the west coast.

Johnathan thought back on the round after round of failures he had endured with his brother before they managed to hit a home run with their current business. There were years of networking events, business lunches, traveling all over the world to meet with clients. Was he going to walk away from his business to start over, all for some woman who didn't even want to share a room with him days before their wedding?

Johnathan picked up a handful of warm sand and let it slide through his fingers. The bartender had been correct about the agitation in his mind. Here he was, sitting in paradise, and instead of savoring it, he was miserable.

Johnathan had stood up to his parents and conquered his fear before; he'd done it when he had rejected their directive to go into business or finance and opted for architecture.

Now Johnathan loved being an architect. Was this another moment in time to stand up to family pressure and go a new way? Johnathan reasoned that he could open up a new architecture office near the beach. So what if his projects turned into designing homes or business complexes instead of skyscrapers and museums? He would still be doing what he loved. If he was honest with himself, he was burning out. He wasn't sleeping well; the deadlines and demanding clients increasingly stressed him, and he spent more and more time in meetings, answering emails, and managing people than doing the design work he loved.

Johnathan hadn't lied to Caroline when he'd said that he was ready to spend more of his time out in the ocean and less time dressed in an Armani suit at an event. It was time to play his own game. He would not let himself be manipulated by his parents into changing his mind.

Sure, he would miss the comfortable lifestyle, the luxury holidays, and the abundant bank account. His ego would miss the title on his business card and how he was treated around town. From somebody to nobody, how would he cope with the reality of that? Johnathan shrugged.

He was beyond caring. His tank was running on empty and his head increasingly filled with a haze of exhaust dust. He needed a new start, and that would be without his family's say-so. A fresh start, in a new place, with a new business somewhere on the California coast.

Johnathan relaxed back onto his back and gazed up at the

blue sky, feeling lighter than he had felt in years. A new start. He let out a big sigh, relaxing his body into the sand.

# CHAPTER 3

Johnathan woke with a start. A figure stood over him, blocking out the blue sky.

"Johnathan. Johnathan? I need to talk to you."

Johnathan blinked his eyes open, sat up, and blinked at his phone as Caroline settled down onto the sand beside him. How long had he been asleep? He waited for Caroline to say something, but she didn't even look at him. She looked as if in a trance, staring at the waves washing onto the beach.

Johnathan took a deep breath. It was now or never. Better sooner than later and get it over with, he reasoned.

"I'm pregnant," Caroline said.

"I don't want to get married," he blurted out a second afterward.

Startled, Johnathan stared at Caroline for a moment in confusion. "What did you just say?"

"You answered my question," Caroline answered, jumping to her feet and hurrying back up the beach.

Johnathan struggled to his feet and went after her. He broke into a run and grabbed her hand. She shook it free and ran up the beach and toward her bungalow. Johnathan followed quickly on her heels. Oh shit, he kept repeating in his head. Johnathan hadn't known she was going to say that. How could he know?

Had Caroline really said she's pregnant? Johnathan prayed

she had said I want to get pregnant, instead of I am pregnant.

Caroline flew through the front door of her hotel room, and Johnathan put a foot in the door just in time. He slipped inside just as Caroline slammed the door to the bathroom. Johnathan went to the door and could hear Caroline being sick.

Johnathan wandered away from the door and sat on the edge of a chair, waiting for Caroline to come out of the bathroom.

Was this why Caroline had wanted separate rooms? No, he shook his head; that didn't make any sense. Caroline knew he wanted lots of kids and to start a family as soon as possible. Why hadn't she told him already?

When had Caroline found out about the pregnancy? How far along was she?

Was it, he clenched his fists, possible that she wanted an abortion and was afraid to tell him? Caroline had insisted she wanted babies, but maybe, once pregnant, she had realized that she didn't want them after all?

Or was it not his baby? Was it another man's, and that's why she was afraid to tell him?

Johnathan sat in agony for thirty-four minutes with his mind spiraling. At last, Caroline emerged from the bathroom, looking pale with red eyes.

She settled carefully onto the edge of the bed, unable to meet his eyes. Johnathan swore in his head a stream of words his mother would disapprove of hearing. It was another man's child. That was and why she didn't want to marry him. She had fallen in love with some new guy. Wait, had Jolan came back into the picture? Or it could be-

"So you don't want to marry me," Caroline told the floor. "You don't love me? Or is that you love the money more?"

"No, Caroline, I mean, I didn't mean it, I think, I mean, did you say you're pregnant?"

"That doesn't matter. It shouldn't change how you feel about marrying me." Caroline perched on the edge of the bed.

"It's another man's baby, isn't it?" Johnathan leaned his

forearms on his thighs, his head handing forward. He hadn't realized how much this would hit him like a fist smashed into the solar plexus. "It's Jolan's baby."

"What?" Caroline looked up from the floor. "No. How could you think that? What would it matter anyway, since you don't want to marry me?"

"Why the hell wouldn't you tell me then? And for that matter, what the hell is your reason for having me stay in a separate room?"

Caroline shrugged, glancing back at the floor. "I spend a lot of time sick in the bathroom these days. I can't keep anything down. Why do they call this morning sickness if it lasts all day?"

"That's not an answer," Johnathan insisted, his jaw gritted. He glared at her. "Why didn't you tell me sooner? How long have you known?"

"About a month," Caroline answered. Silent tears started to slide down her cheeks.

"Why didn't you say anything?" asked Johnathan while beginning to pace the room feeling like a caged white tiger.

"I was scared, okay? I was scared. You kept telling me how unsure you are, about us, about your family pressuring you, how you will need to give everything up if you move out to California, about how you're not sure you're willing to do that for me."

Caroline stood up off the bed and took a deep breath. "I deserve someone who is crazy in love with me. I'd rather raise this baby alone than marry someone who is doing it out of a sense of obligation. It doesn't matter how in love I am with you."

Johnathan bit his lip. Like a kaleidoscope twisted a tiny bit, he could see a new pattern clearly. All the times when she had answered with, 'okay,' or a noncommittal answer about the wedding hadn't been because Caroline didn't care. It was because she was scared; it was because it mattered too much.

"I said I didn't mean it. I want to marry you."

Caroline's lips flattened into a thin line. She took a deep breath. "I want to be with someone who knows, beyond a shadow of a doubt, that they want to be with me. I deserve someone who is crazy about me. Married life is too hard and comes with too many compromises to settle for anything else. It's not your fault how you feel. It is what it is." She placed her hands over her face.

Johnathan could see her shoulders start to move with silent sobs. It was the day before his wedding, his fiancée had just told him she was pregnant, and he had never been so devastated as he was right now. Johnathan wiped his hands down his face and pressed against the sides of his neck. The woman he loved, the woman carrying his baby, was sobbing on the bed the day before their wedding, and it was his fault.

Oh man, I've fucked this up, he thought. How do I fix this?

He went over and knelt on the floor next to the bed.

"Caroline, look at me." He reached up and pulled the hands from Caroline's eyes. He could feel her hot tears wet on his fingers tips.

"I thought you were having second thoughts or that you weren't convinced about me. Sure, I let my family rev me up about the trust fund and the business and whatnot. But I was hoping for you to say that you loved me, and it would all be worth our new life together." Johnathan reached out and pulled Caroline gently into his arms.

Caroline placed her forehead on his shoulder, still sobbing. "It's been so lonely. So hard. I thought I felt all alone after Gram died. It was nothing compared to the last few weeks."

"I'm so sorry, sweetheart. Everything is going to be okay now. I promise. I love you, we have each other, we're going to have a baby, it's all going to be set right. We're going to have a beautiful life."

"But your family," Caroline whispered. "Your business. The money. You said those things were more important."

"Hey, that's not how I feel. I got caught up, you know? I got scared at walking away from the entire life I've known and starting all over. I am crazy in love with you, Caroline, and if it's true your pregnant, well, I couldn't be more thrilled."

Caroline lifted her head and looked into his eyes. "Honestly?"

Johnathan nodded. "Absolutely. And I am not taking no for an answer. I am sleeping in here with you tonight. I've missed you like crazy, and I don't care if you spend half the night throwing up."

Caroline nodded and noticed the clock. "I need to go take a quick shower before teaching tonight."

"You are not teaching tonight. You need to take a shower and get into bed and stay there," answered Johnathan, eying her tear-lined cheeks and the shadows under her eyes. "I'll go talk to Mark. I'm sure he can take over for you."

"And call off the wedding," added Caroline.

"No," Johnathan shook his head. "Hell no. We are getting married tomorrow."

"No, we're not. You told me you didn't want to, and I don't care what you're saying now. We need to give it more time."

"We are getting married in Bali. I want to be your husband and start our life, and I don't want to wait. Listen, you take a shower, and I'll be back in a bit, and we'll talk more, okay?"

Caroline nodded, and Johnathan grabbed her room key on the way out the door. The next day was the rehearsal dinner. Johnathan had one day to convince Caroline of his love and commitment. He only hoped he could find the right words to say.


Caroline lay fast asleep on the bed when Johnathan opened the door, so he returned to his room to shower and get dressed for the rehearsal dinner where he'd left most of his things. They had spent all day alone together, which had been a challenge to keep away from his family and all the friends arriving in Bali for the wedding. Johnathan had given up and asked for a new bungalow room with its own private plunge pool and tipped the hotel receptionist not to tell anyone their real names or their room number.

Johnathan had ordered in food service for all their meals, and they'd spent hours talking everything through. Caroline's tears and recriminations quickly evaporate under the sunlit rays as they ate breakfast on their private terrace. Within an hour, they were both laughing, curled up together on the same lounge sofa.

After one day together, Johnathan felt rejuvenated, the colors of the tropical flowers more vibrant, the smell of the salty ocean, and the feel of the breeze on his skin all pushing him into a near euphoric state. Opting for his outdoor shower, Johnathan looked up at the blue of the sky and sang under the shower. Suited and smelling of his best cologne, Johnathan returned to Caroline's room to find her gone. He dialed her number. No response. Maybe she had headed to the rehearsal dinner without him?

Johnathan made his way to the beach side bar looking for Caroline. Immediately he was waylaid by his aunt. He hadn't expected the prim and proper woman to understand his choice for a bride and had been avoiding her. It took him over ten minutes before he managed to escape her and continue his search for Caroline. He didn't see her anywhere. His family was inter-mixed with friends of his parents, aunt, and other relatives. Cocktails in hand, they mingled under the waving palm trees on the grass lining the white sand of the beach. As soon as he freed himself from his aunt's inquisition, Johnathan was pulled into the conversation by another aunt and uncle. Skin beginning to prickle with sweat despite the cool breeze, he, at last, broke away and headed back toward Caroline's room.

He spotted her drifting along a pathway toward the beach and hurried forward to intercept her before someone could see them.

"Hey, there you are," he called out. "Let's talk before we join the party."

"What do you mean 'join the party? I told you to cancel the wedding."

Johnathan pulled Caroline back toward the direction of her room. She was wearing shorts, flip flops, and a tank top, her hair pulled into a messy ponytail. Her eyes were red and puffy.

"Where are you pulling me? Johnathan?"

"Of course, I didn't cancel. I thought we talked it all through today? I thought we had a perfect day together. What happened?"

"I ran into your brother on the way to talk to Mark."

Johnathan groaned. "Listen, let's just head back to the room, and you can change. I'll wait for you, and we can go back to the rehearsal dinner together."

Caroline stopped walking and pulled her hand away from his. "Daniel said you don't love me and are only doing all this to spite your parents."

"He's lying," spluttered Johnathan.

"Well, he showed me some of your text conversations. I'm not marrying someone who agreed I'm fat and that I'm 'not up to your usual standards, and that 'you weren't sure why you loved me.' What the hell, Johnathan?"

Johnathan swayed, dizzy with regret from having written those texts to his brother. He couldn't lose Caroline. It was as if he had been flung to the edge of a cliff, standing, tipping at the precipice. He could feel his entire life was about to swing in one direction, or the other, and Caroline was the right choice, the only option that would cause everything in his world to shift and rearrange in the correct pattern, like a crystalline grid aligning with the stars.

"There isn't any other woman for me in the world. Please, Caroline. You're my soul-mate. We're getting married tomorrow."

Caroline laughed in derision. "What are you going to do? Go ahead and stand at the end of the aisle and wait for me tomorrow? I'm not marrying you."

"Shh," Johnathan hissed at her. "Please, Caroline. Please.

We'll talk about this in your room."

With a sigh, Caroline marched ahead of him. She slammed in through the door of her room and spun on her heel to face him with her hands on her hips.

"Well?"

"I know the texts were horrible, but I didn't mean them; I was going along with Daniel to shut him up. You are a sexy, gorgeous goddess, and I adore you."

Caroline laid down on the bed on her back and stared at the ceiling. "All I remember at the moment is telling you I am pregnant and you immediately answering you didn't want to marry me."

"Caroline," Johnathan said as he walked forward and wrapped his arms around her. "I didn't know you were pregnant. I thought you weren't crazy in love with me, and I didn't want to marry someone so ambivalent. Especially because you are making me give up so much."

"I'm not making you do anything. That is the point. We're not getting married," insisted Caroline.

Johnathan groaned and sat down in the chair near the window. "So you don't love me?"

"That's not the point right now."

"Of course it is. Do you love me, and do you want to raise this baby with me? That's the question."

"It's about you," Caroline started, but Johnathan interrupted her.

"No. It is about you," insisted Johnathan. "I'm all in here. I want to start all over somewhere new, with or without you, okay? So it isn't about giving anything up because maybe I'm going to do that anyway, with or without you. The truth is this life had been hollow for a while now. I adore you. You know how much I want to start a family. But I'm not going to beg. You need to know you want me and for us to be a family."

"I'll go get ready," answered Caroline.

"Is that a yes?"

"That's a maybe. I need time to think."

# CHAPTER 4

It took only fourteen minutes for Caroline to braid her hair into an intricate style, throw on her turquoise floor-length dress, and put on some makeup. The transformation was remarkable. Gone were the red, puffy eyes, the dark shadows, the sallow skin, and messy hair.

Caroline looked radiant and glowing, just like a happy bride-to-be when she returned from the bathroom. Johnathan pulled her into his arms and breathed in the fresh scent of her perfume. He could feel her body soften against his and kissed her on the forehead.

"I missed you so much," said Johnathan.

She lifted her face to look up at him. "I missed you too." A tear slid down her cheek, and she wiped it away. "Will you stay with me tonight and just hold me like this?"

Johnathan nodded and pulled her back in towards him. He was one step closer. It would be easier for her to decide to marry him if she slept in his arms all night again.

"We need to make it through the rehearsal dinner first," smiled Caroline. "Ready?"

Johnathan forced a smile, his face beginning to hurt from the effort. Who were all these people? When did they arrive? Most importantly, why didn't he know they would all be at the dinner? Johnathan had pictured a beach party with his family and a handful of guests. Afterward, Johnathan had told his Mom he wanted an intimate wedding and dancing until dawn under the stars on the beach. There were over a hundred people at the rehearsal dinner alone. What was going on?

Johnathan saw his sister rushing over to him and held out a hand. "Not now, Mat. I need to talk to Mom."

"I have to talk to you," insisted Matilda. "It can't wait."

"It will have to," he said and plowed forward through the guests holding cocktail classes and tropical drinks with umbrellas.

"Mother, I need to talk to you," Johnathan said as he grabbed her by the elbow and steered her away from someone he didn't even recognize. "When did you decide to invite the entire extended family and not tell me about it? For that matter, who are the rest of these people?"

"You should be thrilled, Johnathan. I had no idea so many would manage to get here in time for the dinner tonight. Now, if you had let me schedule the wedding for Saturday as I wanted, then we could have gotten an even better turnout."

"Wait, what? You invited more?"

"Of course. Most of the guests are coming in tomorrow," answered Alison and pushed her blown-out hair off her shoulder.

"I told you I wanted an intimate wedding. Anyway, most of these people are your friends, not mine."

"Don't worry, love, your friends are coming tomorrow. That's what I'm saying. You should have had your wedding on Saturday, and then they could have come to the rehearsal party too."

"Caroline and I wanted a small wedding," Johnathan insisted.

"I don't see why you care, Johnathan, as your father and I are paying for everything. I didn't want to ruin any of the relationships in our lives, Johnathan; you wouldn't want that would you? Oh, look, it's almost time to go to the restaurant for dinner. You will love the menu I picked out. Just you wait. You're in for a real treat," Alison said. She patted his cheek as she glided past him and over to a nearby group of people.

A hand tapped Johnathan on the shoulder, and he turned

around and gaped at the redhead standing in front of him in a shimmering rose gold Dior dress. "Ariana. What are you doing here?"

"What do you mean. Didn't your brother tell you?" asked Ariana. She smiled in the direction of Daniel.

Matilda strode back forward and grabbed Johnathan's hand. "I told you I have to talk to you. Right. Now."

What did Ariana mean? Where was Caroline, and what was the plan this evening, exactly? He should have paid more attention to his mother and the wedding planner at their one and only meeting together.

"Come with me," Mat insisted, grabbing his hand and pulling him away from Ariana.

"No. Let Brad deal with whatever drama you're going through now. I'm not interested in how the daily meditation time made you cry, how difficult it is to live without the comforts of home, nor how hard it is not to have a daily routine. I don't care anymore about how lonely you've felt since you started on this world tour, or how Daniel has always been the favorite, or how you've realized you have no real friends. I've listened to it all week long, and I'm sick of it," Johnathan paused for breath. "All you think about is yourself. I have my own problems to deal with. Did you think of that? You haven't once asked me how I've been, and you've been a mega brat to Caroline."

"Well, you've never opened up and told me anything you're feeling or going through ever. So why would I bother?" Matilda wiped her fingers under her eyes. "Do you know what? You deserve what's coming. I wanted to help you, but fine. Fine."

Johnathan watched his sister storm off into the crowd as he searched for his mother. Could it be possible that she had invited his ex-girlfriend to his wedding? Alison had always adored Ariana, and to his chagrin, they met for tea and cake every few months and saw each other frequently; Johnathan knew his ex and mother moved in the same social circles.

Johnathan turned his focus back to Ariana. He had to admit

that Ariana had never looked so beautiful. She had grown out her hair from chin length down to her shoulders, and the red curls framed her face in a pretty way. He blinked, pulling his attention away from memories resurfacing of their time together as a couple.

"There you are," called out Daniel as he strode forward and slipped an arm around Ariana. "So, how is the groom? Getting cold feet yet?"

"Daniel. I need to talk to you alone."

"Trouble in paradise? Get it? Hey, everyone gets nervous before heading down the aisle. It's very rare for a man not to want to take flight at the thought of lifetime confinement, and this is not the right woman for you."

Ariana glared at Daniel, shifting away from him slightly and pushing away his arm.

"Not that I will feel like that on our wedding weekend, babe, that you can count on, honey."

"How do you know I won't get cold feet and leave you standing stranded at the aisle?" retorted Ariana with a fake pout on her face.

Johnathan looked from his ex-girlfriend to his brother and back again.

Daniel slipped his arm around Ariana's waist and kissed her cheek. "Admit it, Ariana; you're crazy in love with me and want to have my babies."

"You're still on trial," Ariana laughed and patted Daniel's cheek with her left hand.

The flash of sparkle caught Johnathan's eye immediately. "Daniel? What is going on? Ariana doesn't want kids, and there is no way in hell you are going to convince me you are together."

"You told me he knew. How does he not know? And for the record, I do want babies. I just didn't want them with you." Ariana drowned the rest of her drink and disappeared into the crowd.

Johnathan stood reeling from Ariana's words. She had always

been vicious and capable of hitting him where it hurt most. There had been too many fights to count over starting a family. Ariana had insisted at first that she just wasn't ready to be a mother, then a few years later, she had announced that she never wanted to have kids. It was what broke them up for good the previous summer.

"Listen, I meant to tell you, we wanted you at the engagement party, but then you disappeared without notice to California. When you came back, I was worried about keeping you in New York as my partner, and then there was the ridiculous notion you would move to California."

"Seriously, Daniel? Out of all the women in New York, you chose the woman I dated on and off for seven years? Stop, stop, stop. You may be able to fool all the rest of these people but not me. I'm your brother. I know you're gay."

Daniel grabbed Johnathan roughly by the arm and dragged him away from the party and to a secluded group of palm trees.

"What are you trying to do to me? I am not gay."

Johnathan tried to shake himself free from Daniel's iron grip on his arm to no avail. "You don't need to keep up this lie, Daniel, at least not with me. Listen, I know no one would expect my dashing taller brother, so macho, such the ladies man, to be gay. I've grown up with you. I know."

Daniel squeezed his arm tighter, and Johnathan pushed his brother hard, dislodging his grip.

"I am not gay. Now, I know you don't like me marrying Ariana, but I never did anything while you were dating. Or semi not dating. Or whatever the hell you two were doing all those years until you called it quits for good last Thanksgiving."

"Last Thanksgiving? Are you serious? You've been dating my ex since last Thanksgiving, and you didn't tell me? What the hell, Daniel?"

Daniel blew out a burst of air, his cheeks puffing up in the process. He shifted from foot to foot, his gaze wandering away from Daniel to the sun setting over the ocean.

"Do you still have feelings for Ariana? Is that what this is, Johnathan? Because I'm telling you, Johnathan, you just made each other miserable. Everyone could see that. Remember how often you and Ariana fought? Like every other minute."

"She j said that to hurt me, didn't she, about the kids?"

"Ah," Daniel muttered, bringing his hand to the back of his neck and rubbing. "I don't think so. We're planning on trying as soon as we're married, which is the day after Christmas, by the way, the wedding, I mean."

It was as if someone had sucker-punched him out of the blue. Jonathan didn't care about Ariana; it hurt his ego more than anything else that she'd chosen Daniel, but that his brother could betray him hurt more than he could say. He'd thought Daniel was his best friend. Within twenty-four hours, Daniel had almost lost Johnathan, his bride, by showing her those horrible texts and now this.

Johnathan turned away from his brother and looked out at the sky awash in pastel swirls of yellow, pink, and purple. Allen called out that it was time to go inside for dinner. Johnathan watched the guests make their way up the path toward the restaurant. Gritting his teeth, he turned back to face his brother.

"I had this deep conversation a few days back while everyone was out enjoying the beach and the pool. I was the only one in the bar. Wise dude, this old guy tending the bar I talked to."

"What's your point?"

"Yeah, so anyway, he made me see that I've been playing everyone's game but mine. I have a nice bright wake-up call for you, Daniel. Sure, our contract requires me to stay living in New York, but you forget a pivotal point. I can sell my part of the business at any time. So I think that is what I will do. To the highest bidder. I'll take the money and set up shop anew somewhere with an ocean view and palm trees."

"That's dangerous," said Daniel.

"What? Why?"

"I mean, it's not a good idea to try to sell your share of the company at this point in time," insisted Daniel.

"Why? Because it will make you cry, big brother, that a stranger will have a controlling interest in our company, the company we built tooth over nail up to what it is today?" asked Johnathan.

"You wouldn't do that to me."

"It's surprising, isn't it? What the people you love most are capable of doing?"

"Johnathan, stop; it's not the same thing. You're getting married tomorrow. What do you care if I'm with Ariana?"

"You started dating her before I ever met Caroline."

"You're mad. I get it, brother; I understand. I'll give you some space to cool off, get some perspective. I know you wouldn't go through with doing that to me," Daniel straightened his tie and smiled. "I'll break things off with Ariana if you want; the issues with the project with the Chinese, well, there are some things you don't know, and it would be a bad idea, awful, for you to bring attention to our company right now from the outside."

"What the hell is that supposed to mean?" asked Johnathan. "Wait, don't answer that. I clearly see why you can't understand me giving up my trust fund and potentially cleaving our business in two. You've never been in love. You don't know what love even is, Daniel. If you did, you wouldn't be treating Caroline and me, this way and you wouldn't be willing to so readily toss Ariana aside."

Johnathan walked away. Daniel hustled after him to catch up. Wordlessly they strode toward the restaurant. All Johnathan wanted was to scream some more in his brother's face or punch him square in the jaw and the stomach.

How could his brother be acting like this? Johnathan would feel pity for Ariana, but she was as cunning and ruthless as she was gorgeous, and that was saying something. Perhaps she and his brother would make a good pair; they certainly deserved each other.

Johnathan glanced in Ariana's direction and shuddered.

What had he been thinking? In comparison to Caroline, Ariana looked beautiful but flat, like a two-dimensional magazine cover. Caroline, meanwhile, looked radiant and pulsating with life, as if energy was swirling off of her in every direction.

Johnathan spotted Caroline standing and laughing with her head thrown back and one hand on her belly, which reminded him of their baby.

How many more months did they have to wait to meet their baby?

I'm going to be a father, Johnathan thought. For the first time that day, the news settled down, like sparkling sand, at last, resettling to the ocean floor, leaving the water clear. Delight rushed in, and all thoughts of his brother, Ariana, his mother, and the other guests disappeared.

He'd wanted to start a family for a few years now. To hold his baby in his arms, to play on the floor with his kids, to come home to pattering feet and the smell of homemade cooking. Everything he hadn't had. Johnathan pictured a holiday where he roughed it in the woods with Caroline in a tent and slept with his kids snuggled next to them.

Growing up, Johnathan had hated that his parents were always gone working or at events, eating fancy food, and spending so much time with a nanny. Why had he let his parents and brother talk with their honeyed tongues and convince him he would miss the money, the lifestyle, New York? Daniel could keep his gleaming luxury flat, personal chef, and cold, beautiful wife; he didn't want any of it.

Johnathan looked around at the guests dressed in designer clothes, sparkling with jewels and watches that cost more than some people's homes. He had worried that he would regret the loss of it all.

Honestly, there was fear. Was it possible to be in a family of billionaires, give it all up, and be happy starting a new life fresh and with so much less? So he had been scrambling to find a way to eat his cake and have it too. Johnathan thought, deep down, that he had grown too accustomed to the comforts and freedoms, the privileges and ego-satisfying feel of his luxury life to be able to be happy without the power, luxury, and glamor.

They say money is power, thought Johnathan. Will I lose all mine if I walk away?

There was a fear that he wouldn't be able to make it on his own. That without the wealth, the name, the business, he wasn't enough. But he knew he would be a good dad. He wouldn't control and manipulate like his father and fail to be there, daily, for his kid.

Johnathan observed the thoughts rolling through his mind, but some part of him stood above it, outside it, as if watching himself sitting here in Bali, like a movie.

He saw Caroline was returning from the ladies' room and jumped up to talk to her, grabbing her hand by the bar. He pulled her into his arms. She broke into a smile, and it was as if a dimer had turned down the noise of all the guests talking around him and his own thoughts, uncovering a deep knowing.

He'd known it from the first moment he laid eyes on her. He didn't know for sure if they would be able to make their relationship work or whether he would be able to figure out how to be a great Dad. He didn't know if he would be able to walk away from his inheritance without feeling the loss. What he did know is that he was meant to share his life with Caroline. He knew, deep down, that he was meant to love Caroline, and it would make him a better man.

Johnathan squeezed Caroline's closer to him, leaned in, and kissed her on the cheek, then pressed his cheek to hers. She placed her hand on his other cheek.

"I love you," he whispered in her ear. "I'm crazy about you. I knew the moment I saw you. Please tell me you will marry me tomorrow."

Caroline pulled away slightly to look into his eyes. "Yes."

Johnathan's heart jumped from his chest into his throat. He clutched her to him.

"I was wrong," murmured Caroline in his ear. "About you not being certain about me and also about your family. I talked to your Mom and Dad, and they were telling me how much fun they had with me at the yoga retreat all week. Even Matilda said she hopes to keep in touch with me. And the people at the party tonight, everyone's been so nice. Maybe we can spend half our time in New York. Would that help you like your Mom suggested?"

"We'll see about all that," answered Johnathan and pulled her in tighter. "Right now, I'm so damn excited about our baby and about marrying you tomorrow. That's what's important. Right now. With you."

He was so preoccupied with Caroline that he didn't hear Daniel calling his name until all the guests burst into laughter. Johnathan and Caroline turned.

"Johnathan? Hello? Speech time. Apparently, my brother is so in love that he has lost his hearing. The best-man is trying to give a speech up here. Sit down and Listen up," Daniel said.

Johnathan turned his head and felt the eyes of all the guests on him. He blinked as if caught in the headlights of a semi-truck barreling toward him.

Daniel was legendary in New York for his pre-wedding roasts. He had promised he wouldn't do one tonight. Johnathan had threatened him. But here he was, standing at the end of the table, glass in hand. Johnathan didn't care; let Daniel slay and mock him all he wanted. Nothing and no one could bring him down out of the high of his euphoric mood.

Caroline pulled Johnathan toward their seats as he looked widely around the room for a screen. None was to be seen, and he let out the breath he had been holding as he sat down. At least it would be a photo-free toast. How much harm could that cause?

Johnathan groaned as Daniel took a contraption out of his pocket and pointed it at the white wall behind them. Guests pushed their chairs out or leaned forward to get a better view.

Photos of Johnathan in grade school flashed on the screen, high school, college. All bland and ordinary. Johnathan scooted to his chair's front edge as Daniel talked about Johnathan graduating from Columbia top in his architecture program. He didn't trust his brother. Something must be coming.

A series of photos flooded the screen, one after Johnathan's other at events worldwide, always with a different woman, all of them thin, glamorous, most of them models. The presentation sped up, the photos flowing onto the screen even faster. Johnathan was getting dizzy.

"How many women is that so far?" Daniel asked? "Has anyone been able to keep track?"

The photos continued to flash on the screen. Johnathan standing at s black-tie event in Dubai with a blonde. Johnathan kissing a woman under the Eiffel Tower. Johnathan laying next to a topless redhead on a yacht. Johnathan at the Met Gala with Ariana. Johnathan on a ski lift in Aspen next to a blue-eyed beauty. Johnathan running towards the camera with a dark-haired woman on the Great Wall of China.

Johnathan closed his eyes, not daring to look over at Caroline. They had never discussed much of his previous dating life.

"What a life this guy has had so far, am I right?" Daniel said. "Who is jealous?" The people around the table chuckled.

"But now he is willing to give up the playing and wandering and get married. To whom? So few of you know the lovely Caroline."

A photo came on Caroline's screen lying on her back in a yoga pose, her legs stretched up and her feet resting on the floor behind her head. Her big bum was taking up more than half the photo. The group broke into laughter. The following image was of Caroline smoothing down the front of her dress over her belly at the New York Ballet Gala.

"Maybe she's regretting the second dessert she ate, am I, right, ladies? Especially since she's looking nothing like the previous year's worth of dates this man's been on." The table erupted into laughter as more awkward and bad photos of Caroline flashed across the screen taken the previous week during the yoga retreat.

A dull roar began in Johnathan's ears, and for a while, he didn't hear what Daniel was saying; he could only see the photos of Caroline and the laughter of the room. The photos were all awful, showing her sweat-drenched, makeup-free, with shadows under her eyes and her hair a mess.

"Can you believe this guy got the entire family on a yoga retreat? Who knew the playboy would start downward dogging it every morning, am I right? But really, brother here's to you getting less superficial all of a sudden. Here's to you!"

Daniel smiled like a cat with a mouse trapped as he turned to the wall. A video began to play of Johnathan lounging on the beach with a bunch of his friends. "Seriously though," Johnathan said as he clinked his beer with the others. "I never date a woman bigger than a size two. I don't even care about big tits. I like long and lean."

A friend of Johnathan's laughed and responded, "I want the big boobs. "

"Nah," Johnathan waved a hand at him and slurred, "the skinny bitches look better at events and in all the photos."

"Well, we've seen that's true, am I right?" Daniel roared, and the table burst into laughter and catcalls. "I have to say, I am proud of my brother for marrying a woman for what's on the inside. And when I say that, I mean one's cooking in there."

Johnathan couldn't move. He willed himself to move his feet, look at Caroline, leave the restaurant. He was frozen with shock. Caroline was clutching his hand harder and harder.

Caroline leaped to her feet, stumbling over her chair in her frantic rush to flee. She landed hard on the floor as an audible gasp went out from the group. Caroline lay splayed on the floor, her dress bunched awkwardly high up around her thighs, her belly rolls showing, and her face in a grimace.

"She must be pretty special to change your mind on things,

bro, given that she's a bit on the clumsy side."

Johnathan's heart stopped. His baby. Their baby. He jumped from his seat, scooped her up from the floor, but she fought against him, pushing him away, and ran crying from the room.

Blood thundering in his ears, he strode to the top of the table, calmly took the glass out of Daniel's hand, drank it down in one gulp. "How dare you all laugh at my wife. You all uninvited."

Then he turned to face his brother, smiled, and punched Daniel as hard as he could across the jaw. Screams rang out as Daniel fell to the floor.

# CHAPTER 5

Johnathan ran from the room, blood thundering in his ears. He ran to the front desk, requesting a doctor to come immediately to Caroline's room. Then he turned on his heel. His shoes slapped against the marble floors and down along the path to Caroline's room.

He knocked on the door. No answer. He pounded, frantic, calling out Caroline's name. What if she had passed out? What she was in there in trouble?

The door opened. "Go away," sobbed Caroline.

"I'm so sorry," tumbled over and over again from his mouth, like a torrential river in flood season. He couldn't stop saying it. Caroline allowed him to gather her in his arms. He didn't know how long they stood like that until a knock came on the door.

Caroline looked at him with panic in her eyes. "Don't answer it."

"It's the doctor. We need to make sure the baby is okay. That you're okay. You fell so hard."

Caroline nodded, and Johnathan opened the door.

A tall man with glasses and a case entered the room. After a short inspection, he advised them to go to the hospital for an ultrasound, just to be sure. Caroline was bleeding a bit, and he wanted to make sure everything was fine. Johnathan picked Caroline up and hurried as fast as he could toward the lobby. On the way to the hospital, they didn't talk. Johnathan had his arms wrapped around Caroline, and she clutched his arms, repeatedly squeezing and letting go.

Once in the hospital on a table, Caroline looked helpless lying there, silent tears streaming down her cheeks. "I want this baby so much," she choked out.

"Me too," Johnathan said back, smoothing strands of hair away from her face. He blinked rapidly, his eyes blurry. He struggled to swallow the lump in his throat.

The doctor came in for the ultrasound and, after a quick look, snapped the gloves back off his hands and smiled at them. "Everything looks great. Looks like you're near the three-month mark to me."

Caroline nodded, her body slack. Johnathan had expected to feel jubilant at the news that the baby was okay. Weak with relief, he felt empty and completely drained of energy.

They didn't talk on the way back to the hotel. Wordlessly, they returned to Caroline's room. She went into the bathroom, and he followed her. She didn't even look at him. She just slipped out of her dress and under the shower.

He waited, opening a towel for her to step into when she got out. She hugged the towel around her shoulders, like a small child after a swim at the pool. He returned to the room, lay down on the bed on his back, kicked off his shoes, and took off his tie. He lay starring up at the ceiling when Caroline lay down next to him, putting her cheek on his chest.

He got up and pulled back the sheets for her to get into bed, then lay back down next to her, wrapping his arms around her. Within a minute, they were both fast asleep.

They both awoke with a start to a fist banging on their door. "Johnathan, are you in there? Open up right now. Caroline? Johnathan? Johnathan!"

Johnathan looked at his watch. It was almost twenty past ten. They had both slept over ten hours. Caroline rolled out from under his arms and made her way to the bathroom. He could hear her being sick. He ignored the hammering on the door, hoping his mother and father would go away. The last thing Caroline needed was his mother coming into her room this morning.

The knocking didn't stop, so Johnathan stumbled out of bed with a sigh and opened the door. Before he could blink, his parents pushed past him into the room.

"Here you are. When you weren't in your room, we were worried you left without telling us. What are you doing in last night's clothes, son?" asked Alison.

"Did you just wake up?" Allen looked over at Caroline, who had snuggled back into bed with the sheets up to her chin looking pale.

"The events of last night were exhausting," spoke up Caroline. "I think we slept ten hours. Now, if you don't mind, I'm going to go get dressed."

Johnathan ushered his parents out of the room and into the corridor.

"What the hell is going on, son? You have some explaining to do," said Allen.

Both of his parents stood standing in front of him. Johnathan stared back at them wordlessly. Something clicked inside him, and there was stillness. Silence. Johnathan had the strange urge to laugh, but then the glimpse into the deeper knowing vanished again, and the thoughts began to stick back into the drama story of his life.

"Well, answer your father," insisted Alison, her hands rolling the pearls around her neck. "What do you have to say for yourself?"

"What do I have to say for myself? Are you serious?"

Alison pressed her lips together in a thin white line. "Punching your brother like that, such a scene, and in front of all our guests.

You know a few people got the entire thing on video? Can you imagine how this will hurt your father's business, your business, not to mention our family's reputation?"

Johnathan laughed. "You can't be serious right now. You saw what Daniel did last night, you were sitting there, you heard his speech, saw the photos."

Allen waved a hand in front of him as if swatting away mosquitoes. "He was just having a bit of fun; it did get a bit out of hand. That video he showed of you went too far, I'll admit. It didn't cast you in a good light."

Alison ran her fingers over the diamonds encircling her neck and pursed her lips. "He really must think of the family image. Sure, these people are family and close friends, but still, you know you can't trust them. Some would love to see your father and I knocked off the pedestal."

"I can't believe what I'm hearing," Johnathan pressed his hands to his ears. "Have you thought about how Daniel hurt Caroline? She'll never marry me after last night."

"Oh, of course, she will. You're Johnathan Arrozzini," retorted Alison. "Or it not, well, perhaps it is for the best. You two hardly know each other. What is this nonsense about marrying someone you've known for a few months? She doesn't even come from our world. Look, did you get her to sign the prenuptial agreement? You know we talked about this, Johnathan. Over and over again. She could just be after your money. I mean, what woman doesn't care about any details of her own wedding? That's strange. You have to admit it, honey."

Allen set a hand on Johnathan's shoulder, turning him to face them.

"She's not wrong."

"I told you I'm giving up my rights to my trust and moving to California," answered Johnathan. "I'm selling my half of the company, and I'm walking away from all your manipulation and games."

"Look at what nonsense you're thinking since taking up with

this woman," said Allen. "We're your family. Who has always had your best intentions at heart? Who has supported you every step of the way? We have, and we will continue to do so, son. I can't let you throw away the business you've built from the ground up like this. If you sell your half of the company, then you will spook investors and destroy the business. With the critical project with the Chinese, well, it couldn't come at a worse time, and it will look like a loss of confidence or hint to internal fighting. I know what Daniel did was deplorable yesterday, but does he deserve to be ruined because of it? You've been more than brothers and partners; you've been best friends since kids. Don't you love him enough to give him a chance to make things right? What about your team? Do your employees deserve to lose their jobs?"

Johnathan's thoughts immediately turned to his team of architects, and his stomach turned over at the thought of their sometimes twelve or even fourteen-hour days when completing projects. His team had families, Anna was pregnant, and Joe had bought a new house he'd saved up to purchase for his family for twelve years. Could he walk away knowing they could lose their jobs because of him?

Alison nodded and said, "You must question how this woman is turning you against us, Johnathan? Surely? Frankly, I think you should take more time to think things through. Calling off the wedding is a good idea. I'll see to it and tell all the guests."

"No," shouted Johnathan. "Don't cancel the wedding. You couldn't get your money back now anyway, right? So what if we wait a few hours to cancel? That will be more than enough time for me to do some thinking."

Alison began to argue, but Johnathan interrupted her. "If the wedding doesn't happen, then you can go ahead and enjoy the party afterward with all your guests," Johnathan concluded. "Why waste all your party planning efforts and the money, Mom?"

Allen looked at his wife, and she nodded. "Well, that is true.

You always were the most practical child, Johnathan dear."

Allen took a step closer to Johnathan and lowered his voice. "In the meantime, you can talk with the yoga instructor about the prenuptial agreement and moving to New York. I'm not letting you walk down that aisle without it."

"The bride walks down the aisle dear, not the groom," answered Alison. Allison took an envelope out of her bag and held it out to Johnathan.

"You know what I meant," growled Allen.

Johnathan gritted his teeth. The best way to get rid of his parents was just to agree with them. Otherwise, they would keep hunting him down and terrorizing him into capitulation. The steady drip of disapproval, disappointment, and undermining his confidence would be mixed with just the right amount of dashes of insight and affection. Johnathan knew his parents were both master manipulators in their own right. As a team, it was near impossible not to relent to their will.

He held out a hand for the envelope containing the prenuptial agreement and nodded at them. "See you later. I need to talk to Caroline."

Alison kissed his cheek, and Allen patted him on the back. Johnathan waited until they started walking away before he went back into the room. Caroline was gone.

Johnathan rushed to the closet and let out a sigh of relief. Her clothes hung neatly from the hangers, and her suitcase was still inside. Where would she go?

He checked the turquoise infinity pool, the sun deck, the restaurants. He wandered through the lobby and outside along the paths under swaying palm trees, past bright pink and orange tropical flowers towards the beach. A half-mile away from the hotel, he found her standing shin-deep in the water, looking out at the ocean.

Johnathan pulled off his sandals and stepped into the water. He slipped his arms around her and brought his hands over her belly, feeling a sudden onrush of relief. His baby was okay. Caroline leaned her head back against his chest and laughed out loud.

It was the last thing Johnathan expected after the evening they had just gone through the night before. "Why are you laughing?"

"I thought I was over my stuff. You know that I'd worked through my body image issues and my need to be liked. My attachment to how other people see me and feeling good enough. I thought I was this radiant, mystically awakened person. Turns out I was wrong, and my pain body is very much with me. I can still get triggered. Looks like I'm normal after all" She turned to face him and wrapped her arms around his low back, resting her face on his chest.

"You're anything but normal, my love."

Johnathan didn't understand this woman. He had expected tears, recrimination, anger, hostility. Perhaps a demand his family never come near her or her baby ever again. He had been mentally preparing, thinking up how he would answer her recriminations and agonizing about ways to talk to her since he woke up that morning.

Was Caroline in shock? Was the storm of anger on its way? Well, he would take a break before the storm came. He nestled his head on top of hers and closed his eyes, taking in the feel of the cool water on his feet, the sound of the waves, the feel of the warm salt breeze on his skin.

"I think we're meant to be together," Caroline said. "I love you."

"I think so too. You're beautiful, Caroline. Fun, light-hearted, and you know, deep and still. I want to be by your side for the rest of my life."

"Let's do it then," said Caroline, lifting her head from his chest to look at them. "To hell with all of them. Let's get married today, and afterward, come home with me. Let's start our life together. Right now."

It was Johnathan's turn to laugh out loud. It felt good. He hadn't been expecting her to say that, either. "I canceled it. I didn't think that after last night we would be getting married. You were on the fence before my brother."

Caroline shook her head and closed her eyes. "Let's not talk about it now."

"Caroline, we should talk. You can't pretend it didn't happen."

Caroline sighed and replaced her head on his chest. "Maybe if we don't talk about it and can just go away, last night, your family, the weight of the money fighting, and all of it will magically leave us alone."

"Hey, money is beautiful. I love money. Just not like how I love you."

Caroline laughed again, and Johnathan led her out of the water towards the shade of a palm tree. They sat down side by side, looking at the azure blue of the ocean sparkling in the sun. For a long time, neither of them spoke.

"Matilda did try to warn me," said Caroline, still looking out at the ocean. "I didn't believe her that it would be that bad. Okay, and maybe I thought I had become so chill that I could just handle whatever Daniel said in his speech and not get upset." Caroline laughed again. "I was wrong. But that's great that Mat cared about me, about us, enough to try to help. You know? Here I thought she was going to be the one to watch. Just goes to show," she shrugged her shoulders and smiled over at Johnathan.

"You know, now that you mention it, Mat tried to tell me something last night too, but I was a jerk." Johnathan rubbed the back of his neck, recalling what he had said to his sister.

"You know; I think this yoga retreat has been more transformative for Mat. We've spent a lot of time together meditating and talking. She's come to the edge of a cliff. Matilda says she can't turn and go back to her old life and how she used to live, and she doesn't know what's next."

"That's how I felt," answered Johnathan, instantly. "I can't go back to my old life now that I've been with you."

Caroline nodded. "Except with Mat, it's the reverse. I think she's questioning whether she should stay with Brad. She told me she has this weird vibe about him now and doesn't know what to do. They've been together for so long, and she is confused about how she feels."

Johnathan didn't have space to think about his sister's troubles.

"Let's do it. Let's get married today. There is a prenuptial agreement my parents are insisting you sign. Do you feel up to that?" asked Johnathan.

Caroline shrugged. "Let me read it."

"You're sure?"

"Sure. What's in this prenuptial? Let's read it before we get upset because it might be completely reasonable. Then again, maybe there's a clause that if you die, I get nothing, or we have to live in New York forever. Who knows. Hand it over."

Johnathan smiled. Sometimes he forgot how rationally and logically Caroline's mind operated; he had been sure she would be angry at the mere mention of the prenuptial.

He pulled the envelope he had stuffed in his pocket and smoothed it out, and began to read it himself before handing it to her. She tore it from his hands.

"You haven't read it yet?"

Johnathan shrugged. "I didn't think we were getting married, so what was the point?"

Caroline turned her focus to reading the document.

After twenty minutes, Johnathan's stomach began to growl so loudly that Caroline looked over at him with a smile. "You're hungry."

"We need to eat. I haven't eaten since lunch yesterday," declared Johnathan.

"I should try to eat too," Caroline answered as Johnathan helped her up to her feet. "I'm not crazy about talking to friends or relatives we might run into in the restaurant."

"Then we'll order room service."

On the way through the lobby, they were intercepted by Alison and Allen.

"There they are. All packed and ready to go?"

"Not quite," answered Johnathan.

"Wait, what? Where are we going?" asked Caroline.

"Well, that all depends on what you want, dear. We may as well use the villas though, come what may, they aren't refundable on such short notice," answered Alison with a small laugh. "And am I ready to stay somewhere decent! It's been great, don't get me wrong, Caroline, a wonderful yoga retreat. But it will feel good to stay somewhere with a bit more luxury."

"Don't mind her," Allen winked at Caroline. "Once you've stayed in five-star hotels, it's hard to stay anywhere else. Right darling?"

Caroline looked at Johnathan with confusion and shook her head. "So we're leaving? You canceled our wedding?"

"I didn't cancel the wedding."

"Well, then how can we leave?" asked Caroline.

"You didn't think we were doing the wedding here?" laughed Alison. "Wait. Is that what you thought? No, of course not, Caroline; if I organize a party, it will be done with style, with grace, with elegance. We're having the wedding at the Mulia. Now personally, I would have opted for the eternity chapel for the vows; I told Johnathan more than once that no one wants sand in their shoes and to sit out in the heat. But he did insist on it being on the beach. Really. On the beach. In the sand. Good heavens."

"The Mulia? What's that? I thought we were having a small wedding on the beach here and having dinner afterward on the patio together, you know, just your family and Mark."

Johnathan looked over at Caroline and grimaced. Had he forgotten to tell her that the wedding would be at a different location? He had said something, hadn't he?

"No dear. All the relatives and friends are coming," said Alison. "Didn't Johnathan give you the invitations? Who do you have arriving?"

Johnathan watched Caroline's face go stony as she crossed her arms over her chest. "No one."

Johnathan rushed in to explain that Caroline's best friends Annie and Daniel couldn't leave their bakery to fly to Bali for the wedding, and Mark couldn't afford the trip. Even Adrienne, Caroline's employee and beloved friend, couldn't make the wedding because she was eight months pregnant. Caroline had no family since her Grandma died.

"Good heavens child. Well, that explains your choice of bridesmaids. Why else would you select Johnathan's ex-girlfriend as one?"

"I didn't," said Caroline.

Johnathan experienced a rush of guilt as he realized that Caroline would have no friends and no family at her own wedding except Mark and his wife. Why were they getting married in Bali?

Really, Johnathan reasoned, it wasn't his fault. When his mother had offered to help plan the wedding and pay for it, Caroline had been pleased. She had told Johnathan that she was so swamped at work that she would be super grateful to just need to show up on the day of the wedding and enjoy it all. Alison had even sent a designer to Caroline to make her a wedding dress.

Alison looked from Caroline to Johnathan and back to Caroline again. "Well, how can you not know? Johnathan?"

"It's not his fault. I was so sick all those mornings and had so much work to do; I was so exhausted that I probably didn't hear him properly on the phone this summer."

"About your own wedding?" Alison blinked rapidly. "It is peculiar, you not wanting to have a say on anything to do with any of it." Alison exchanged a look with Allen. "Perhaps you've decided to call it off?"

"No," declared Caroline instantly. "In fact, if you will wait here for ten more minutes?"

Johnathan watched as Caroline disappeared around the corner. He stood shifting from one foot to the other, not wanting to be left alone with his parents.

"What is going on, son?"

"Can you tell Caroline I will be right back too? I just need to grab something from my room."

Johnathan rushed back to his own hotel room and packed faster than he ever had before. Either they were getting married, or they weren't, but either way, he was ready to get out of this place.

The week had been torture. Caroline's refusal to tell him why she was staying in a separate room and avoiding being alone with him had been horrible. Then he had called off the wedding just as she had told him she was pregnant. To top it all off was the drama of his own brother humiliating his future wife and their rush to the hospital in fear of their baby's life. This hotel had no good memories for him except the day trips with his family.

Also, Johnathan reconsidered; he had ended up enjoying all the yoga on the beach, even the meditation sessions. Yes, the day tours had been exhilarating and fun. The waterfall tour day had been a highlight and perhaps one of the best days of his life to date; he'd never experienced his family being so loving to each other and having so much fun together. His Dad had even hugged him. It had been a week of high highs and low lows, he decided as he threw the last of his things in the bag and zipped it closed.

Grabbing his suitcase, he rushed back down to the lobby, surprised to see Caroline rolling her bag across the lobby with her head held high. She had changed out of her shorts and a baggy t-shirt. Caroline's hair was now braided down her back, and she had put on some light makeup, golden flip-flop sandals with a small heel, and a pretty soft pink floor-length dress with a long multicolored necklace. Her face broke into a big grin when she saw him.

"Great minds think alike. So. You ready to marry me, Mr. Arrozzini?"

Johnathan let go of his bag and pulled Caroline into his arms, bringing his lips softly to hers. "Yes," he said, pulling away, his heart beating faster in his chest as he looked down at her.

"Come on," Caroline said to him, and grabbing his hand, she led him back over to his parents.

"We are ready to go get married," declared Caroline. "Here's the prenuptial agreement you wanted. Signed and delivered." She handed the envelope over to Allen. "Note that I did make three small changes."

Allen crossed his arms over his chest. "What changes?" Caroline handed them the document with a bright smile. Alison moved closer to Allen on the sofa, her back still perfectly erect as she read over his shoulder.

Johnathan grabbed Caroline's hand and gave her a quizzical look. He was kicking himself for not reading the prenuptial before giving it to her. What had his parents cooked up? What changes had Caroline made? After another five minutes, Johnathan couldn't handle the anticipation anymore.

"Well? Are you happy or what?"

Both his parents shushed him and continued to read, every few moments looking at each other with strange expressions on their faces before returning their eyes to the document.

Johnathan's stomach was rumbling, all the drama and lack of food were making his head throb with pain, and he wanted nothing more than a cold beer, hot meal, a refreshing swim in a pool, and then a nap. He may have slept near ten hours, but he was still exhausted.

He decided he didn't care about what was in the prenuptial anymore, nor whether his parents were satisfied with Caroline's changes. He just wanted to leave.

"Are we getting out of this place or not? You two can read that on the drive over to the Mulias," declared Johnathan.

"Yes. Yes, let's go," answered his mother with a quiver in her voice. Johnathan jerked his eyes back from the people swimming outside in the pool. Alison took a pen from her purse and signed below Caroline's scrawl and then stood up and wrapped her arms around Caroline. Allen bent over and added his signature to the document as Alison hugged Caroline.

Johnathan barely heard his mom murmur, "thank you, Caroline."

Johnathan stood in shock. He hadn't seen his mother hug anyone outside the family this long, not even Ariana, and she had spent holidays and vacations with the family for years. What the hell was going on? This morning they hadn't wanted him to marry Caroline, and now Alison was hugging her?

Allen cleared his throat. "We may have been a bit hasty, with the finer details in here. We just wanted to protect Johnathan. I'm sure you understand."

"And didn't want to lose him," added Alison as she pulled her arms away at last.

"Okay, give me that," Johnathan said as he grabbed the document out of his father's hands. "I need to read this."

"You mean you haven't read it?" asked Allen. "Son." Allen shook his head.

Johnathan waved his hand at him, trying to read, but Caroline gently tugged the paper away from him. "You can read it after we get to wherever we're going, and you've had something to eat. You haven't eaten in over twenty-four hours now."

"Johnathan, why ever not? We can go to the restaurant here."

"No, the sooner we get out of this place, the better I'll feel," answered Johnathan.

# CHAPTER 6

Johnathan insisted on pulling back out the prenuptial agreement on the way to the new hotel. The steam and heat began to build within him while reading the first few lines. The prenuptial was insane. Not only did it preclude Caroline from receiving any of his current wealth in the event of a divorce, but it also prevented her from accessing any of the money he would earn during their marriage.

If they divorced for any reason, then she would walk away with nothing. Caroline had changed this sentence to read, 'In the event of a divorce, for any reason, Caroline will forfeit all rights to any wealth acquired previous or during the marriage except for gifts given during the course of the marriage, such as anniversary and mother's day presents.'

To add gas to the fire, the document also required her to live in New York. Here Caroline had amended the line to read, 'to live in New York three weeks per year' and added two more lines. The first was that Johnathan would have no access to any of Caroline's current or future wealth in the event of a divorce. The second was that any and all of Caroline and Johnathan's children would be under the guardianship and care of Alison and Allen Arrozzini in the event of their deaths.

Johnathan looked at the bottom of the page at the three signatures, panting like a bull ready to charge a waving red flag. Caroline held out a pen in front of his face.

"Are you crazy? Why did you sign this? What are you doing?"

"I don't need your money, Johnathan. I make my own," she shrugged.

"I can even see you forfeiting the money made before our marriage, but all money earned during the marriage? That's insane, Caroline."

Caroline grabbed the document and tugged gently. He resisted. "Johnathan, give me the papers."

With a growl, he let go. "I do not agree to this. It's nuts. We're not living in New York three weeks a year just because my parents are controlling and manipulative."

"And they're your parents," Caroline finished his sentence. "You love them. Listen, they are who they are. Who cares if they like me? Who cares about the money? We've found each other. We're having a baby. We have more than enough of everything we could possibly want, and if we lose it all, well, we could just start over. Together."

"Well, I think it's time I broke away from being a piece in their game and start living my own life. Without them."

Caroline placed a hand on Johnathan's shoulder and held it there for a minute, looking into his eyes. The silence settled in, hot and pulsating with his anger. Johnathan let out a sigh and looked out the window. Some women dressed in bright colors caught his eye, each carrying a bowl on their head filled with fruit.

"I wonder sometimes, you know," Caroline said in a soft voice. "What it would be like to have parents who fight to protect me, who want desperately to be near me, who want my dreams to come true." Caroline let her hand fall back into her lap and looked out the window. "Even if they did drive me crazy with antics like this."

Johnathan looked at Caroline's profile and let out a sigh. "I'm your family now, Caroline. And believe me, you're better off not having parents like mine, controlling and manipulating your life at every step."

"Okay, first of all, it seems to me that you're good at getting what you want in the end. You did study architecture. They didn't want that. You did start a design and building company with your brother, which they didn't want for either of you. Did they cut you off from financial support then? No. They even helped you find additional investors since you had trouble finding them on your own after three? Or was it four failed businesses?"

Johnathan tilted his head, considering. She wasn't wrong.

"I was in New York with all of you. Remember? You love them. We had so much fun together at those dinners. They'll come around back to how they were this past spring. They're full of fear of losing you. It will be okay. And you know what? Part of you doesn't want to leave New York, at least not forever. Why be extreme, all or nothing? We can go live in their world for a few weeks of the year. I can work from anywhere."

Johnathan smiled, his shoulders relaxing down away from his ears. "What did I do in a past life to deserve you?"

Caroline laughed out loud. "You don't believe in all that."

Johnathan grinned back. "Nice touch, by the way, giving our kids to them in the event of our deaths. That really got them."

"Yeah, no," Caroline's smile faltered. "That was for me more than for them. I want to know they have someone to love them if something happens to us. They would, wouldn't they?"

Johnathan nodded. "They would, Caroline. They would love them in their crazy way."

Caroline rubbed her hand over her still flat belly and closed her eyes. Johnathan leaned over and put his arms around her, kissing her cheek and closing his eyes.

"I think we're going to need a vacation from our vacation. I'm exhausted," Johnathan said.

"Speak for yourself, dude. I've been either working on my laptop, teaching yoga classes, or throwing up in my bathroom all week. I haven't had a vacation except for yesterday."

"Who's fault is that? You missed out on some amazing day tours this week."

"With Daniel? I'm so sorry I missed out," smiled Caroline. "Forget all that. The next week I am completely one hundred percent on holiday. The yoga retreat came to a successful close, and I have placed my business in trustworthy hands while I enjoy my honeymoon in Bali."

"We're not having a honeymoon in Bali," Johnathan said as he shook his head. "Have you listened to anything I've told you on the phone the past few weeks?"

Caroline turned to look at him with big innocent eyes. "Yes?"

"Caroline. Where are we going for our honeymoon?"

"Back home?"

"Switzerland."

"Switzerland? I would have remembered you mentioning Switzerland."

Johnathan let out a sigh of exasperation. "You told me you've always wanted to go hiking in the Swiss Alps. Remember? And I told you, okay honey, we'll do that for our honeymoon."

Caroline's mouth dropped open. "Really? Really we're going to Switzerland? Right after we get married? Straight to Switzerland?"

"Yes, and we'll finish with some days in Paris. I've always wanted to spend my honeymoon in Paris. Now we'll both get what we want."

"Paris," breathed out Caroline as the car pulled to a stop. "Bali, Switzerland, and then Paris. I'd never traveled out of the country until this week, not even to Canada or Mexico. Wow."

Johnathan ran around the car and helped Caroline out. They stood, gazing at the resort entrance as Alison and Allen climbed out of the car behind them.

"Well, what are you waiting for? We're late. I already called ahead to the spa to reschedule your missed treatments. They didn't know how to squeeze in a massage, facial, manicure, pedicure, hair styling, and makeup in just two hours, but I convinced them. So let's go, Caroline. No time to waste. And you," she paused and kissed Johnathan on the cheek, "I have a massage booked for you and someone to do a facial and clean shave. You're looking scruffy, son. I expect you to look your best tonight. Now, say good-bye to your future wife. Next time you see her, she will be on her way down the aisle to you."

Johnathan pulled Caroline into his arms. He could feel her heart hammering in her chest.

"Okay, let's go, you two; we're late," declared Alison.

Johnathan entered the lobby behind Alison, Caroline, and Allen. Within minutes he was escorted to his villa and shown around by his dedicated butler. He was just kicking off his sandals and stepping into his private infinity pool when he heard a voice that made his skin crawl.

"Brother, it's the big day. How are you feeling?"

Johnathan turned around. "Daniel. Get the hell out."

"Is that how you talk to your best man?" Daniel strutted into the room with two of Johnathan's friends and groomsmen behind him.

"Get out." Johnathan climbed out of the pool and stood face to face with his brother. "Change of plans. I don't need a best man or anyone standing with me at the top of the aisle today."

"Mom will not be pleased," answered Daniel. "She'll have your head. Just wait until I talk to her."

"Go ahead, Daniel. Or do what you want. You want to stand there and pretend? Go for it. But we're done. The friendship. The partnership. All of it. It's over."

"You need me," Daniel answered, slipping his hands in his short pockets and rocking back on his heels.

"The hell I do. We're done. I would start looking for a new partner and a new venture. Our business is about to go to the highest bidder."

"I'll never sell," shrugged Daniel.

"Well, then get ready for a new boss because I'm selling my controlling share of the company." Johnathan took a breath and consciously forced himself to relax his hands, which had clenched into fists by his sides.

"Johnathan, Johnathan, Johnathan, why get so upset over some nobody getting her panties in a twist over some harmless jokes? You know, I think Mom's right. She's probably just after your money. Perhaps you want to reconsider and find someone of a certain class to marry. I can go and inform everyone the marriage is off. It's all part of the best man service," said Daniel.

Johnathan rolled his head around, loosening the tension building in his neck. He turned his back to Daniel and gazed out at the view of the ocean. Johnathan decided that he didn't need to give his power away anymore. He wasn't going to rise to Daniel's baiting, as he always had.

"Or is this all about Ariana? I knew that would get under your skin. That's why I kept it a secret for so long. I knew you couldn't stand to see the woman you love marrying me, having my babies, being in the top tier of the social scene."

Johnathan could feel his shoulders settling down away from his ears, his skin body softening, and his pulse rate slowing. Matilda said Daniel was the favorite, but deep down, they all knew the truth. Johnathan knew he was the favorite, and not just of his parents. He was the quiet, calm, and reliable solid center in the midst of the entire family; Johnathan could see that now as if a dark pair of glasses had been pulled from his eyes.

Jonathan's passion for architecture was the bedrock of their company. Why had Matilda gone on her world tour? Johnathan had made a few off-hand remarks that getting away from the New York social scene could do her good, help her grow up, settle her into more sustainable happiness.

Who had stopped his father from making a mistake with the twenty-year younger socialite? Who had guided his mother into a detox program when two daily glasses of wine had become four?

Johnathan gazed out at the waves, and a smile came to his face. Here he had thought his brother was the beloved, charismatic golden boy his parents favored. He had envied his sister's flare, her ability to talk to anyone and hold the attention of everyone in a room. Suddenly, he didn't feel inferior, nor superior to either of them; he didn't see the sense of being confined to the pre-ordained role of the reserved deep-thinker who loyally supported everyone's drama at his own cost.

Yes, he decided, he would love them all no matter what, despite their flaws. He just wasn't going to be a pawn in their drama games anymore.

Johnathan felt a hand on his back. "Hey man," Brad spoke up. "Sorry about last night. I hope the wedding's great. Would you prefer some time alone and we see you at the altar? We'll give you some time to work things out with your brother."

Johnathan nodded.

"Looking forward to tonight," spoke up Dylan. "I'll see you beach side."

Johnathan shook their hands and pulled them in for one-armed hugs. A young man entered through the door as his friends left the villa.

"I'm here for the facial and shave?"

"Hold on just one minute, would you? Take a seat," gestured Johnathan toward the sitting area inside. He watched as the man settled onto the sofa, then returned outside by the pool. He slid his hands into his pockets, a smile floating up from his mouth to reach his eyes as he turned to look at his brother.

All at once, the entire situation was comical, and he burst into laughter. Here they were, in paradise together, his wedding was in less than two hours in a luxury resort in Bali, and he was fighting with his brother. He had spent the morning in anguish about his parents' manipulation, efforts to control him, and insistence they knew what was best for him better than he did. It hadn't been about him at all.

"It's all a game," he laughed. "It's all a game, Daniel. Don't you see?"

"It's a game I'm willing to play. If you think you can take my company away from me, push me down under the thumb of someone else, then you're in for a nasty surprise." Daniel's nostril's flared as he leaned forward, his jaw clenched. "You can't put your share up for sale. Please, Johnathan, I'm begging you. You don't know the high stakes and what could happen. I wish I could tell you everything." Johnathan watched Daniel's facial expression completely change. A mix of terror and tenderness played across Daniel's face as he looked at Johnathan.

"Tell me what?"

Daniel turned away, shaking his head as if pulling himself together, and Johnathan thought perhaps Daniel, like he had, was thinking about all their employees' well-being and livelihoods. Something in Johnathan shifted, and he softened. One way or another, Johnathan was walking away from the business. An internal voice, fainter before, but now insistent, insisted that he walk away from the company and start over in California.

Johnathan grabbed Daniel gently by the shoulders and looked into his brother's eyes.

"Have it. Have it all, Daniel. Here," Johnathan strolled inside to his laptop bag, pulled out a paper, and quickly wrote out a note, signing and dating it. He returned outside and handed the paper to Daniel.

"The company is now yours. I am gifting it to you and walking away." Johnathan threw his arms up in the air. "I am now a free man. Good luck with finishing that project in Huaxi Village in China. I'll send over my progress so far, and you can find someone to take over that and, well, all my projects. Now, if you will excuse me, I'm getting married soon, and I want a swim and a shower after my facial and shave."

Daniel picked up the note and held it in his hand. "You think this is funny? You know this isn't legitimate. We need a witness."

"Great, call up Dad or Brad to run over. They can sign it too."

"You're making the right decision," said Daniel.

Within minutes Brad came back in through the door, and they all signed the document.

"Okay, well, I'll see you at the top of the aisle then, brother."

"No way in hell, Daniel. Either you go and grovel for forgiveness from my future wife, or you don't come within twenty feet of either of us for the rest of the day," said Johnathan. "Now get out."

Daniel and Brad left, Johnathan enjoyed his facial and shave, and then, at last, he was alone.

Johnathan stripped off all his clothes and jumped into the infinity pool naked. He enjoyed the soothing sensation of the cold water against his skin as he glided from one side of the pool to the other. Johnathan waited for loss or any kind of emotion to surface over giving away his company.

To Johnathan's surprise, all he experienced was a relief.

# CHAPTER 7

Johnathan took a rain shower outside on the deck in an alcove surrounded by bamboo with the sound of the ocean waves and tropical birds calling around him. After eating the lunch delivered to his room, Johnathan was ready to put on his tux. He wasn't sure if Daniel would be waiting for him on the beach or not, and it didn't bother him.

Johnathan wandered toward the lobby and asked for directions to his own wedding, which he found amusing. He followed the guide down the steps and through the gardens. When he arrived at the back of the garden overlooking the beach, he stopped and thanked the young woman, insisting she had led him far enough.

Johnathan wanted a minute to take it in the sweeping view of the green lawns and palm trees down to the beach, where his mother had chosen a smooth white carpet to be placed underneath a latticework of cherry blossom tree branches covered in white and pink flowers. At the top of the aisle stood two cherry trees in full bloom, standing close enough together to create an arch-like feel.

"Do you like it?"

Johnathan turned to see his mother and father behind him.

"Your first date was walking under the cherry blossoms. I remembered. It was a fortune to find cherry trees in blossom and import them from Meghalaya this time of year, but worth it, I think."

"It's spectacular, Mom. Thank you," Johnathan leaned in and kissed her cheek.

"Ready for this son?" Allen clapped his hand on his son's back and looked out at the guests starting to take their seats in the white chairs. "Time to go and greet our guests. Where is your brother?"

"Behind you."

Daniel strode forward, his hands thrust into his pockets, his mouth in a thin line. "Though I would be joining you in the crowd instead of at the altar by his side."

"What's all this," declared Alison. "Don't tell me you two are still fighting. Now don't be silly. Makeup, and let's go and have a wonderful wedding."

A smirk twisted the corners of Daniel's face. "Sorry."

"There now. It's all settled. Let's go say hello to everyone," Alison said as she wrapped her arm through Johnathan's and looked out at the beach.

"No," answered Johnathan calmly, refusing to be pulled forward by his mother. "I expect a real apology and for you to go and ask my bride for forgiveness."

"Really, Johnathan, people are beginning to stare. They'll wonder what all the fuss is about back here. Let's go. He said he was sorry."

"No," Johnathan looked at his mother, his voice completely relaxed, his breathing slow. "He didn't apologize to Caroline."

"I thought you wanted me to stay twenty feet away from both of you?"

Alison looked from Johnathan to Daniel, then back to Johnathan. "Allen?" Alison turned to her husband.

"Now Johnathan, I'll admit that Daniel took it too far yesterday; it was in terrible taste. Yet here we are, on your

71

wedding day. Isn't that what is important? Enjoying the wedding? Let's put it all behind us now."

"No. What he did was not just in bad taste. It was vicious," said Johnathan while slipping his hands in his pockets. "Caroline is pregnant. When she tried to jump from her chair and flee the humiliation, she crashed hard to the floor. Do you remember? We spent hours worried about the safety of our baby last night at the hospital until we could get her checked out."

Alison's jaw dropped. "Caroline is pregnant?. How awful. How utterly awful. Well, that's why she's been running away from us all week. Morning sickness."

"It's all making sense now," laughed Daniel. "You're marrying this nobody because you knocked her up. It's exactly what I thought! You always were too good for your own good."

Johnathan looked from his mother to his father and then at Daniel.

"Daniel, that is quite enough," Alison smoothed the sides of her teal dress down.

Allen turned to face Daniel while crossing his arms over his chest. "Apologize, Daniel. We need to tend to our guests."

"Oh, come on," Daniel shook his head. "You two are cowards; you as much as admitted you feel the same way I do. The woman isn't one of us. Didn't you say Caroline has neither the grace nor elegance necessary to be Johnathan's wife, Mom? Dad, you commented minutes ago on the veranda that Caroline doesn't have the social finesse to entertain business clients and host charity events."

Alison circled her diamond bracelet around her wrist as Allen's smile tightened into a thin-lipped grimace.

Allen's jaw tightened. "I recall a much different conversation on the veranda, and it involved you and me and the promise we both made."

Johnathan laughed out loud, making both his parents startle and look up at him. There was no fighting Daniel. The effort was futile. He just managed to find a new angle to create drama and feed in the resulting negative emotions. His brother could stand by him at the top of the aisle, apology or no apology. The breeze was warm and fragrant with the smell of the ocean and the tropical flowers nearby. He had found his person to travel through life with and was ready to start his life with her. Nothing else mattered.

"They're right, Daniel. You're right. Caroline may be a nobody without money, family, or fame, but I prefer her company to yours," said Johnathan.

"Yes, now, you're in love, and it's like being drugged. Are you quite sure you want to do this, son?" asked Alison. "We can stop it right now. You don't need to marry her because she's pregnant."

"That's not why I'm marrying her. Caroline is fun and playful. She's quiet and deep thinking, taking time to consider different perspectives, always willing to unravel things so she can come up with a new innovative position. She jumps into new things, trying them out, always learning by action and reflection. I feel uplifted, more energized, and relaxed all at the same time around her. I can be me. I can just be. We're getting married."

"Well, if you're that smitten with the woman, what are we waiting here for?" Daniel's lips lifted in a smile that didn't reach his eyes. "The wedding starts in twelve minutes."

"Are you going to ask my wife for forgiveness?"

Johnathan discovered that all at once, it wasn't a matter of him being right and Daniel wrong. He no longer felt the urge to play the victim nor make demands. His perspective expanded, taking in the panorama of where they stood on the lush green lawns flowing down to the blue of the ocean. Curious, that's what he was. Just curious. What would happen next?

Daniel hesitated, then lifted his shoulders and let them fall, running his fingers along his jawline. "Why not? A small price to pay," a gleam came into his eye, "for sole ownership of our company. Excuse me, I mean my company."

"Daniel, what on earth is he talking about?"

Allen took a step forward as Alison grabbed Johnathan's elbows.

"This isn't acceptable, Johnathan. Whatever game Daniel's playing, I will put a stop to it," insisted Alison.

"It's for the best, Alison," said Allen. "Let it be."

"Let it be? Are you insane?" Alison turned to glare at her husband. "What's gotten into all of you?"

Johnathan put his arm around his mother and guided her forward toward the wedding ceremony venue on the beach. "Everything is okay, Mom. Just relax and enjoy this beautiful wedding you created for us."

Alison started to say something, her body coiled, but then she snapped her mouth shut, and her body went lax in his arm. "I should, shouldn't I?"

"We all should." Allen looped his arm around Alison from the other side. As a threesome, they strode toward the sun beginning to set over the ocean, painting the sky in lavender, rose, and peach.

# CHAPTER 8

Moments later, Johnathan stood at the top of the aisle, watching Daniel and Matilda walk down the aisle together as pink cherry blossoms floated down from the trees overhead. Next, his cousin and Brad strolled down the aisle. Johnathan blinked twice, his jaw tightening as Ariana began the walk down the aisle on Dylan's arm.

What the hell was Ariana doing in the wedding? He couldn't imagine Caroline being thrilled at having his ex-girlfriend standing beside her at her wedding.

Matilda caught his eye and winked. It was as if she was reading his mind. She nodded and then shook her head and smiled. That must mean Caroline knew, and everything was okay. Johnathan winked back at his sister and blew out a big breath of air. Where was Caroline? Wasn't she supposed to follow right behind the others?

Motion at the back of the aisle stole his attention from the lawn where he had been searching for the appearance of his bride. Two staff members, one in front of Johnathan and the other at the other end of the chairs, picked up the aisle.

The two men in front of him gave a shove, and the two men at the back pulled the aisle as a segment up and away back out of sight. Johnathan smiled.

So Alison had worked out a way to let Caroline walk down on the sand as she'd wanted, Johnathan thought with a smile.

The two staff in front of Johnathan quickly hurried to join those at the back and carried the flooring away.

When Johnathan looked back, he let out a noise of surprise along with the guests. The solid white aisle the guests had walked down to take their seats was gone. There was no sand underneath. Instead, a turquoise container, empty except for some randomly placed rocks, stood in its place.

"Your shoes, sir," spoke up a voice beside him.

"My shoes? What?"

"Your shoes," insisted the man. "And please roll up your pants, sir."

"Go ahead, Daniel. It's a beach wedding, after all," called out his Mom from the front row.

Johnathan looked at his Mom in shock. He took off his black leather shoes, stuffed his socks inside, and handed them to the man waiting patiently at his side. He rolled up his pants.

As Johnathan straightened up, he noticed movement. The sight of Caroline walking barefoot down the green lawns toward him took his breath away.

He had expected her to be dressed in a floor-length gown. Instead, she sprung towards the beach in a strapless white wedding gown with a lace embroidered bodice cinched at the waist with a ribbon. The smooth silk organza floating flange skirt swished playfully just above her knees as she bound forward, holding her bouquet of pink peonies and cherry blossom branches. A diamond tiara sparkled in her hair, which was swept up in a messy bun with wisps of a few curls floating down toward her shoulders.

As Caroline approached the beach, the band began to play.

*One calm day. I saw you standing there. And in one breath I knew, I'm meant to flow to you.*

As the singer sang, *Like a stream will go, gliding to the sea, so will my love flow, darling we're meant to be,* water flowed into the aisle, splashing down and around the rocks, and cascaded down to fill the pool in front of him. His cousin's four-year-old twin little girls stood holding their baskets at the back of the aisle and giggling began to hop from one stone to the next while dropping in handfuls of pink rose petals and cherry blossoms. The crowd chuckled as one of the little girls ran out of flower petals and splashed down off the rock to try and scoop some petals out of the water to refill her basket.

*Take my heart, take all of me, for darling you're the start of my everything,* sang the band.

The other little girl noticed and splashed into the river to help her sister. Johnathan's cousin appeared, laughing, at the top of the aisle barefoot and urged the girls to continue their journey forward.

The girls ended with a splash in the pool in front of Johnathan. The two little girls, still giggling, each took one of his hands and pulled him forward. Understanding took hold of him, and the crowd laughed as he stepped into the water, which now reached up to just above his ankles and searched out his Mom. A radiant smile beamed back at him, and he laughed out loud. How had she come up with this?

Johnathan's eyes returned to Caroline.

*Take my heart, take all of me, for darling you're the start of my everything,* sang the band.

Just like the girls, Caroline stepped from one rock to the next down the river aisle towards him, the silky layers of her dress swishing around her long legs. Johnathan's eyes blurred, and he blinked.

*One calm day. I saw you standing there. And in one breath I knew, I'm meant to flow to you.*

Caroline splashed into the pool beside him at the bottom of the human-made river with a giggle, looking radiantly happy.

*Take my heart, take all of me, for darling I love you; you are my everything.*

Johnathan reached out his hand, and Caroline placed hers in his.

As Caroline and Johnathan turned to face the officiant, the sun was slipping towards the ocean. Johnathan looked over at Caroline, behind him at the splashing river, forward at the sun beginning to set over the ocean, then closed his eyes, trying to let the images be branded into his brain. He reopened his eyes as Caroline began her vows.

"Johnathan, you are my best friend. You are the love I always wanted. In your arms, I feel like I've come home, wrapped in the most incredible love. I know, down deep, that you are my soul mate, the one with whom I'm meant to go through the highs and lows of life. I feel a connection flowing between your heart and mine, an understanding, a knowing. You are both powerful and protective. I admire your creativity, passion, and loyalty to those you love. Today in front of all these people, I vow to cherish you, to support you in going after your dreams, and to fill your life with tenderness, playfulness, and love."

Caroline slipped the ring onto Johnathan's finger, and his mind went completely blank. What had he wanted to say?

Caroline squeezed his hands and beamed up at him. He looked into her eyes and took a deep breath.

"Caroline, I can't imagine living my life from this day forward without you. I love how much fun you are, so vibrant and playful, and at other times quiet and introspective. I've known you just a short time, and some may think we're fools to rush into marriage so quickly. But I love that about you, that you rush forward into trying new things with faith and hope. You told me the best way to learn is by doing. Well, I believe love is a verb, not a noun. I promise to act to show my love to you every day for the rest of my life. I promise to honor you, respect you, take care of you and fill your life with laughter and love."

Caroline had tears in her eyes as Johnathan slipped the ring onto her finger. The wedding officiant declared them married as Johnathan swept Caroline into his arms, leaned her backward in a grand romantic gesture to kiss her deeply. Taken by surprise, Caroline clutched at Johnathan, her feet slipped out from under her, and she reached out wildly in her panic and grabbed Ariana's arm to keep from falling. Ariana clutched Matilda's arm to keep from tipping forward into the pool, tittering precariously on her ridiculously high heels.

Johnathan fought to gain purchase on the slippery floor of the splashing pool beneath his feet and failed. The guests let out a gasp as he fell, which set off a lightning-fast chain reaction. Caroline pulled Ariana forward, who pulled Matilda off balance. The heels gave out beneath both women as they crumpled with a splash onto their bums in the water. Johnathan had managed to twist so that Caroline landed on top of him.

Heart racing, Johnathan took in the sight of both bridesmaids sitting in the swirling water next to him and his wife. His arms were still wrapped around his bride, preventing her from falling into the water.

The hem of Caroline's silky dress swirled around her legs in the water as she looked down at him with round eyes. Caroline tried to struggle to her feet, fighting to find purchase on the slippery floor. Daniel reached out a hand to first help Caroline, then offered a hand to help Johnathan to his feet.

Suppressing a grin, Johnathan took his hand and pulled hard as he stood up, pulling Daniel into the water. Daniel landed with a splash, took a deep breath, and pulled his jacket down as he looked down at his soaked shoes and trousers. Brad burst into laughter, as did Dylan.

"Oh, you think that's funny, do you?" Daniel growled. He reached out like a slingshot, grabbed both men by the arms, and pulled hard.

Brad and Dylan toppled into the water next to him. Johnathan stood next to the wedding officiator with his arms wrapped around his wife, laughing at his groomsmen standing in the water and the bridesmaids still trying to get to their feet.

Brad slid forward through the water and pulled Matilda into

his arms. She threw her arms around his neck and kissed him. Ariana slipped and fell again with an even bigger splash into the water. Her mascara was running, her hair a wet dripping mess; she slapped the water with both hands as her bouquet drifted past her.

Daniel snatched the bouquet up and reached out a hand to Ariana, who took it and exited the pool. Ariana attempted to storm off toward the hotel the moment she reached dry land, but Daniel held tight, pulled her in, and gently wiped the mascara away from under her eyes before pulling her into his arms.

Caroline pulled Johnathan forward back into the water and snatched up her bouquet. They splashed up the river aisle together, arm in arm, where Alison waited for them.

"Good heavens, I am sorry, what a fiasco, I thought it was brilliant, the river, I guess I didn't think it through, how slippery it would be. Of course, I didn't know Caroline's pregnant. I would never have had her hopping from stone to stone down the aisle. Can you imagine? What if she had slipped and fallen while walking down? Or God, I just thought, she has such marvelous balance from all the yoga, it would child's play, but now I see it was a colossal disaster."

Caroline threw her arms around Alison and hugged her tight. "I thought it was marvelous. I loved it, all of it: the river, the cherry trees, my bouquet. It was all romantic and perfect. I'll never forget it, Alison."

"You did good, Mom," Johnathan nodded with a smile at his Mom.

"Well," Alison placed a hand on her chest and took a deep breath. "Now I need to apologize to the bridal party. Ariana looked like she was out for murder on her way back toward the hotel."

Caroline gave a snort of suppressed laughter. Johnathan chuckled, and then even Alison couldn't help grinning before she pressed her lips together.

"You two head up to the hotel to freshen up in your villa, and I will be sure to send some champagne. Oh, Caroline, I will be sure they send your shoes and dress as well."

"I can't go barefoot to the reception?"

"Oh, good heavens no. No, no, Caroline, we talked about this, and you agreed."

Caroline giggled and placed a hand on Alison's arm. "I'm just teasing you, Alison. I'll follow all your instructions."

Johnathan held out his arm, and Caroline wrapped hers through it. "Instructions?" he asked as they started walking back up to the hotel.

"She wrote me a list," Caroline said. "I'm sure she will send it over with the dress. And the shoes."

"A dress?"

"Yes, there's a second dress for the reception. She tolerated the dress I picked out and bought for the ceremony but insisted on buying me a dress from Vera Wang for the reception and fancy shoes."

Much to Johnathan's disappointment, there was more than champagne and shoes awaiting them in the Villa. Caroline had sent over someone from the spa to retouch Caroline's makeup and hair and help her put on the designer wedding dress.

Johnathan allowed himself to be shooed out of the bedroom with exasperation while his wife changed and got ready. He slipped on a new pair of pants, new socks and shoes, and then sat down to sip a glass of champagne. Johnathan grew impatient waiting for his wife on a sofa overlooking the infinity pool, private gardens, and ocean waves below him. He'd loved the short playful wedding dress and resented his mother for interfering and insisting on controlling everything and everyone around her. Why on earth was she making Caroline put on some dress she hadn't even picked out for herself? Who needed two wedding dresses?

The woman from the spa came out of the bedroom and announced that her work was done and Caroline would be out shortly. Johnathan tipped her and scooted forward on the sofa, his elbows on his knees.

"Caroline? The golf cart is here to take us to the reception."

"I'm coming," she called back.

She pushed the door open and walked toward him in a white floor-length mermaid dress with a lace overlay that rose to a straight line just below her neck. The dress hugged in tight at her waist, showing off her curves in a sexy way. Johnathan was secretly relieved that she wasn't in a cupcake pouf wedding dress, nor did she have a long tail on her dress. Caroline looked elegant, glamorous, and tasteful, just the things his mother valued most.

Johnathan rose to his feet. "You look, glamorous honey. Here, let me pour you a glass of champagne to drink together on the way."

"No, I'd better not," Caroline smiled at him.

"Oh, of course not. I forgot for a moment. You're pregnant. A juice then?"

"In this dress? Let's get me in one piece to the wedding reception, and then I'll drink something."

"Okay," nodded Johnathan. Let's go."

Caroline turned and walked in front of him toward the door, and Johnathan's eyes widened. The dress was entirely backless, the button at the back of the neck sweeping open in a smooth oval that extended down to just above her bum.

Caroline looked back at him over her shoulder. "I love the dress."

"No complaints from back here," agreed Johnathan. Taking her hand, he helped her into the golf cart.

# CHAPTER 9

Johnathan paused before entering the wedding reception and pulled Caroline in for a quick kiss. He took a deep breath and let it out. If it were up to him, he would order room service and savor having his new wife all to himself. As if reading his thoughts, Caroline squeezed his hand.

"Only a few hours to the honeymoon."

They both stepped into the room and looked past the guests beginning to take their seats at the view through the large windows and the ocean beyond.

Alison rushed forward. "There you two are. Didn't it turn out lovely?"

Johnathan took in the candlelight's soft glow on the tables, the turquoise plates, and the restrained and elegant Ikebana Japanese floral arrangements. In the center of each table, a turquoise vase held a single cherry blossom branch. Two smaller white vases had been placed next to the cherry blossom branch, each containing nothing but a tree branch with bright green leaves just beginning to unfurl.

"Each cherry branch is a different color." Caroline's eyes swept the room. "I love it."

"Yes, did you know there are over six hundred different cherry variations? I had no idea," Alison turned to look at her handy work, placing her hands on her hips.

"I wasn't expecting something so restrained from you," Johnathan grinned.

"Ah, well, you haven't seen the after-dinner venue. I did indulge there in some arrangements featuring over two hundred branches of cherry blossoms."

Caroline laughed out loud. "There's another room to go to after this?"

"Well, of course. We need a dance floor. How could you have your first dance as a married couple? What kind of wedding would that be? We could have set up the dinner in there, of course, but I thought it's a pity to be in a windowless room all evening when there's a view like this to enjoy."

"What's going on here?" Allen said as he approached them. "Let's have a toast and start dinner. I'm starving."

"Yes, yes. I lost my head. We must take care of our guests. Go on, you two, back out the door, and we will properly introduce the arrival of the couple."

Johnathan began to protest and gave in as Caroline tugged on his hand. They stepped back out the door and immediately back through it as they heard Allen's voice magnified by a microphone announcing their arrival.

Alison escorted them to their table, and Johnathan settled into his chair next to Caroline with an internal sigh of relief.

Alison had sat Adam directly next to Caroline, so she had a beloved person next to her. Adam's wife, Josie, sat across from Adam. Sitting beside Adam and Josie were Daniel and Ariana.

Johnathan was relieved to have Brad placed to his right. Matilda sat across from Brad, intently talking to their cousin in hushed tones while Dylan took up the conversation with Brad. Johnathan accepted a champagne glass as his Dad pulled out the chair for Alison to sit across from him and Caroline.

"Well, son, I hope you're hungry."

Johnathan looked across the table at his father and nodded,

but before he could respond, he heard his brother's voice.

"It's time for me to give the best man's toast. First, I would like to thank you for traveling here for this auspicious occasion on behalf of my family. We are honored and delighted to have you here to celebrate the wedding of my brother to Caroline."

Caroline attempted to hold Johnathan's hand under the table, but it was clenched in a fist. She hit his hand with hers. Distracted for a moment, he looked down, blinked, then allowed her fingers to intertwine with his own.

"Now it's true that Johnathan has followed me everywhere I've gone since he was a little kid. He even followed me to college at Columbia, even if he insists it was because the architecture program is one of the best in the country. He even refused to move into the dorms and instead into my apartment. Most of you know we lived together up until just a little over two years ago. When I decided to open my own business, it came as no surprise to anyone that Johnathan joined me as my partner. Sure, it took a couple of tries to get it right. For anyone who invested with us on those first failed attempts, well, drinks are on me tomorrow poolside."

Johnathan hardly heard the crowd laugh around them. Any moment now, he thought, Daniel is going to blow everything up, like he always does. Why were his parents allowing Daniel to give another speech?

"We shared endless twelve to fourteen-hour workdays in the early years of our business. Now we have built up a successful multi-million-dollar architecture and real-estate company. I couldn't have done it without the determination, resilience, passion, and creativity of the lucky groom. Johnathan, there is no one else like you. Thank you for your loyalty, love, and dedication to not only our business and family but to me as your brother. I wish you and Caroline an abundance of wealth, success, and happiness together. Words can't express my gratitude to you for your gift to me of your half of our company as you set off on into new, uncharted territories on your new adventure with your beautiful bride at your side. Here's to the beautiful couple." Daniel raised his glass, and everyone began to clap but Allen and Alison.

"What kind of game is your brother playing now?" muttered Allen. "We agreed to keep Johnathan leaving the company a secret."

"Now, Allen, let's not ruin the lovely dinner that's on its way out to us. I thought it was a lovely speech." Alison leaned back as the waiter placed the first course in front of her. "We can straighten this all out tomorrow, whatever it is. Tonight we enjoy ourselves."

Allen looked over at Alison and nodded.

Caroline leaned in close to Johnathan's ear. "What did you do? You didn't give your company up?"

Johnathan just nodded and then reached out to take a sip of the white wine the server had poured for him to go with the first course.

"Don't make any hasty decisions. I don't want you to do anything you will regret because your brother has triggered you," whispered Caroline.

Johnathan smiled at his wife in response. "Let's focus on our new grand adventure, starting with the honeymoon. Did you pack hiking shoes?"

# CHAPTER 10

After dinner, Johnathan and Caroline rose to cut the multi-tiered cake iced in white with a few sugar cherry blossoms, the only decoration. Caroline and Johnathan held the knife together as they sliced it into the cake. Caroline inhaled as they pulled out the first piece and placed it on a plate. The inside of the cake was a rainbow, each of the six layers a different color.

"I love it," breathed out Caroline. "How fun and not at all like your mother."

"But very much like what you would like," spoke up Alison beside them.

Johnathan scooped a bite of the cake up with the fork and held it out for Caroline to taste.

"It tastes divine. Here try some."

Johnathan half expected Caroline to smash some of the cake into his mouth with her fingers, but she didn't. Instead, she lifted the fork to his mouth. Caroline cut another piece of cake, carried it back to the table with her, and then pulled at his sleeve, gesturing at the tiered tea trays the waiters placed on each table containing miniature pastries petite-fours, macaroons, strawberry tartlets, and chocolates.

After espressos and coffees, some of the party began to drift outside to breathe fresh air. Caroline joined Johnathan outside on the terrace under the starlight for only a few moments before Matilda informed everyone it was time to go dance. Half the crowd ignored her announcement and continued to sip their after-dinner drinks and chat in small groups.

Matilda and Daniel moved around the terrace to usher people inside. When everyone had disappeared, Johnathan pulled Caroline in close for a kiss, his hands sliding up and down the bare skin of her back.

"Come on, you two. Time for your first dance," insisted Matilda and urged them to follow her inside.

Despite not having any practice dancing together, they glided smoothly around the floor to the band playing "Falling Like the Stars." He had taken countless dancing lessons growing up. He had hated the experience but now silently thanked his mother for insisting he learns to dance.

Caroline looked up and almost stopped dancing.

" Is that James Arthur is up on stage singing this song? Is that possible, Johnathan?"

Johnathan nodded with a grin. In the middle of the song, cherry blossoms started falling from overhead onto the dance floor. Caroline's smile in response was breathtaking. When the dance ended, Johnathan pulled Caroline in for a soft, quick kiss, and then she giggled as a hip hop song came next.

An hour of dancing later, Caroline insisted she was fine, but Johnathan saw the exhaustion in her eyes. Grabbing her hand, he led her away from the dance floor and straight over to his parents.

"It was the most beautiful wedding Alison, thank you," exclaimed Caroline and threw her arms around her new mother-in-law.

Alison patted Caroline on the shoulder awkwardly. "Of course. I'm so happy you liked it. Meanwhile, I am mortified. People will be talking about the entire wedding party falling into my raging river for weeks."

"I wouldn't have changed one moment of it," insisted Caroline with a grin as she released Alison. "You call me tomorrow, and we will straighten out whatever nonsense your brother is up to now."

"I'll talk to you after the honeymoon, Mom. I'm going phone and Internet free for a few days."

Allen reached out a hand. "Son. I will see you back in New York."

"Sure thing Dad. Thank you, Mom. Goodnight."

"Wait. You can't just leave. Everyone will want to see you off." Alison looked around. "We'll just announce you."

Johnathan reached out for his Mom's hand. "Please, Mom. Just let us go. The wedding has been perfect."

Alison nodded. "Okay. I love you, Johnathan."

"I love you too, Mom."

Johnathan leaned in, kissed his mother on the cheek, and then shook his father's hand before slipping out the door with Caroline and into the moonlight.

The wedding may have been perfect, but the day following was anything other than happy, at least for himself. They had gone for a refreshing nude swim in their private infinity pool their first morning as man and wife.

Johnathan had been just finishing his request for brunch to be delivered to their villa when they had been surprised by a knock on their door.

Johnathan hadn't been surprised to see his father standing on his doorstep. Luckily Caroline was in the bedroom for a quick ten-minute meditation. Johnathan had gotten rid of him by promising to meet him after lunch at the sky bar.

Johnathan had pushed all thoughts of Daniel and his parents out of his mind for the rest of the morning. He joined Caroline for brunch on the patio in the sunshine and then returned to the bedroom until lunchtime.

After a light lunch, it took some convincing to usher Caroline off to the spa for a facial, body scrub, pedicure, and manicure. Johnathan had just asked what would take a couple of hours and accepted all the spa receptionist's recommendations; his Dad had said they'd need time to work through some serious matters.

By the time Johnathan showed up at the sky bar overlooking the regal statues lining the turquoise pool and the ocean below, he was sweating. His heart had been palpitating irregularly every few beats, and he was regretting his choice to give away his share of the company the day before.

On the day of the wedding, it had been as if someone had pulled dark glasses away from his eyes. It had all seemed so clear, so blissfully obvious how he should act and what he should do. The day after the wedding, the dark glasses had returned. When his father settled down next to him and just looked at him in silence, Johnathan knew something was terribly wrong.

"What were you thinking in throwing away your life's work? Your company? Because some woman was humiliated? You're less of a man than I thought you were."

Johnathan sat looking at his father. He didn't know what to answer. What had been his reason for giving Daniel his majority share of their company?

"I was getting bored. It's time for a fresh start. If I can do it once, then I can do it again. On my terms. I'm ready to work alone, without a partner, build my own ship."

Johnathan didn't believe the words even as he said them. He hid his uncertainty from his father and purposefully took on an attitude and body position of nonchalance and relaxation. Allen leaned forward, resting his elbows on his knees.

"You made the right choice. We'll figure out a way to get you the investment capital to start whatever the hell you have in mind next when we can."

Johnathan stared at his father in surprise; he'd expected Allen to tell him he'd made a terrible mistake and plead with him to change his mind.

"I didn't want to bring a stranger into the company. Let Daniel run it. He's always wanted to be the top boss. Now he can have his chance. And I have enough capital without it."

"About that son. I have to tell you something." Allen paused and finished the rest of his drink in one go. "We aren't exactly liquid these days."

Johnathan waited for his father to continue.

"I may have invested the majority of our fund into some rising technology aerospace companies. There's an upside to double our money in as little as five years."

"That is insane. Why would you take such a risk? Have you talked to Brad about this?"

Allen shook his head, gritting his teeth. "He needn't know. Brad has a few million that I gave him to boost his investment fund and get new clients, but he's made some bad choices, and the fund is in trouble. Brad is certain he can turn things around, but it will take time. Brad has our name invested with him. We can't pull money from his fund now either. It would spook his other investors; it wouldn't be sending the right message."

Johnathan shrugged. "I have my trust fund."

"I may have leveraged the money in you kids' trust as well," answered Allen with a grimace.

"You took our money and invested it without talking to us?"

"Keep your voice down, Johnathan," said Allen while looking left and right if anyone was listening in to the conversation.

"I'll take the money I personally gave to Brad to invest out then," said Johnathan.

Allen shook his head, "it isn't a good idea. It will spook the other investors and cause his fund to collapse."

"So? So what? I need my money. I can take a loss on the investments," said Johnathan.

"You'd take a huge loss. I already talked to Brad," answered Allen. "I'm sorry, son. You need to be patient."

"So. I can? What? Start a new business with monopoly money?"

"You have a few vintage cars as well as the Lamborghini Veneno Roadster and the Bugatti Divo. Sell those. Don't you have some gold? Any properties?"

Johnathan leaned forward. "You aren't serious. Is this some kind of a joke?"

Johnathan looked around for his brother. He was probably over in a corner laughing it up at his expense right now.

"I wish it was a joke," answered Allen.

"Haven't you told us our entire lives that we'll never know what it's like to build something up from nothing, with no one backing us? Well, it looks like here's my chance."

"Don't be ridiculous. You don't have nothing, Johnathan," said Allen. "You have assets to sell, but it will take time, that's all. Be patient. Now do me a favor, son. Don't tell your mother about our lack of access to cash right now."

"Dad. You have to tell her. What if she starts giving away money to charity again, buying impressionist art, or something?"

Allen gritted his teeth, a furrow deepening between his eyes. "Of course I'll tell her. I wanted to let her relish the wedding. I'll speak with her as soon as we return home. Now get back to your honeymoon and relax. We'll talk more in a few days."

Johnathan's body shook as he walked back to their villa. No company. No trust fund. No investment portfolio to access. What was happening?

Caroline shook Johnathan awake as she pulled the eye mask off of his face. "Johnathan, you have to see this. Wake up."

Johnathan blinked his eyes against the light pouring into his eyes. He shook his head and focused his gaze on his new bride. "What's wrong?"

"Everything is right. That's the point. Look out the window at the sunrise over the Swiss Alps. Is that not the prettiest thing you've ever seen?"

Johnathan smiled and leaned back in his seat. The hostess walked by, and Johnathan ordered a flat white coffee with an extra shot of espresso. They hadn't even landed yet, and he had jet lag. Johnathan resolved to get a workout as soon as possible to counteract the time change and all the alcohol he had consumed the past two days.

"What is a flat white John?"

"No one calls me John."

"Can I be your exception?"

"No."

"What about Than? Can I call you that?" grinned Caroline.

"No."

"You're pretty grumpy for a man sitting in first class next to his bride and looking out at rolling green hills, mountain peaks, and a spectacular sunrise."

"But first coffee." Johnathan accepted the porcelain coffee cup gratefully from the hostess.

Caroline ordered a flat white as well and an orange juice.

As the last sips of coffee hit his system, Johnathan let out a sigh of contentment. The hostess brought them their breakfast and both of them another flat white coffee. Ignoring the food, Johnathan sipped his second cup of coffee first and watched Caroline. She had a child-like quality about her that he still found mesmerizing. She tried a little bit of each type of food in front of her, smiling with delight at her first taste of Swiss birchermüesli. Johnathan accepted a spoonful of the birchermüesli and shrugged.

"Not bad."

"Not bad? It's delicious. This is what I'm eating for breakfast from now on. Let's find out how to make it while we're here. Anyway, what's the plan once we land? Where are we going? Do I get to see Zürich?"

"You can see Zürich the night before we fly back to Paris. I've rented a car to drive us straight to St. Moritz."

"Is it nonrefundable?"

"What?"

"The car Johnathan. Can you get your money back? I'd love

to go by train. I've never been on a train before. And anyway, I get carsick even when I'm not pregnant. Though the morning sickness has disappeared."

"Maybe it was getting married that fixed the morning sickness? Gather your things love. We're a few minutes away from landing at the airport."

Caroline clapped her hands together and squirmed around in her seat. "I'm so excited."

"I can see that," Johnathan laughed. "Okay. You have yourself a deal. The train it is, but we're taking a private car to the hotel."

Johnathan took a deep breath of the fresh air as he stepped out of the private car that had driven them from St. Moritz to the Waldhaus hotel in Sils Maria. He looked up at the five-star Swiss hotel and smiled. His family had stayed in the hotel when Johnathan was twelve, and he had never forgotten the experience. He just hoped nothing had changed.

Caroline threw her arms around him, vibrating with excitement. "Look at this hotel. Smell that air. I was right about the train, wasn't I? Didn't you love it?"

Arm in arm, Johnathan ascended the steps with his wife. They stepped up to the reception and were asked to wait just a moment. The owner himself appeared behind the counter to welcome them to the family-owned hotel. Caroline wanted to explore the entire hotel, but Johnathan insisted they go up to their room first and then go down to the pool for a refreshing swim. When they walked in through the hotel room doors, Caroline ran to the series of windows to look out at the view.

Speechless for the first time in hours, Caroline looked out at the alpine peaks, the lake glimmering in the afternoon sun, and the clouds drifting through the valley. The rest of the day went by in a happy blur for Johnathan. First, they headed down to the terrace surrounded by pine trees swaying in the breeze for lunch, coffee, and cake. After lunch, Caroline begged Johnathan to go try out the spa with her. Caroline couldn't enjoy the sauna being pregnant but was delighted in the luxury pool area with the massage pool. Johnathan enjoyed time in the sauna to sweat out the toxins he'd accumulated in the past few days of celebration and misery and then rejoined his wife to announce it was time for their couple's massage.

After a nap, Caroline and Johnathan dressed up for dinner and descended to the dining room. Over dinner, they talked about the wedding, the yoga retreat, and all of the day tours Johnathan had experienced while Caroline had been battling morning sickness back at the resort. The food was delicious, the wine he chose interesting and complex, and the experience just as he had remembered as a boy. After dinner, Caroline heard music playing and pulled him into the bar where a trio was playing.

"It's like we've entered a different time," mused Caroline. "What a grand, charming hotel. How did you know about this place?"

"I came here on a ski holiday with my family when I was a boy." Johnathan swirled his drink in his glass, remembering how at peace he had felt during that trip. "I spent hours each evening before and after dinner in the library reading and sketching. I came across a stash of books on architecture and spent hours devouring them at the wooden desks. It's when I decided what I wanted to do when I grew up. Here. In this hotel." Johnathan looked around him at the old-world charm of the vaulted ceilings.

"Do you know, it reminds me of that movie, the Budapest Hotel, only this hotel is still in perfect condition," Caroline said as her eyes grew heavy with sleepiness. "I just can't get enough of the views. And it smells so good outside." Caroline's eyes drifted closed, and she snapped them open again.

"The views are spectacular, aren't they? I can't wait to take you out hiking tomorrow. Now I'm taking you up to bed. You're falling asleep sitting up."

"I'm fine," protested Caroline. "We had that long nap."

Johnathan winked at her in reply. "There wasn't much sleep happening during that nap."

Caroline smiled at him as he finished his drink and then helped her to her feet.

Johnathan tossed and turned in the night. At two in the morning, he gave up. Careful so as not to wake up Caroline, Johnathan threw on some clothes and left their hotel room.

He descended the stairs and sat starring at the empty lobby for a moment before turning and wandering toward the comfort of the library. It was just as he remembered it. The wooden floors, walls, and desks gave the room a warmth as he clicked on the light. He settled down in a chair, smoothing his hands over the desk as he let out a sigh.

Johnathan's mind continued to loop in spirals of self-recrimination and fear. He kept playing the conversation with his father through his over and over again. Johnathan had thought when he gave up his company that he was still a rich man. Now it felt as if he stood on a hill of mud, with the ground literally melting out from beneath him. What awaited him when he returned from his honeymoon?

# CHAPTER 11

Johnathan stood up and wandered over to the bookshelf. He didn't want to go to outside investors to start his new business; he'd learned the hard way with the first few failed businesses. It looked like he would be selling his cars to make a fresh start in California.

His office wouldn't be the all-white gleaming space with bright, vibrant accents that he had envisioned building. Instead, he would need to rent a space as is and level up once they became profitable. He'd done it once, hadn't he? He could do it again. He didn't need Daniel's charm to close big deals, as Daniel insisted. His work would speak for itself.

Johnathan pulled out the same architecture books he had looked at as a child. Turning the pages, he soon became soothed by the familiar words and photos. His eyes became heavy, and he stood up yawning, at last quieted enough to go back to bed.

In the morning, Johnathan dined alone for breakfast. Caroline felt sick due to the altitude change, and she asked that Johnathan leave her in peace for a few hours to sleep longer. The mountain air and late-night rambling in the hotel had given Johnathan a huge appetite. He ordered two picnic lunches to take with them on their hike and returned to the reading room with his laptop.

The first email he saw when he opened his laptop was from a colleague, including a link. Johnathan shook his head in dismay. Daniel had moved fast. The article in the Wall-street announced

Daniel's new sole ownership of their company. Johnathan groaned and shut his laptop again; he didn't understand what was going on with his family.

Why had his Dad insisted it would be horrible for Johnathan to sell his half of the company if Daniel was going to turn around and announce his sole ownership? None of the conversations he'd had with his family were making any sense. Had he made the wrong decision in signing over his half of the company? What had he been thinking?

Gazing out at the pine trees moving in the breeze outside the window, Johnathan took a deep breath in and let it out. Johnathan reminded himself that he was on his honeymoon. Johnathan decided that he would tackle the plan to start his new business when they returned home. He resolved that he would use this time as a digital detox and spend more time with his sketchpad and pencils dreaming up new designs.

Gritting his jaw, Johnathan reopened his laptop and wrote to his team explaining his decision to leave the company. He sent a few personal emails naming specific architects on his team as the new heads for the various projects he had been leading. The last email went to Daniel and his family, announcing that he was going off-line for the next ten days. He was finishing his email when Caroline found him.

"What a beautiful place to work," she whispered, glancing across the room and at a man typing away at his laptop at a desk by the window.

"Are you ready for our hike?"

"Yes. I just managed to grab a bowl of Bircher muesli as they were cleaning up the breakfast. I'm ready to go."

Johnathan looked Caroline over. "You're wearing your yoga clothes on the hike? Do you have a backpack? A water bottle? A rain jacket?"

"It looks warm and sunny outside."

Johnathan gathered up his things and left the library. "We're in the mountains, love. Unexpected showers are a real possibility."

"I didn't pack for a hiking holiday," Caroline answered as they took the elevator up to their room. "Because you kept it a surprise."

"Then you relax, and I will stroll down into town and buy you some things. I could use a new baseball hat anyway."

Johnathan left Caroline protesting in the door frame of the hotel room. He assured her she would have plenty of walking by the time they completed their hike and hurried down the stairs. Walking down the hill, Johnathan took a deep breath of air and quickened his pace. He didn't want to start hiking too late in the day. He had scheduled another massage for Caroline after the hike.

After a trip to two different sports stores, he climbed the back up to the Waldhaus perched on top of the hill overlooking the valley. After he packed their water bottles, lunches, and rain jackets into his backpack, he straightened up to see Caroline step out of the elevator.

Hand in hand, they stepped out of the hotel and turned left, following the road up the hill. A distant roaring reached their ears after a few minutes.

Caroline insisted on stopping for ten minutes to sit on the park bench and watch the waterfall crashing down. Johnathan urged her onward with the promise they could return. Following his map that the hotel owner had given him in the morning, he made a right onto an inclined road, and they began to climb their way toward the Muott' Ota.

In silence, they wound their way up above the tree line of the forest and looked at their first view of the two lakes sparkling in the sunshine below with Sils Maria nestled in between them. At the top of the Muott' Ota Caroline let out a sigh of relief and fell onto the blanket Johnathan laid out on the grass for them.

"Why was that hike so hard?" asked Caroline

Johnathan began to pull out the picnic lunches and search for his camera in his backpack. "Well, Sils Maria is already at around 1,800 meters. Up here, we climbed to 2,458 meters. You're also pregnant, which means that the high altitude could be affecting you more intensely."

"It's worth the view," smiled Caroline as she placed a berry in her mouth and grinned. "But you didn't pack enough food."

Johnathan laughed. "You've got your appetite back. There's a restaurant on the way back to the hotel. We can stop for a snack."

Johnathan looked out once last time on the lake plateau. He tried to point out the various alp peaks of Piz Duan, Lagrev, Julier, Güglia, and Corvatsch to Caroline, but she shrugged.

"I don't care what they're called. I like to soak up the beauty of this panorama view."

Holding out a hand after another few minutes, Johnathan needed to urge Caroline back to her feet. They crossed in silence over the top of the Muott' Ota and then began the gradual winding descent through the forest. Caroline stopped every few steps to admire the butterflies dancing among the wildflowers and rocks along the path. The beautiful hiking trail descended into Curtins in Val Fex, and they stepped onto the narrow paved road.

"Is that a glacier?" Caroline pointed behind her at the blue ice on the mountain peak at the end of the valley.

Johnathan nodded and took her hand. They walked along the road, listening to the river flowing through the valley down from the glacier. Caroline pulled Johnathan into a small mountain church next to the road. After taking in the frescoes inside, Caroline said she was ready for another break and more to eat.

Johnathan agreed, and they stopped at a hotel and settled at a table on the green lawn, looking up at the glacier. After some cake and coffee, Caroline was at last fortified and rested enough to talk.

"You're hiding something from me. Why couldn't you sleep in the night?"

Johnathan took a sip of his white beer and looked out at the glacier, avoiding eye contact. "It was just jet lag, love."

"What happened with your brother? Why did you send me off to the Spa the afternoon after our wedding? Anyway, what did you say to get him to come begging me to forgive him before our wedding?"

Johnathan's lips twisted to the right. He shrugged and took another sip of his beer. "I gave him my half of the company."

"You sold him your half of your business? Why?"

Johnathan let out a gust of air. "No. I gave it to him." Johnathan looked over at Caroline. She blinked, shook her head, then bit her lip.

"I'm sure you can change your mind."

"No. No, I had time to think while in Bali. I talked to this wise old dude. Do you remember that guy serving drinks in the bar?"

He shook his head and laughed. "You're pregnant. You weren't ever in the bar. We had a long talk. It made me realize I was ready for a change. I was scared as hell to do it. But yeah, ready. Ready to get light, you know? Start fresh in every way. With you," he added with a smile, taking her hand in both of his own.

He did not find Caroline's furrowed brow heartening. He released her hand and let his head roll forward toward his chest, trying to loosen the kinks in the back of his neck.

"Okay, so the truth is I have a feeling something strange is going on between my brother and my dad and our business, and I want no part of it."

"What do you mean?"

"I don't know," Johnathan shrugged. "But our conversations and the way Daniel was acting in Bali was insane. He isn't an ass, Caroline. I know he was acting like one, but he isn't. I don't know what the hell is going on with him."

Caroline sipped her lemonade and asked, "Was your Dad acting strange?"

"No. Dad's always like that, except he told me he made a risky investment with most of his money, which isn't like him. And he took our trust fund money as well to invest without asking. To top it all off, Brad seems to have made a mess of his hedge fund, and I can't get my money out."

"Does Matilda know?" asked Caroline.

"I'm sure," said Johnathan.

"I'm not sure she does. What if Brad is hiding it from her?"

Johnathan shook his head. "She would know if something was wrong real quick because she wouldn't have money to spend," said Johnathan. "She gave him most of her money to invest."

"Your ego isn't going to like you not being the head of a multi-million dollar successful company," commented Caroline. "Marriage is enough of a change, let alone moving across the country. Having everything in your life change at the same time, well, I don't know if that's a good idea."

"Well," Johnathan lifted his palms to the sky. "What's done is done."

"Also, I didn't want to tell you this while on the honeymoon, but we'll have to modify our living standards when we go home. Cash isn't readily available, and what I do have will need to go into my new startup."

Caroline shrugged. "You mean you'll need to modify your living standards. Mine will be the same." A grin spread on Caroline's face from ear to ear. "Let's see how tough you are. No more couple thousand-dollar suits, expensive meals out, and I don't know, what else do you splash out money on?"

"I may not be able to go skiing in Aspen this year," Johnathan mused.

"You were planning on leaving your super pregnant wife to go skiing?"

Johnathan shook his head. "That's right. I didn't think of that."

"Just teasing, honey. I'm not due until March, remember? Well, we will take it all one day at a time. You probably should start meditating every morning again. You know, to maintain some balance in the face of all the change?"

Johnathan groaned. "You're probably right. Ready to hike

back down to the hotel?"

"I'm exhausted. Oh Johnathan, look at the horse-drawn carriage."

Caroline walked over to admire the horses. The driver asked them if they were climbing in to ride down through the valley back into Sils Maria. Johnathan took one look at Caroline and agreed. They climbed up into the coach, and Caroline slid under his arm. He pulled her in tight, taking a deep breath. She smelled like strawberries.

Turning his face up to the sun, Johnathan let out a sigh and leaned back to enjoy the sound of the river and the bird song. Caroline kissed his neck and then snuggled closer as they passed by houses with quaint river stone-tiled roofs. By the time they passed the waterfall again near their hotel, Johnathan had needed to shake Caroline awake.

"It's been a perfect day, hasn't it, love?" she asked, sleep still thick in her voice. "Let's remember this day if things ever get hard, okay?"

Johnathan kissed the top of her head and agreed with a sinking suspicion that those hard times were soon to come.

# CHAPTER 12

"Paris is always a good idea," insisted Johnathan.

Caroline wasn't so sure. Johnathan had just spent half the morning trying to arrange for the sale of his cars and had difficulty getting anyone to buy at full price on short notice. He had decided to sell one at a lower price than he had wanted to free up cash but wasn't happy.

"We could just cancel Paris and save the money." Caroline grabbed his hand as they walked toward the lake glittering in the sunshine in front of them. "Our honeymoon could not have been more perfect. Yesterday's hike around the seven little lakes on the top of that alp was my favorite so far."

"You've said that every day," Johnathan laughed as he pulled Caroline in and wrapped his arm around her waist. You've also said that about every meal."

"Well, it's true. The food has been divine. I'm so thankful I don't feel like throwing up the whole damn day anymore. Just in time, right?"

Johnathan nodded, once again distracted by the thoughts swirling in his head on how to finance his new startup and how many people he should hire to begin. What kind of office should he rent? It would be better to buy, but he wanted to be on or near the beach, and he didn't think any commercial real-estate would be for sale. He made a mental note to contact a real estate agent as soon as they returned to the hotel. Or did they need to stay in the little beach front town?

"What if we moved somewhere else in California? Say somewhere near LA?"

Caroline shook her head. "Give it a try for one or two years with the traveling, and then we'll talk about it. I don't want to move while pregnant or with a brand new baby."

"It won't be easy to get new big clients in a little town on the Californian coast," commented Johnathan.

"I believe in you. Now, let's go hike this peninsula the waiter recommended at breakfast this morning. I'm ready for our picnic."

Johnathan didn't bring up the topic of the new business he wanted to build, his hesitation at living in her little town, or his refusal to answer any of the distressed texts his mother and sister had been sending him. The last thing he wanted was to have a storm cloud mar their honeymoon. Johnathan did his best to smile, laugh, and cuddle in all the right places for the rest of the week until they were boarding the plane to Paris.

"I know you're agitated. You can try and hide it, but I know."

Johnathan settled into his airline seat with a sigh. "I'm not in the mood to talk about it. We'll have plenty of time after the honeymoon to deal with it all. Right now, I want to enjoy flying to Paris with my new bride."

"Did I hear new bride?" asked the airline host. "Congratulations. Can I bring you some champagne?"

"Sure," Johnathan agreed.

"A cherry coke for me, please. In a champagne glass if possible."

"I thought you didn't drink soda," Johnathan commented as the host moved away.

"I'm craving it. A little won't hurt the baby. Right? You're right. I'll just go and catch him."

Caroline jumped out of her seat before Johnathan could respond. He wasn't worried about Caroline drinking a little soda. With amusement, he watched Caroline settle back into her seat and felt his phone buzzing in his pocket again.

"Aren't you ever going to answer it?" asked Caroline. "You can't outrun your family and everyone forever. Maybe if you talk to them for a few minutes, then they will leave us alone until we go home."

Johnathan pressed his lips together.

"At least look at the texts."

The host brought Johnathan his glass of champagne. He took a few sips, considering. At last, the curiosity was too much. He had spent a week not looking at any emails, texts, or incoming calls.

The vast majority of the texts were all from his mother, father, and sister, urging him to call them as soon as possible. The last few texts were panicked with rows of exclamation points.

Letting out a big sigh, Johnathan leaned back in his chair. What drama had the cooked up now? With his family, it was always something. Why couldn't they kick back and enjoy all that their luxury life had to offer? But no, it had never been like that for his parents. They had always resented not being able to keep up with their friends.

Some of his parent's friends had private jets; others had fancy yachts; one couple owned their own private golf course and resort in the Maldives. Why did his father always need to feel lesser than just because they had less money? It was never enough for Allen, and he was continually irritated at how much money Alison insisted on giving away to all her charity work.

"I made the right decision, walking away," mused Johnathan. "It's time to feel the real ground under my feet and feel as if everything is enough. Do you know what I mean? No more frantically working, pushing, wanting more and more. My family is intense; if you knew them, understood them, then I hate to think how you would feel."

Caroline shrugged. "There's nothing wrong with your family. There's a natural human inclination to have those same problems. Look at the gorgeous wedding they just planned and gifted us. It seems to me as if you are the one being ungrateful and always wanting more. You've been fussing over giving up your company and that lifestyle all week. I think you overestimated your ability to change."

"That's not true," Johnathan snapped back. "Anyway, you're my wife. You should be taking my side. You should think better of me than that. Look at what I'm doing for you, giving up everything in my life, just to make you happy."

Caroline let out a laugh of consternation. "For me? Are you? And taking your side against whom? Is there some competition or fight I don't know about yet? But then again, how would I, since you refuse to talk to me about what the hell is going on with you? Instead, I am dealing with your moody silences and introspection all week."

"I showed you a world-class honeymoon, and that's the thanks I get? I thought we had a week of a lifetime. Every day you acted were delighted and grateful. Maybe it's you who should tone down all the enthusiasm. Try acting less like an over-excited child bounding all over the place, clapping her hands, and act more like an adult."

Caroline closed her eyes and took a deep breath. She blew it out slowly, looked at him again, took her juice, and finished the rest of the contents.

"Johnathan. I am on your side. I had a dream week with you, and getting excited about things is who I am. Your family loves you. They are like most people I know in being self-involved and feeling like nothing is ever going quite enough. They do loving things for you all the time. And I am asking you if you will let me be on your team. Can you do that? Can you let me know what the hell is going on with you? I want to help."

Johnathan felt his body soften. "I'm used to handling things on my own."

"I noticed," laughed Caroline.

"Let's wait until we get to the hotel in Paris to talk it all through, okay? Not in the plane?"

Caroline nodded and handed him back his champagne glass.

# CHAPTER 13

Johnathan's phone rang as soon as he turned it back on in the Paris airport.

"Daniel. Stop calling me. I'm on my honeymoon."

"I want you to come back to New York today and sign away your half of the company."

"What's the hurry? Scared I'll change my mind?"

"You can't?"

"Is that so?"

"No."

"You must come, Johnathan. I wouldn't insist unless it were important. We're short on cash because of that China project, and if I don't get a new infusion of cash from investors, then we're done for."

"What do you mean we're done? We had our most profitable year to date."

"About that. I may have finessed the numbers a bit."

It was as if Johnathan had just swallowed an enormous ice cube. The cold stuck in his throat then slid down to the pit of his stomach.

"What did you do?"

"Nothing to cause worry. Nothing at all. Just get on back home, and come straight to the office. I'll have the attorney here and all the paperwork ready for you to sign," Daniel soothed.

Johnathan just couldn't believe what he was hearing. After all the times he had talked to Daniel about the importance of keeping costs low, avoiding excess, the importance of playing straight and true. What had he done? Or what was he planning to do? Johnathan didn't know, and he was done fighting his brother.

"I'll take the next plane out."

Johnathan ended the call and turned to his wife. "Caroline, I promise, I'll bring you back to Paris someday. Right now, we have to get back to New York immediately. I can't spend one day longer tied to that ass of a brother of mine."

"What's going on?" Caroline asked, her mouth full of a croissant.

"Hell if I know, darling. The point is that I don't want to know. I'm done playing babysitter for my brother. He can learn from his mistakes in the future. I'm out." Johnathan threw his hands up in disgust.

"Do we get to fly first-class home?"

"For the last time, babe. After this, all the cash I have is going into my new business."

"Fine by me. I have my own money." Caroline gave him a bright smile, but Johnathan didn't see it. He was already working with the airline representative to change their outbound flight.

### One year later

Johnathan rolled over, trying to reclaim the oblivion of sleep to reprieve him of reality in vain. Opening his eyes, the shame and self-loathing took up their usual residence.

All gone. Everything. He was no one.

Worse than nothing started up the voice in Johnathan's

head. You smell. You haven't showered in days. What good are you lying in your own filth? The world should be free of you. Johnathan buried his face in the pillow and then reached for his phone to drown out the punishing internal dialogue.

"Good morning, honey," Caroline called out cheerfully as she pulled the curtains back and let in the late morning sun a few hours later. "Time to get up."

Johnathan buried his head under the cover. "I was up in the night three times. Let me sleep."

"Oh no. No, you aren't doing this anymore." Caroline held a cup of coffee out to Johnathan as she sat down on the bed beside him. "It's time to pick yourself up and dust yourself off. I've let you wallow in self-pity and despair long enough. I'm putting you on a new regimen. Yoga every morning at the studio, and then you go to work. I've rented you the tiny office under the Yoga studio. You can design houses for normal people. I already have you a client."

Johnathan sat up, his eyes blinking in the bright light. He took the turquoise coffee mug out of her hand and took a sip.

"It's not self-pity. It's humiliation. Regret. Disbelief. How did I lose everything we have? We have nothing. I'm worth nothing." His eyes stared vacantly into the distance. The bright, flashy office, the team of twenty architects, their support administration and marketing team, all those employees hired and let go in under a year. How did he do that?

Why couldn't he land any big clients? Johnathan asked himself for the thousandth time. He had been so confident that his projects and that his work would speak for itself.

"It looks like I needed Daniel's salesmanship all those years. Alone I was a failure: a miserable failure. I'm a failure," said Johnathan. What good is any of it?"

"The good is your baby, who you haven't so much as looked at in weeks. Why don't you shower and watch him today so I can get some work done in peace and quiet? You know we can't afford a babysitter."

"Because I lost all your money too. I know, okay? Stop terrorizing me about it, Caroline. I get it, okay? I'm a loser, and you'd have been better of not having married me."

Caroline rolled her eyes and sat down on the bed with a sigh. "I only pointed out that I need your help today. Please take a shower, eat some breakfast, and watch our baby today. I have a bunch of back-to-back video conferences today."

Johnathan stared at Caroline, not hearing her. All he could think about was that he had put his new wife into bankruptcy with him. All Caroline's years of hard work building up her business from scratch and all the money she had earned, gone.

"The worst was when they came for the house," said Johnathan.

"That was a bad day, but it's over now, Johnathan. It's time to start again."

Johnathan cringed at the memory of Jolan showing up on their doorstep with the news that he'd bought Gram's house from the bank.

"You can live in it rent-free until you get yourselves on your feet. Then you can work at repurchasing it from me. It's what Gram would have wanted me to do. I love you, Caroline. Let me do this for you."

Caroline had stood on the doorstep, tears sliding down her cheeks until Jolan's daughter held out her arms because she wanted Auntie Caroline to hold her. Caroline had melted into a million pieces.

"I've missed you, princess. Come see my new baby. Come with me.' Cooing to the little girl, Caroline had disappeared down the hall towards the kitchen.

"Hey Jolan," Johnathan had rubbed the back of his head with his hand, looking down at the floor, unable to meet Jolan's eyes.

"It'll work itself out. I believe in you, John."

Johnathan hadn't corrected Jolan that no one called him that. Why should he have? Johnathan had wanted to crawl back under the covers of their bed and hide there but couldn't until Jolan left a few hours later. The entire visit had been torture.

"Are you even listening to me? Hello?"

Johnathan took a sip of the coffee and looked up at his wife with resentment. Whereas he had fallen to pieces at the failure of his startup and their resulting bankruptcy, she laughed out loud more often than she ever had before. He just couldn't understand it. Caroline had lost all the hard-won money from her business. Shouldn't that hurt all the more if you started with next to nothing? He had almost lost Gram's house, for God's sake, and what did Caroline have to say? Nothing.

All Caroline talked about was her gratitude that they had people to whom they could turn to help them. Hearing about Jolan, the hero, set Johnathan's teeth on edge.

"Are you going to talk to your parents?"

"No."

Johnathan cringed at the memory of their fight the previous night over accepting his father's offer for financial help. Caroline had urged him to accept their offer. Something deep inside Johnathan could not take the money. He wasn't sure why he refused Caroline even a few thousand dollars to have some liquidity for her business. Caroline called it pride. Johnathan wasn't so sure.

Johnathan had lost contact with his family. Despite the prenuptial agreement clause, they hadn't been back to New York for about a year. After the wedding, Johnathan flew alone to New York to sell all he had to invest in his new life. He'd gone out to dinner with his parents and Matilda, who had just returned from her world trip with Brad. Then he had flown back to his new bride in sunny California.

"Why won't you let them help us?" asked Caroline. "I can't get any loans. I need financing for my business to grow."

"Uh, perhaps because my parents didn't come to see our baby until he was four months old? When they did arrive, Mom spent the entire time berating us for living in a tiny town in the middle of nowhere instead of coming back to New York. She held Leo exactly twice the entire trip. Remember? They haven't offered to come back to see us since. Every time I talk to my mother, she complains bitterly that we never come to visit."

"Does she know we don't have the money to fly out right now?

"I can't tell you how many times I've said nothing is stopping her from coming and staying with us for a visit," said Johnathan. "It's always the same. She answers that she can't possibly get away because she is so busy organizing something or other."

Johnathan's parents hadn't tried to come and visit since the bankruptcy, nor had his sister or brother. So much for family, thought Johnathan. After all the times he had helped them, when he needed them, where were they? He was out of sight and out of mind. That was the truth. They hadn't missed him, and they certainly didn't want to deal with the hollow failure of a man he was now. There was no way in hell he was taking any pity money from any of them.

"Hello? Johnathan, I'm talking to you." Caroline shook Johnathan's knee.

"If only I hadn't given away my half of the company."

"Johnathan," sighed Caroline. "We've been through this a million times. I can't do it again."

"Why the hell did I rent that expensive space and spend all that money renovating it? Why did I start with such a large team of architects? I could have started smaller, with less overhead; it would have given me more breathing room, more time to make it work."

Caroline blew out a gush of air and fell backward onto the bed with a thump.

"This shouldn't be happening. Should it? I mean, no, I am talented. I have awards in architecture, Caroline. I've designed massive projects. Sky scrappers, museums, libraries, luxury villas all over the globe. Why couldn't I make that business work? Why? Over course, if I hadn't spent so much straight away and created all that overhead."

"Johnathan. You're talking in circles again. Stop focusing on it.

Move forward, start over, and build something new. Sitting here mulling about it isn't going to turn you back into a successful millionaire. In the meantime, I need help. I've been doing it all alone. We can't afford daycare now, let alone the nanny we had hired to be here with Leo before we lost everything. Taking care of our baby all alone, running my business strapped for cash, doing all the cleaning and the cooking and the shopping while you lay up here for hours every morning and then drift down to the beach until the sun sets each night? I can't stand it anymore."

"I was going to be a billionaire, Caroline. I was on my way before I gave it all away to my brother and rejected my inheritance. If it hadn't been for you."

"Not this again. Look, I didn't ask you to do anything. You made your own decisions. And yes, you know what? It is your fault that you put us into bankruptcy. You are one hundred percent right that you shouldn't have created so many fixed overhead costs before you were at least past the break even point."

Johnathan punched his fists down into the bed. "At last. Finally, After three months of you being little miss crazy sunshine, the mask slips. God help me, it has been so annoying having you flounce around smiling and humming every damn day as if we haven't lost everything."

"Are you kidding me right now?" Caroline popped back up to sitting. "We have a baby, Johnathan. A baby who needs us and needs me to pull myself together and take care of him as best I can. I can't just fall to pieces like you, you egotistical, self-involved mess of a man. And you smell! I've had enough. Enough! All you do is create extra work for me to do and bring me down like you're sucking the energy out of me. You need to leave. Now. Pack your things and get out. Come back when you've found Johnathan because I have no idea where he went. This isn't the man I fell in love with and married."

"Caroline."

"No. Get. Out. I mean it, Johnathan."

"I'm not. I'm not leaving. I have nowhere to go."

"You have family, unlike me, Johnathan. I can't stand living with you anymore. If you won't leave, then Leo and I will have to leave."

"You have nowhere to go either."

Caroline slipped off the bed and pulled out a packed suitcase from the closet. "I've had this packed for over a month. I've kept thinking, just one day more, maybe he will pull himself out of it, maybe things will change. He'll start taking care of Leo, and I won't need to bring him with me to the office every day. Or I'll come home, and he'll have done some cleaning, or shopping, or laundry, or just something, anything, to help out. But no, it's the same story, and I can't let myself be pulled down into your quicksand. Leo needs me too much. I need me too much. You have my number. Call when you get your act together. Oh. And Happy Thanksgiving."

Caroline took a last long look at Johnathan. With a start, Johnathan saw the dark blue smudges under her eyes, the new wrinkles creasing between her eyebrows, how skinny she had become.

Johnathan watched as Caroline picked up the suitcase and lugged it down the stairs. His gaze fell on the wedding photo on the bedside table. Where had his radiant voluptuous bride gone? He heard Leo crying, Caroline soothing him, the slam of the door, and then silence.

Nothing but silence.

# CHAPTER 14

Johnathan still wasn't sure how long he laid in bed. Was it two days and nights? Three? Four? The misery was throbbing in him with such intensity that he could barely breathe. He hadn't even thought about who was taking care of Leo or realized that the nanny was gone.

When had Caroline fired Ella? He hadn't seen the piles of laundry or the dishes in the sink. Johnathan hadn't seen the exhaustion in Caroline's face. Not only had he bankrupted them and almost lost Gram's house, but he had neglected Leo. When was the last time he had held his son? It had been months.

Johnathan told himself that he was worse than nothing. Caroline's words reverberated again and again in his head. 'I can't get pulled into your quicksand—you egotistical, self-involved mess of a man. I've had enough. Enough! All you do is create extra work for me to do and bring me down like you're sucking the energy out of me.' Her voice kept circling round and round until he grew dizzy and faint despite lying down.

He slipped down onto the floor, stumbled to his feet in the pre-dawn twilight, and down the stairs. Seized with frantic desperation, he ran out the porch door and towards the beach. His feet sunk into the sand, and he slipped and fell. Immediately he pressed himself up and ran into the waves.

Johnathan hurled himself into the ocean, the cold giving him a moment of pause, taking his breath away. After a moment, he began to swim. All his focus was on swimming out as far as he could, then allowing himself to sink. At last, he stopped, completely out of breath, and allowed himself to sink.

An arm clutched around Johnathan's throat, gagging him, forcing him to the surface. Johnathan was too exhausted from swimming out into the ocean to fight off the arm clutching at him. Johnathan felt himself being heaved face down onto a surfboard, a strong arm holding him fast to the board's surface. A few minutes later, Johnathan felt the board slide up onto the sand and rough hands turning him onto his back.

"What? What the hell, man," gasped a face framed in wet blonde curls down at him. "Say something."

"Who are you?"

"The dude who just saved your life, brother. What the hell were you doing swimming so far out in December?"

Johnathan's mind began to wake up slowly. "Mark. You're that yoga guy. From the place. In the town." Johnathan struggled to sit up. "What are you doing here?"

Mark collapsed onto the sand, still breathing heavily. "I was out for my sunrise run when I saw your crazy ass thrashing into the ocean."

Johnathan's teeth began to clatter together. "You should have left me."

"Dude, that's crazy talk there. Come on, let get you inside and warmed up." Mark held out a hand to help Johnathan up.

Johnathan hesitated, the numb of the cold settling like ice into his bones.

"Get the hell up. Now," ordered Mark, his teeth also beginning to chatter violently together.

Johnathan grabbed Mark's hand. Mark pulled him forward toward the house and pushed him straight upstairs.

"You got two showers in this place, man? I've never been so cold," stammered Mark.

"Yeah, yeah, down the hall." Johnathan pointed to the guest bathroom.

"I'll t steal some dry clothes. Got any sportswear? I need to go teach a yoga class in thirty-two minutes."

Johnathan pointed at the master bedroom. "Anything clean you can find is yours."

Mark hurried into the bedroom and grabbed some sweatpants, a sweatshirt, and a t-shirt and then ordered Johnathan into the shower.

"I'll see you downstairs in fifteen minutes," Mark called over his shoulder on his way out the bedroom door.

Johnathan staggered into the shower and stepped in before it had a chance to warm up. The cold spray was still warmer than the ocean had been. As the water became warmer, he melted into the heat. A few minutes later, he stepped out of the shower in a waft of steam and threw on some clothes and wool socks. He grabbed a second pair of wool socks for Mark and went downstairs to the kitchen, where he could hear cupboard doors opening and shutting.

"Where's the coffee, dude? I don't see any."

Johnathan pressed the button on the automatic coffee machine and added fresh water to the tank. He grabbed two mugs as the machine warmed up and then pressed the button. Mark pulled on the wool socks Johnathan had given him as the machine ground the beans and filled the cups with coffee.

"That smells good. Have any milk?" Mark opened the fridge. "Yikes. You have nothing in here. Not even pickles."

Johnathan just shrugged. Mark walked into the living room and sat down on the gray textured modern designer sofa Johnathan had brought with him from New York when he moved in. Mark pulled one of Caroline's turquoise wool blankets around himself.

"So. You want to tell me why the hell you did that this morning?"

Johnathan shrugged again and sat down on Gram's rocking

chair that Caroline had refused to get rid of and looked down at the dusty wooden floor.

"No offense, dude, but this place is a mess. And it smells. What's with all the dishes in the sink and all the piles of laundry all over the floor in your room?"

Johnathan didn't answer, pressing his lips together.

"Listen, brother, I heard about what happened. I mean, the whole town knows, of course; it's a small place. Tough break, man. Tough break. But listen, you need to pull yourself together. Where is Caroline?"

"She left," Johnathan mumbled at the floor.

"Ah. That makes sense. I can't imagine Caroline letting the place get like this. Where's she staying? She's still teaching her morning yoga class. She didn't even say anything to me. Although she does look like she has the world on her shoulders when she thinks no one's looking."

Johnathan's eyes flitted up to look at Mark when he mentioned Caroline.

"Is there someone I can call to come to hang here with you? I can't leave you alone after what just happened. Or didn't happen." Mark pulled the blanket tighter around him as he finished the last of his coffee.

"I have no one. And nothing. No one and nothing."

"Dark. When did she leave?"

"Thanksgiving."

"Shit. Well. When was the last time you had something decent to eat?"

Johnathan shrugged. "I haven't been hungry."

Mark let out a big sigh and stood up. "Come on. Up you get. You're coming with me to yoga class. Let's go, or we'll be late. And I've never been late, so today is not going to be an exception."

Johnathan continued to sit staring at the floor until Mark grabbed him roughly by the arms and hoisted him to his feet. "Come. Now. Let's go."

Like a robot, Johnathan marched to the front door. Mark threw him a jacket and took one for himself before pulling the door shut behind him.

After a sweaty power yoga class, Mark ordered Johnathan to take another hot shower and put on some fresh clothes he threw at him. After showering, Mark took Johnathan down a flight of stairs and let him into his tiny studio flat, where he cooked up two heaping bowls of hot oatmeal, two plates of eggs, and multiple slices of multi-grain bread he had baked himself the previous day. After breakfast, Johnathan had warmth and an aliveness spreading back into his belly and extending outward like a wave. His brain started to wake up.

"Thanks," Johnathan sighed as he accepted his second coffee from Mark. "What is your name again?"

"Mark. So. You ready to talk. Or do I need to take you into the hospital now and tell them about your morning one-way swim?"

"God no. Please no," Johnathan shook his head.

Mark crossed his arms and leaned back in his chair. "I'm all ears."

Johnathan looked at Mark blankly. He blinked. "What do you want me to say?"

"What the hell is going on with you, man? Why is your home look like that? Why'd you go running like a maniac into the ocean trying to get yourself drowned or something? Or are you just a member of the polar bear club?"

"You already know my story. I lost everything. I lost Caroline and Leo. They're better off without me."

Mark punched Johnathan hard in the arm, making some of his coffee spill on the floor.

"What the hell? That hurt," said Johnathan.

"I hope it hurt. Wake the hell up, dude. How is Caroline better off raising her son completely on her own without any kind of help from you? Pull your shit together. You need to help that woman. She's an angel, that gal; you know that? If I could tell you how she's changed my life for the better, we'd be here all day. Now you listen to me. You're moving in here with me, and you're sleeping on the couch. I'm going to call Caroline to move out of Annie and Dan's place and back home with Leo. I'm putting you on a new regimen. You're getting up and going running with me in the morning and then to power yoga. Afterward, you're going to work with me on the building site. In the evening, it's more yoga, and then we enjoy a big dinner together before bed. Well?" Mark paused, raising his eyebrows at Johnathan.

"Okay," Johnathan answered.

"Okay? Okay." Mark nodded, looking surprised at Johnathan's acquiescence while crossing his arms over his chest. "We start right now. It's Saturday, so we have some time free. I'm hauling you back to that house, and we're going to scrub that place until it's sparkling. I'm not having Caroline go back to a place looking like that, brother. Then you can pack your things, and we come back here in time for an early dinner before the yoga meditation workshop this evening."

Johnathan began to protest.

"Hospital?" Mark asked.

Johnathan shook his head.

Mark stood up and headed toward the front door. Johnathan followed him while letting out a deep breath. On the way back over to the cottage, Mark stopped at the store and picked up some sandwich materials, tea, milk, mixed nuts, apples, cucumbers, carrots, whole grain pasta, green smoothies, and a bunch of fresh flowers. As soon as they walked through the door of the cottage, Mark began ordering Johnathan around.

"Go start a load of laundry."

Before Johnathan could even press the start button on the laundry machine, Mark found him and pressed rubber gloves and a spray Clorox bleach bottle into his hands.

"Go scrub down all the bathrooms from floor to ceiling. I'm

talking about everything. Showers, floors, tub, toilets, sinks. Yeah?"

Johnathan could hear Mark filling the dishwasher in the kitchen as he headed upstairs to start with the master bath. Once in his bedroom, he found his phone and looked up how to clean a bathroom. He hadn't wanted to admit to Mark that he had never cleaned a bathroom before in his life. Mark found Johnathan standing with his phone in his hands, watching a video on YouTube on bathroom cleaning for the second time.

"What the hell are you looking at, dude? I'm serious. Get your ass into that bathroom and stop scrubbing." Mark tore the phone out of Johnathan's hands and looked at the screen. "Do not tell me you don't know how to clean a bathroom."

"I do now. I think," replied Johnathan with a shrug.

"Oh man, oh man," muttered Mark as Johnathan headed into the bathroom and began to pull on the yellow rubber gloves.

Johnathan scrubbed each bathroom and then went to find a cloth to wipe them down. He found Mark dusting in the living room. "Do we have something called a microfiber cloth?"

Mark turned off the vacuum. "How the hell should I know? Look in the drawer. Try them out."

Johnathan opened and shut the drawers in the kitchen until he found one with a plastic box of clothes labeled 'for cleaning' next to another box labeled 'kitchen.' Once he had wiped down all the bathrooms until they gleamed, Johnathan found Mark, who was vacuuming in the living room.

Mark directed him to change the sheets on the beds, including the baby's crib, and to start another load of laundry.

"There's almost nothing a woman likes more than getting into clean sheets after a long day," commented Mark. "Don't tell me that's something you need to look up how to do too."

Johnathan trudged back up the stairs, his stomach beginning to growl. He didn't know how long he had gone without eating anything and had experienced no appetite for weeks. But the yoga, breakfast, and cleaning had woken up his stomach. He was finishing pulling new sheets onto the last bed when Mark showed up in the doorway.

"Let's make some sandwiches, John. I don't know about you, but I'm hungry."

Johnathan nodded. "Me too." He followed Mark down the stairs and into the clean kitchen. Mark handed Johnathan some vegetables to peel and cut up as he made two sandwiches for each of them and placed two green smoothies on the counter next to the fresh flowers he had put in a turquoise vase.

"Let me guess. Caroline's favorite color is turquoise; it's everywhere."

"What? Oh, yeah, turquoise," Johnathan muttered as he added the cut-up veggies onto the sandwich plates.

"I've been thinking all morning about your story. You need to change your glasses. Put on some new frames. See the picture with new eyes."

Johnathan took a big bite of his sandwich and looked over at Mark. What was he going on about now?

"I don't wear glasses."

"No. I mean how you're looking at your life story."

"There's only one way to look at it," muttered Johnathan.

"Don't be too sure there, friend. Don't be too sure. Now the way I see it, you've never been freer than you are right now."

"Is that right?"

"Yeah. Money can be heavy, brother, like a dense weight."

"I don't buy into that yoga bullshit Mark. I love money. Money buys you freedom. What are my options right now without a cent to my name? I couldn't even pay for our groceries."

Johnathan's solar plexus clenched at the recent memory of standing by Mark's side as he paid in the store. There was a time in the not too distant past when he could have afforded to buy the whole damn grocery store, and now he couldn't even afford some food and flowers.

"Your options are endless. That's what you're not seeing. It's right in front of you. You get to start over fresh. Start from the beginning and do it right this time?"

"Look, I'm grateful for what you're doing for me. I'm still not sure why you're doing it, but it seems like you're a good guy. Caroline seemed to think so when she talked about you. You even watched Leo once or twice for us, right? Caroline's a lioness about who she lets take care of him, so you must be quality. I know you're trying to help, but I'm no yogi pal. I love money. I loved my life. Being a millionaire is amazing, and being broke is shitty. That's all there is to it. I'm a failure and have nothing. I'm nothing. There are no rose-colored glasses on the planet that can filter this into something beautiful."

"Well then, saddle up, dude. Last I checked, they didn't take away your architect license. You don't like being a broke man? Then go get a job or start knocking down doors to get some work."

Johnathan shook his head. "That's how I went bankrupt in the first place. I couldn't get enough clients."

"Oh yeah? It seems that it would only take one client's project to buy us some groceries next time we swing by the store. The truth is you're a boy born with a silver spoon in his mouth who's a bit of a lazy bastard."

Johnathan almost choked on his sandwich. He swallowed a big gulp of the green smoothie. No one had called him lazy, not ever. He had always had the top grades in his class. He had always been the last person to put out his light in the office.

"That's not true," he shot back once his airway was clear. "I'm a hard worker."

"Oh yeah? Looking around this place this morning made it hard to believe that," retorted Mark.

"Yeah, but that's different, that's not my..." Johnathan began to say.

"Job?" finished Mark. "Not your job? But it's Caroline's, Just like a said. Spoon in the mouth. I bet you've never even changed one of Leo's diapers."

Johnathan starred at him in response.

"Just as I thought," nodded Mark. "I got your number, dude. But the good news is, you can leave that version of Johnathan in the past! Get light, brother, get moving. Let that shit go and start showing what you're made of now. Start cleaning toilets, changing diapers, watching Leo, knocking down one door after another until you've had fifty slammed in your face in one day. Then show up the next day for fifty more doors slammed in your face. Sooner or later, someone is going to hire you to design them a pretty little house. Right? And there you go. You'll be back on your way. Maybe you'll be able to get the next client after having only thirty doors slammed in your face. See what I mean?"

"It won't matter. Caroline won't ever take me back."

"Who the hell cares about that dude!" roared Mark. "Right now, you have a son, who needs a dad, and you need to find the courage and start showing up for that kid. Start hustling and don't stop so you can earn some money to take care of yourself and your kid and spend time being with him."

"Yeah. Yeah, maybe you're right," Johnathan said as he leaned back into his chair. For the first time in longer than he could remember, he could feel himself sitting in a chair with his body. He was sitting in a chair in the kitchen, and it was as if his awareness had been pulled out of the spinning tortuous thoughts and into his body with a whoosh.

"You're probably just doomed to stay a lazy, spoiled, self-involved arrogant jackass." Mark shrugged. "Either way, you're coming to stay with me, and you're following my routine to the letter, or I'm hauling your ass to the hospital, and they can deal with you."

"Hey, what the hell, man? No need to get aggressive."

Mark shrugged. "Being nice wasn't working on you."

"Anyway. You're wrong for sure on one point: I'm a hard worker."

"What's that?" Mark raised his eyebrows as he took a sip of his smoothie. "Didn't hear you."

"I'm a hard worker," Johnathan spoke up louder. "I'm going to try. I'm going to try to make things right for Leo."

"Try? You a wimp or what? What's with this try?" Mark crossed his arms over his chest.

"What the hell Mark? What's your deal?"

"I want you to wake the hell up. That's why I keep telling you over and over again."

"I'm going to do it."

"Do what?"

"Hustle?"

"Are you asking me a question?"

"I'm going to hustle," Johnathan said. "I'm just not sure how to start. Or what' doors to knock down'. I've always had a sales and marketing team to bring in sales leads. I'm not sure how to go about it." Johnathan's lips twisted to the side.

"Mark waved a hand away. "Don't worry about that. We'll take it one day at a time. First, you're starting on the building site with me first thing Monday morning. It'll do you good. Now I'll clear up here and watch some TV while you fold that laundry and pack. We need to be out of here by six so Caroline can come home. We have dinner plans at eight. You can meet my girlfriend, Jenny."

# CHAPTER 15

Over the next few weeks, Johnathan's days fell into a regular rhythm created by Mark. They went running together each morning. Johnathan attended Mark's power yoga class, and they cooked a huge breakfast before heading to work on the building site.

Attending Mark's evening meditation class was a prerequisite for enjoying a big dinner together. Mark went out with his girlfriend Jenny most evenings after dinner, and Johnathan did the dishes and then collapsed into bed exhausted with a book. He had never been so physically tired or slept so deep in his life.

Christmas came and went with no response from Caroline. Johnathan had tried to call and text her a few times, but she had remained silent and distant.

In February, Mark declared Johnathan's work on the building sites had come to an end, and it was time for him to start hustling and knocking down doors, explaining that he had placed an ad for him on a local real-estate website and billboard in town.

"Start answering your phone, man. Also, I talked to the owner of the real-estate shop on the boardwalk. You have an appointment in one hour and twenty minutes. She wants to talk to you about designing home renovation projects in the area. I'll walk over there with you as soon as I go clean up the studio real quick. Be right back."

Johnathan thanked Mark. His heart hammered in his chest as he dialed Caroline's number yet again.

"Johnathan."

"Caroline. You answered."

"Well, you won't stop calling."

"I want to see Leo." Johnathan cleared his voice. "I want to see my son."

"Okay."

"Okay?"

"Yeah. I talked to Mark. He thinks you're ready. You can care for him this Saturday. I'll pack him a bag."

"Great. How are you two doing?"

"I'm filing for divorce."

Johnathan slid to the floor onto his knees and then sat down.

"I'm not saying there isn't any hope for us someday. I can't be tied to you financially. I can't go through what we just went through last year all over again. I work too hard at my business, and I want to buy back Gram's house. I want to protect Leo."

Johnathan swallowed loudly. "Yeah," he cleared his throat. "Yeah, I understand."

"I'll give the paperwork to Mark for you to sign. Please give it back by Friday. Leo misses his Dad. This will be good. We can go to breakfast together first, so he has time to readjust to being with you. I'm sure Annie and Dan will be happy to see you again. We'll meet at their café at nine. Does that sound okay?"

"Yeah. Yeah, it sounds great."

Johnathan said goodbye, and leaning his elbow into his knees, he pressed his fingertips into his eyes. A few minutes later, Mark found him.

"What are you doing? Get up, brother. We're going to be late."

Johnathan rushed into the bathroom and shut the door. He splashed some cold water on his face and took some deep breaths before joining Mark at the front door.

"You got this, John."

Johnathan forced a weak smile on his face.

The real estate agent was obviously smitten with Mark. For

most of the meeting, her eyes kept drifting back over to Mark, even when Johnathan was talking. Johnathan found the situation oddly irking, and it took him over half an hour to figure out why. He couldn't remember ever being in a room and not having all eyes on him.

Johnathan began to laugh internally. What did he care if this pretty woman was into Mark instead? Johnathan realized he hadn't known how addicted he had been to not only the money and the prestige but also the attention of his previous life.

I used to be someone and had everything. Johnathan shook his head at himself and let out a sigh. Now I'm nobody and have nothing; no wonder Caroline is filing for divorce.

"Something wrong?" Cindy stopped in mid-word to stare at Johnathan.

"Not at all. Just anxious about getting this gig."

Nobody and nothing, his mind repeated, but a quieter voice insisted that it wasn't true. I am feeling good in my body; he thought, Real good. All that running, work on the building site, and the power yoga had made him strong and feeling aligned.

Nobody and nothing.

Someone and everything.

Nobody and nothing.

The words kept circling around and around in his head. Only this time, it wasn't torturous as it had been last fall. It was like taking a few elements out of a busy design, only in his head. All of a sudden, there was more space. It should make him feel awful. Instead, it was as if he was expanding in every direction, getting lighter, and grounding down all at the same time.

"Johnathan?" Cindy tilted her head to the side. "Did you hear me?"

Mark placed a hand on his arm.

"Sorry," chuckled Johnathan. "Those nerves just won't let up."

Cindy swished her long hair over her shoulder, smiled again at Mark, and then turned her focus back to Johnathan.

"No need to be nervous, Johnathan. How cute. A man of

your talents being nervous. No, no, of course, I'm thrilled I'll be working with a world-renowned architect. Can you just imagine?" Cindy laughed as she tilted her head to the side. "Of course, if Mark recommends you, that's all I needed anyway."

"So I'll be remodeling homes in town?"

"And showing some homes as well to start. I could use a hand helping with the real estate work. I don't sell only in town, you know. I've got projects going all over in a two-hour radius from here, isn't that right, Mark? That's how I can afford all those private yoga classes with you. Once, I even sold a home to a celebrity. But of course, I can't tell you who. Go on. Ask me who. No, no, I can't tell you." Cindy laughed again.

Johnathan cleared his throat. "Ah, don't you need a license for that? To sell real estate? I'm an architect Cindy." Johnathan glanced at Mark. "I mean. I could try to get licensed?"

Cindy waved a hand at Johnathan. "No problem, I would do all the final work and be the one selling the properties. You have no idea how many times people want to walk through a place before getting serious. You can help with all that. And, of course, it would be the perfect time to pitch how you could renovate a property for them. You know, they walk into a home and say, 'blah blah I love this, but I don't like that,' and you could say, 'hey, I'm an architect, and I can change that for you. If you're serious, then I can create a proposal and send it right over. Let's make this your dream home.' Oh, I like that. 'Let's make this your dream home- the perfect fit unique for you.' That's going on the marketing. Yes. Yes, this will be good. And then don't worry, because I also sell tracts of land for new construction, and then you can be building up dream homes from scratch."

"I'm so grateful for this opportunity, Cindy. I can't tell you what it means to me. I'm happy to work on getting that real estate license if that would help."

"Look at that. He's a team player. You know I like you," Cindy leaned in and looked with her full attention at Johnathan for the first time since the meeting started. 'I heard you were this arrogant ass, but I don't get that vibe at all."

Mark spoke up, "At least he isn't anymore. I'm sure you can forgive the man for who he used to be. Being a billionaire can go to a guy's head, you know?" Mark laughed and slapped Johnathan on the back and then left his hand on Johnathan's shoulder. "You're not what you own or your job or whatever dude. You are you. And everyone else? They are them. No high, no low, and all is mellow."

Johnathan found himself laughing. "Ah Mark, the fact that I understand what you mean is so funny. But yes, I see everyone at eye level now. Everyone."

"Look at that brother," Mark shook Johnathan's shoulder. "What a mindset shift. Do you mean that?"

The smile faded from Johnathan's face as he looked over at Mark. He could feel a tingling from the tips of his toes all the way up through the top of his head. "You know something? Johnathan reached up, interlaced his hands behind his head, and leaned back in his chair. "I think I really do."

Cindy leaned over her desk towards the two men. "I can't blame you about how you were. Goodness knows what I would be like if I could buy anything I wanted, whenever I wanted, do anything I wanted. Think of the shoes I could buy. The real estate empire I'd build." Cindy's eyes grew vacant for a moment; then, she shook her head. "Anyway. I'll be part of your fresh new start, and if you can repay some day in designer shoes." Cindy laughed and winked at Mark. "The whole being non-materialistic part of yoga isn't my thing."

Mark winked at Cindy. "You think I don't know about the money you donate? It's a small town. People talk."

As Cindy beamed at Mark, Johnathan spoke up. "Tell you what. Mega rich or no, as soon as I get my financial feet under me again, I will be gifting you some new shoes."

"Well, Mr. Arrozzini, you are hired. Welcome to Dream Lifestyle Realty. All we have to do now is draw up a work agreement that makes us both happy."

Johnathan smoothed his blue striped colored shirt down for the fifth time as he paced back and forth in front of the studio's front door. He could feel Mark's eyes watching him from a stool at the kitchen bar.

"Dude, relax. You'd think the run and the power yoga this morning would have calmed you down. Come eat something."

"We're eating together at the bakery."

"You're going to the bakery? Good for you, man. You haven't been in there with me once since you moved in here. Relax. Annie and Dan will go easy on you." Mark took a sip of his coffee and grinned. "Maybe."

"It's not Annie and Dan I'm worried about."

The doorbell rang, and Johnathan whipped the door open.

"Johnathan." Caroline looked startled at the instant opening of the door and took a step back.

"Caroline."

Johnathan swallowed, taking in Caroline's red dress cinched at the waist with a turquoise belt and her dangling blue earrings. Caroline's face was rounder again, softer than it had been the last he had seen her on Thanksgiving; she looked prettier. The shadows under Caroline's eyes weren't completely gone, but her skin was glowing, and her smile looked real, if hesitant.

Johnathan had seen Caroline only from a distance over the past few months. Once, he had been running with Mark and had seen her with Leo on the beach. Another time he had spotted her in the grocery store. More times than he would ever admit, he had walked past her office to catch a glimpse of her through the window.

"You look better. I mean beautiful. You look great. Ready to go?"

"Sure."

"Hey, Caroline. Hey Leo." Mark peeked his head around the door frame. "You going to come to hang with your Dad and me today, little man?"

Leo reached out his arms to Mark, and Mark scooped him up

and twirled him around. Leo burst into giggles as he held him upside down.

"Careful, Mark." Caroline smiled. "Do you want to come to breakfast with us?"

"I think you two need to talk," Mark answered as he pulled Leo back up and held him out to Johnathan.

Johnathan moved to take Leo, but Leo burst into tears. Johnathan froze with his arms out, his heart thundering in his chest. Caroline stepped forward and pulled Leo into her arms.

"That's your Daddy Leo. Daddy," she said, pointing at Johnathan. "Daddy. Let's go, Johnathan. See you later, Mark. Oh, hey, I left the papers you wanted on the table upstairs in the studio."

"Thanks for that. Maybe you want to think about co-leading the retreat and come along."

Caroline shook her head. "I have no one to watch Leo."

Mark looked over pointedly at Johnathan. Caroline shook her head.

"Ready? Johnathan?"

"Yeah." He took a last look over at Mark, smoothing his sweaty palms down his pants legs.

Mark nodded his encouragement, and Johnathan pulled the door shut behind him.

When he reached the street, Caroline was already placing Leo back into his stroller. They walked to the bakery in silence. Johnathan's mind had no idea where to start. Ask her to forgive him? Tell her that he'd changed more in the past few months than he had in his entire life? Ask for another chance? Plead with her not to go through with the divorce? Tell her about the new job?

"Mark told me about saving your life yesterday. Don't you ever do something stupid like that ever again, you hear me?"

Johnathan stopped walking in mid-step. Why had Mark told her about that? He'd promised not to tell anyone, ever.

Caroline stopped and looked over her shoulder. "Johnathan?"

"I'd like to take Leo on the weekends from now on," he answered.

Caroline instantly shook her head. "I'm not giving my son into the care of someone who just tried to drown himself in the ocean. No way."

"Caroline. Could you keep your voice down, please? And I would appreciate it if you didn't go running your mouth about that to anyone."

Caroline nodded her head, her posture softening. "I'm sorry. I'm sorry I left you. If Mark hadn't been there, if he hadn't been there, then I," Caroline didn't finish her sentence. Her eyes filled with tears, and she closed her eyes. A few tears slipped out from under her closed eyelids and fell down her cheeks.

Johnathan shifted from foot to foot uncomfortably. Every fiber of his being wanted to pull his wife into his arms and comfort her. Yet, Leo had rejected him moments before. Johnathan wasn't sure if he could handle Caroline pushing him away right now as well.

"That's not going to happen. I'm in a good place now, Caroline. Really. I'll do what I have to do to prove it to you. I want a relationship with my son. I'm going to figure out a way to help support both of you. How are you anyway? How's your business?" He began to walk in the direction of the bakery again, and Caroline fell into step beside him

Caroline nodded. "Business is perfect. I've hired two more people to my team, actually, and a new nanny. It's Annie's Mom, Anna. Leo is happier with her than he was with Ella. The only downside is she wants me to eat a freshly baked piece of cake or pie with her every time I come to pick Leo up. I've gained a bunch of weight again." She let out a sigh,

"You look better. You look like you," Johnathan commented.

"The second time being skinny, and I was too miserable to enjoy it," commented Caroline. "But I feel great and energized and more like my old self again, and that's good."

Johnathan couldn't help it. He slipped an arm around her

waist. "I've missed you both so much."

"You didn't call," Caroline said with her eyes still fixed forward as she pushed the stroller.

Johnathan paused. "I wasn't in a good place. If Mark hadn't taken me in and forced me onto his routine, bossed me around, then I don't know where I'd be now."

"He's a good guy."

"The best," Johnathan nodded. "Hell, he even found me a job. I don't understand why Mark is doing all this for me."

They took a few steps in silence before Caroline spoke up. "You can't tell anyone I told you this." Caroline looked over at Johnathan, and he nodded in agreement.

"Mark lost his Dad that way. The way Leo almost lost you. He told me it put something right inside him, knowing he had saved some kid that kind of pain."

Johnathan swallowed a knot in his throat. "He's never mentioned his Dad. Or his family, for that matter."

"He doesn't want you to know. Anyway, he doesn't get along with his Mom and sees her maybe once a year. She lost her head after she lost her husband and joined this cult in Oregon where they grow their food and live off the grid."

"Is that where Mark lived? In a commune with his Mom?"

"No, went to live with his Dad's Mom in New York City right after he lost his dad. How do you not know any of this?"

"He always changes the subject when I ask him about his family," Johnathan replied as they came to a stop in front of the bakery.

"Yeah. Mark adored his Grandma. They lived in this big gorgeous flat near Central Park that was still rent-controlled. She passed away when he was twenty-two, though. Mark's Grandma didn't have much to leave him because she had run through almost all of her savings by the time she died. He used what he inherited to pay for his first year of college but dropped out when he was almost done because he had run out of cash. He traveled across the country doing odd jobs a few months at a time and then started working in construction. He saved up enough to do his yoga teacher training."

"Wow," Johnathan shook his head. "I had no idea."

"Of any of it? You've been running together daily, working together, living together, and you had no idea of any of his life story? How is that possible?"

"We don't talk a whole lot," Johnathan answered with a shrug. "We just enjoy being together. It's nice. Unless Jenny is with us, then she does all the talking."

Caroline laughed. "She is quite the chatterbox. She isn't who I pictured Mark choosing."

"Come on," Johnathan pulled the door open. "Let's go eat some brunch."

The mood lightened over croissants, omelets, and fresh berries. Caroline talked about Leo and tried to catch Johnathan up on what he had missed over the past few months. Every once in a while, she pointed to Johnathan and repeated, 'Daddy.'

Caroline laughed at Johnathan's jokes about his first attempts at working on the construction site when he had accidentally nailed his glove to the wall, dumped a whole can of paint over another man's head, and fell through a newly plastered wall.

Maybe it was seeing his Mom relaxed and laughing. Perhaps it was seeing his Mom reach out and squeeze Johnathan's hand a few times during brunch. As Johnathan was just finishing his latte, Leo toddled over and leaned his head against Johnathan's knee.

Slowly and carefully, Johnathan reached down and smoothed the brown curls away from Leo's amber skin and patted him on the back. Leo stayed there leaning against Johnathan's leg until his eyes began to droop closed. Gently Johnathan reached down and pulled Leo up into his arms, bracing himself for crying. Leo snuggled against Johnathan's chest and drifted off to sleep.

Johnathan sat there, holding his one-year-old baby in his arms, looking at how much he had grown in four months.

When had he started walking, or crawling, for that matter? He had missed it all. He cradled his baby closer to him, and as he looked down at his peaceful little face, and couldn't hold it in. Silent tears started sliding down his cheeks. Until that moment, he had managed to push it all down and store it all away. Johnathan had missed his baby so much it hurt. In that instant, something hammered into place. Johnathan wasn't ever going to lose connection with his son again.

When Johnathan returned to the studio with Leo, Mark was waiting for them. When Leo woke up, there were a few minutes of crying for mama, but Johnathan was able to distract him with a brightly colored present and a chocolate cupcake. Johnathan may have missed Leo's first birthday, but he'd decided that wasn't going to stop him from recreating the day.

"I didn't anticipate just how much of a mess he would be able to make with one chocolate cupcake," laughed Johnathan.

"This kid needs a bath. He even has it in his hair," chuckled Mark. "And his ears. How did you do that, Leo? Did you get any of it in your mouth?"

After a bath and a new set of clothes, Leo was at last ready to open his birthday present, which was a set of wooden painted blocks and a matching wooden train set. When Caroline showed up just before dinner to pick up Leo, all three of them were still on the floor playing with the toys. Leo would wait patiently while Mark and Johnathan built up houses and towers along the train track. Once finished, Leo would take the train, pushing it on the track, sometimes having it fly like a plane, and crash it into each structure, sending everything cascading onto the floor.

Caroline tried to scoop Leo up to take him home, but Leo twisted out of her arms and toddled over to where Johnathan was lying on the floor and put his little arms around his neck.

Johnathan sat up and scooped Leo into his arms. "It's time to go home, Leo. I'll see you soon. Caroline, give me a second, and

I'll pack this together for you to take home."

"Leave it. Then you have something to play with him when he's with you."

Caroline tried to take Leo from Johnathan, but he started crying and clung to his Dad.

"No. It's Leo's birthday present. I want him to take it home."

"Well, then you deliver it sometime after dinner this week, okay? Right now, I just need to get him home and into a bath."

"He already had a bath," spoke up Mark.

"Well, then he'll have another one. It's part of his nighttime routine," declared Caroline as she reached out her arms for Leo.

Johnathan was too busy putting Leo's jacket on to notice.

"Here, I'll walk you two home," said Johnathan. He reached down and grabbed the diaper bag.

Without waiting for a response, Johnathan walked down the stairs and placed Leo into his stroller, and tucked a blanket in around him. He didn't wait for Caroline. He started pushing the stroller in the direction of home.

Caroline came rushing up out of breath beside him and tried to take the stroller handle from him, but Johnathan held on tight.

"Johnathan. You don't need to walk us home."

"I want to."

"Well, I don't want you to."

"Please, Caroline," Johnathan looked over at Caroline without stopping. "Seventy-five percent of the way. How's that? Then I'll turn around."

Caroline let out a big sigh. Johnathan took that as agreement and continued forward with his eyes alternating between watching his son and looking ahead. He just got his son back. He wasn't ready to let him go for another whole week.

Within five minutes, Leo fell fast asleep in the stroller.

"Great," Caroline sighed. "Just great. Why is he falling asleep right before dinner? Didn't he sleep well during his afternoon nap?"

139

"Nap?" Johnathan looked over at Caroline.

Caroline's hell fell back, and she growled n her throat. "You didn't give him a nap? Now what? It will be impossible to wake him up to feed him dinner, and he'll probably sleep through and wake up in the middle of the night."

"I'm sorry. Hey, listen, I could take Leo back to the studio with me. Mark won't mind. And then you can come and get him in the morning instead. Then you can have a good night's sleep, and we can go out to brunch all together again in the morning."

"No, I don't think that's a good idea."

Johnathan stopped and reached out for Caroline's hand, "Please. Let me make this right. You saw Leo. He's fine with me. Mark's in the studio, and he's great with him too. We'll be fine. And you look tired. You deserve a night to rest."

Caroline inhaled deeply and held it, then let it out slowly. "Okay. Okay. But call me if he gets sick or starts crying for me and won't stop, or you don't feel like you can handle it, and I will come right over."

"Chill, lady. I've got this," smiled Johnathan as he saluted her. "You can count on me. Now go home, have yourself a nice hot bath, and tuck into bed with a glass of wine and a book."

"That does sound good," murmured Caroline.

Johnathan gave Caroline a quick kiss on the cheek and turned the stroller around. "See you tomorrow. Not earlier than nine."

Mark was surprised when Johnathan carried the still sleeping Leo back into the studio. "Looks like we have him for the night."

"That's great, man, but I was just head to take Jenny out and then stay the night at her place. Should I call and cancel?"

"No, no, I'll be fine. You go on. It's probably better anyway. Caroline seems to think this little guy will be up in the night. You'll sleep better at Jenny's."

"Okay, well, if you need anything, don't hesitate to give a call,"

Mark answered as he pulled on his jacket.

Johnathan sat down on the sofa and gently pulled off Leo's coat, and then took his own off as well. He laid down on the couch and stretched his legs out long, pulling a pillow under his neck and a blanket over Leo. Within minutes he was fast asleep.

Johnathan startled awake, confused as to the heavyweight on his chest that was beginning to squirm. Leo. It took him a moment to realize where he was and how he got there. Twilight was seeping into the giant floor-to-ceiling windows overlooking the ocean. Leo pushed his hands onto Johnathan's chest and struggled to sit up. He took one look at Johnathan and burst into tears.

"Mama, mama, mama," he began to cry.

Johnathan tried to soothe him. He sat up, holding him close, and repeated, "It's okay, Leo. You're with Daddy, little guy. Are you hungry?"

Leo's crying began to calm as Johnathan stood up, still holding Leo, and checked the time. It was a quarter to six in the morning. They both had slept on the sofa together through the night.

"I haven't slept over ten hours in a long time, buddy. Let's get you something to eat. Are you hungry? I'm super hungry. But I'll get you your bottle first, yeah?"

Johnathan warmed a bottle and settled onto a high-backed chair in the corner, and pulled a blanket around both of them. As he fed Leo, he watched the sunrise over the ocean. The warmth of his son pulled close to his chest, the over ten hours of sleep, the sky painted pink and yellow with the rising sun, and the quiet all fused together.

Johnathan felt joy and a deep sense of contentment roll through his whole body. Johnathan could have stayed sitting like that for ages, despite his growling stomach. Yet Leo struggled to climb down out of Johnathan's lap, and it was only then that Johnathan remembered he should change Leo's diaper.

The diaper change went awry. For some reason, Leo decided

to pee as soon as the diaper was taken off, which went all over Johnathan. Johnathan swore, Leo started to cry, and Johnathan scooped his naked son up and carried him into the bathroom, where he eyed the shower but decided it would be too slippery. He ran the water for a bath instead. Leo toddled around the room naked as Johnathan shed his clothes and climbed into the tub. A quick soap and he was just rinsing off while keeping a close eye on Leo when Leo wandered over to the side of the tub and held his arms out.

"Da. Da."

Johnathan reached out carefully and pulled his son into the bath with him. Leo splashed the water happily. Once the water began to grow cool, Johnathan sat Leo on the bath rug and climbed out of the bath himself. First, he wrapped Leo up in a towel and placed him back down on the mat. He dried off and carried Leo out to the living space, where he put on a new diaper, some new clothes and then got dressed.

With a clean diaper and a tray full of cheerios, Leo was happy. Johnathan made himself a cup of coffee. He ate a handful of nuts and a quick piece of toast as he scrambled some eggs up for himself and Leo as he sipped his coffee. They were both eating eggs and English muffins when Mark peaked his head in the door.

"You two okay?"

"Yeah, we're great."

"You look good. Listen, I came for a quick shower and a change of clothes. I'm meeting Jenny for breakfast at the Café."

"Oh yeah? We're going there for brunch later too. Maybe we'll see you there."

Caroline walked through the open door behind Mark.

"Caroline. What are you doing here so early?" Johnathan felt a pang or regret. He wasn't ready for her to take Leo."

"It's nine-thirty."

"It can't be," Johnathan began until he saw the clock on the oven. Where had all that time gone? They had gotten up at quarter to six.

As Johnathan sat continuing to mull over how the hours had flown by so quickly, Caroline came in and kissed Leo and then helped herself to a cup of coffee. She sat down at the kitchen counter next to Johnathan.

"Do you two still want to go to brunch? It looks like you just ate."

"Sure we do. We didn't eat any dinner, so two breakfasts sound great," replied Johnathan.

"Bye, guys," Mark called out at the door. "Maybe I'll see you at the café."

"You didn't feed Leo dinner?"

Johnathan shrugged. "We slept through dinner until around five-thirty this morning."

"Five-thirty. You must be feeling that."

"I fell asleep with Leo and slept over ten hours. I feel great," smiled Johnathan.

Caroline took a cloth and began to wipe Leo's face. "Well, I have to admit that I needed the break. I did almost fall asleep in the bath last night. I slept nine hours myself. Shall we go? I'm hungry."

On the way to the café, Johnathan experienced a lightness of being he hadn't felt in a long time. He wasn't sure if he had ever felt this light. Sure, he was still sleeping on the sofa of a friend and only had forty-two dollars in his bank account. Somehow it didn't matter. His son was back in his life, he had a new job, and he was walking down the street feeling strong and full of energy.

A desire had come over him to sit down and sketch. He resolved to settle at on a patio beach side and design in the afternoon. Just for the fun of it again, like he used to do when he was a kid.

"Why are you grinning from ear to ear like that?" Caroline asked as Johnathan pulled open the door of the café for her and Leo to go inside.

"I'm happy. I missed you guys so much."

Caroline started to say something and then stopped. Johnathan saw her hesitation and added, "look, Mark and Jenny are over by the window."

Caroline headed in their direction, and Johnathan followed. He could be patient. Jo would sign the divorce papers, but he wasn't going anywhere. Johnathan had noticed the way Caroline kept looking at him when she thought he wasn't looking. She still loved him. He could tell. There was fear mixed with hesitation and disbelief in how Caroline dealt with him now as if he was a ticking bomb that could explode at the wrong touch or a mirage too good to be true.

Johnathan watched as Caroline threw her head back and laughed at something Mark said, and it made his heart warm. He decided right then and there that he was going to win back the woman he had lost. Jonathan didn't just want his son back in his life. He wanted his wife too. He wanted them to be a family again.

Johnathan carried his last box out of Mark's place down to the street where Caroline waited for him with the car. It had taken a few months of consistent effort, but Johnathan had won Caroline back. Today he was moving back home.

Johnathan was content and profoundly happy in a way he'd never experienced. Caroline was once again in his life. Sure, they were no longer married, which pained Johnathan, but he understood Caroline's reluctance to fuse their financial lives together again. They were back together and a joyful little family, and that's what matters, Johnathan told himself as he picked up Leo and kissed his plump little cheek.

Johnathan's work with Cindy was going well, and he was working on acquiring his real estate license. He had a waiting list of clients for his home renovation work and two new home designs on which he was working. Sure, he wasn't working on designing skyscrapers or museums anymore. Yet, he was happier than he had ever been at work.

If someone had told him five years ago that he would find it more rewarding to design the perfect home remodel or a middle-class three-bedroom house for a new family, he would have laughed in their face, but he was.

It was so much more satisfying. Johnathan could see his clients' faces light up when they walked into their newly renovated or built home. He could imagine all the happy moments they would spend together.

Johnathan saved each thank you card and gift he received from his thrilled clients and pasted them up in his office.

Johnathan carried the few boxes of his belongings inside and stacked them near the door.

"Good to have you home, Johnathan." Caroline wrapped her arms around him and squeezed him tight. "I never want to lose you out of my life again."

"You won't, and that's a promise," said Johnathan.

"Happy birthday Leo," Johnathan picked Leo up out of his crib and hugged him close. "It's your birthday, it's your birthday, happy birthday, it's your birthday," he sang as he danced around the room with his son. Caroline peeked her head in the door while pulling her hair back into a ponytail.

"Happy birthday, sweetheart," she called out. "Do you know how old you are today?" She held up two fingers. "Two. Two years old. I can't believe it. The past year has gone by so fast. Now you two have fun. I'll be back from teaching yoga and running errands in around two hours. I'll be picking up the C-A-K-E, but you need to go and get the balloons for the party."

"Sure thing, boss lady," Johnathan said and kissed her on the cheek and rubbed his hand over her belly. "You feeling nauseous this morning?"

"Yeah. But the ginger mint candies are helping. I'll make it through yoga."

"You could ask Mark to take your class."

Caroline shook her head. "He's already done that for me five times. I'll be okay. Happy birthday Leo. Maybe Daddy will make you pancakes because it's your birthday."

Leo clapped his hands, and Caroline smiled. "Bye, my beautiful men. See you soon."

Johnathan waited until he heard the front door close downstairs. "Forget making her wholegrain pancakes. It's your birthday. I'm taking you to pick out a donut. It'll be our secret."

Johnathan managed to get himself, and Leo dressed in record time, but it took four times as long as necessary to get from their front door to the café. Leo kept insisting he wanted down to walk, which entailed him stopping every few feet to look at something or pick something up. At last birthday or no birthday, Johnathan put a struggling Leo back into the stroller and buckled him in.

"I haven't had a cup of coffee yet, little man. Let's get some coffee in me and some oatmeal in you, and then we'll both enjoy our donuts, and then I'll take you to the playground."

Leo heard the world playground and clapped his hands. "Mama?"

"Nope, mama's at yoga. It's just you and me this morning."

Inside the café, Johnathan ordered his coffee and oatmeal and made sure Leo had some bites of it before they returned to the counter.

"Okay, Leo. Which donut do you want?"

Leo pointed at a vanilla cream-filled chocolate glazed donut.

"Good choice. That's my favorite. Hey Annie, two of these, please," he said, pointed at the display.

"You know Caroline's going to kill you when she finds out you fed him a donut," replied Annie as she placed the donuts on a plate.

"It's his birthday. Don't tell on us, Annie."

"He'll want one every time she comes in here with him."

Johnathan shrugged. "Maybe he won't like it."

Annie laughed and handed over the treats. "It's on the house.

Happy birthday Leo. So when are you two flying to Paris?"

"In two days. Your Mom is an angel to watch Leo for a week for us. Are you sure she's up for it?"

"Dan and I will stop in and make sure she has some downtime to relax, don't you worry. You two just go and have the time of your lives."

"Thanks, Annie."

Johnathan laughed at the expression on Leo's face when he took a bite of his donut. Johnathan had never seen him eat something so fast in his life. He tried to slow him down, but there was no taking the donut out of his little hands. By the time he was done, vanilla pudding and chocolate icing were all over his face and hands.

Just then, Caroline came into the café and immediately spied both of them sitting in the sunshine in the corner.

"Johnathan. What in the world? Did you already feed him a cake? You let him eat his birthday cake without me?"

"Donut Mama," spoke up Leo. "Donut." Johnathan just managed to grab Leo before he reached out to hug Caroline with his sticky hands.

"Donut? Johnathan! You know how I feel about feeding him sugar."

Johnathan took a wet wipe and began to clean up Leo's hands and face. "It's his birthday Caroline. He wanted one."

"You mean you wanted one. He didn't know what a donut even was until today. How am I going to ever bring him in here with me? He'll want one every time now instead of his oatmeal and berries."

"What are you doing here? Sneaking a donut, yourself maybe?"

"I'm here to pick up his cake for the party. But since you're both here, I may as well have a tea."

After Caroline finished her tea, they went to the gift store to pick up the helium balloons together. Leo's reaction to the helium balloons was priceless. They tied the big bunch of balloons in all the colors of the rainbow to the front of his stroller and a mylar balloon of a dragon to his wrist. He kept shaking his wrist up and down and laughing the entire way home.

It was impossible to take the balloon off his wrist even to eat lunch. He struggled and cried, so they let him eat lunch with it still on his wrist. After lunch, Caroline took him outside while Johnathan set up for the party. He could see Leo running around the garden with the balloon streaming out behind him. At nap time, they, at last, managed to get it away. He was so worn out he didn't struggle.

Annie, Dan, and their twin four-year-olds, Mark, Jenny, Anna, Cindy, and her new boyfriend Evan all showed up for the birthday party at three. The house was filled with voices and laughter. Leo was thrilled to have the twins over, and both girls were sweet at how they played games with him. Anna was doing a good job taking care of Leo and the twins. Johnathan could see that she treated Leo as if he was another one of her grandkids like the twins, which touched Johnathan deeply.

Johnathan's thoughts strayed uncomfortably to Leo's grandparents, who Leo hadn't seen once in the past year. Caroline didn't know that Johnathan had called and almost begged his parents to come and visit so they could be here for Leo's second birthday party. His Mom's answer was the same as it had been every time he'd talked to her for the past year.

"We can't possibly get away at the moment. Your Dad is swamped at work, and then there's the Ballet Gala soon, which I'm helping to organize this year, did you know? Why don't you fly to New York for a visit with Leo instead? We would be thrilled to see you. Why don't you ever come to visit us, Johnathan? You promised you wouldn't disappear to California and never come back home."

"Mom, you know that for a long time, I didn't even have the money for the ticket."

"Well, that is just nonsense. I'd buy you a ticket any time.

All you had to do is ask. Speaking of which, why you wouldn't accept the money from us after the bankruptcy, I will never understand. It's pride; that's what it is, Johnathan. Foolish pride. Why have all this money if you can't help the people you care about most when they get into trouble? Now you talk to Caroline and decide when you're coming for a visit. I won't take no for an answer this time, Johnathan. I will buy you the tickets. Or better yet, I'll arrange to send Daniel's private jet to pick you up. You text me when you want to come."

Johnathan didn't know how his Mom always managed to make Leo's lack of a relationship with his grandparents all his fault. He hadn't told Caroline about his Mom's offer to buy the plane tickets and certainly didn't mention his brother's acquisition of a new private jet.

After closing his first new home build on a beach front lot two weeks ago, Johnathan, at last, had some considerable money in his bank account. The first thing Johnathan had wanted to do with the money was to surprise Caroline with a trip to Paris. Sure, they would be economy seats and a rented flat instead of a five-star hotel, but it would still be Paris. The critical thing, Johnathan kept reminding himself, is that he would be kissing Caroline on a boat drifting down the Seine, gazing up at the Eiffel Tower.

Johnathan's rumination was interrupted by the sound of the doorbell and then a voice from the hall.

"Where's the birthday body?" Jolan walked into the kitchen holding his daughter Melody. Astral floated into the room behind then in a soft pink dress and gold kitten heels.

A combustion of different emotions rolled through Johnathan at the sight of Jolan. Jolan had been Caroline's best friend for years. It was no secret that Jolan and Caroline almost became a couple before Astral showed up unexpectedly nine months pregnant and still in love with Jolan. Johnathan still wasn't sure if it was Jolan who had chosen Astral or Caroline who had chosen him instead of Jolan. Whatever the case, Jolan had moved to New York to be with Astral and his baby girl.

After a series of nude photos had landed on Instagram of Caroline, Johnathan had been confident that Caroline was finished with Jolan for good. But then Jolan had swooped in and saved Caroline from losing her Gram's house in Johnathan's bankruptcy.

Johnathan knew he should feel gratitude to Jolan for that, but he hated it and being beholden to him. The day Johnathan could afford to repurchase the house from Jolan outright would be a day to celebrate. In the meantime, they were paying him to rent the cottage every month. Johnathan had a spreadsheet with calculations of how many home renovations and new building projects he would need to finish before he could afford to buy the house back pinned on his office wall.

Jolan stretched out his hand. "Hey there, Johnathan. How are you doing?"

Johnathan offered a firm handshake and a smile. "Never been better. Your little girl gets prettier every time I see her."

Both men turned their gaze down at the floor, where Leo was happily playing with three-year-old Melody. Astral walked up and kissed Johnathan's cheek.

"Hi, Johnathan. Good to see you again."

"You're looking lovely as always. So you managed to get away from the office? How's the law treating you these days? Still working the twelve-hour days?"

Astral cringed and looked over at Jolan. Jolan's eyes remained fixed on his daughter.

"It's not easy balancing being a partner in the firm and being a Mom. We're lucky Jolan is such an amazing father. Otherwise, I don't know how it would work. I'm indebted to him."

Jolan turned to face his wife. "That's dumb. She's my kid. It's your problem if you miss out on being around for Melody."

Astral glanced over at Jolan and back at Johnathan. "We do have beautiful weekends together. It isn't as if I'm missing out on everything, Jolan."

Johnathan excused himself gratefully as the doorbell rang again. Just as he reached the hall, the door swung open, and a head peaked through.

"Mat?"

"Surprise!" Matilda dropped a big present wrapped in mickey mouse wrapping paper, threw her arms open, and hugged Johnathan around the middle so hard it knocked the wind out of him. Matilda hugged him even tighter then lifted up on her toes to kiss his cheek. "Now, where is that nephew of mine!"

Johnathan didn't get a chance to answer. Matilda had already grabbed her present and pushed past him toward the kitchen.

"You didn't tell me Mat was coming," said Caroline as Johnathan rejoined the party.

"I didn't know. Why didn't you tell me that Jolan was coming?"

"I didn't think I needed to. They're here to get ready for the wedding."

"What wedding?"

"Oh, for goodness sakes, Johnathan. Their wedding? The invitation is on the cork-board in the kitchen. It's the day after we get back from Paris. The ceremony is on the beach and the reception at that private villa on the cliffs overlooking the ocean. You know what one I'm talking about?"

Johnathan watched Astral and Jolan talking to Mark and Jenny. "They didn't act like two people about to get married when I just talked to them, that's for sure."

"What's that supposed to mean?"

"Jolan seems furious that Astral works around the clock and is never home with him and Melody."

"Well, that is something I can sympathize with," commented Caroline.

Johnathan's jaw dropped. "I pick up Jolan from Anna every evening. Nine-times out of ten, I'm the one who makes dinner. It's you who doesn't get home until I'm tucking Leo into bed."

Caroline laughed. "Easy tiger. I'm referring to the time before the new and improved Johnathan."

Johnathan crossed his arms over his chest, but Caroline loosened them and pulled him in for a hug. "Forget I said anything, okay? Look at how happy Leo is."

Johnathan watched Leo and Melody running through the pile of balloons on the floor and laughing as Matilda blew bubbles over their heads.

Matilda helped to clean up after all the guests had left. At last, Leo had calmed down enough to eat some dinner and let Caroline take him up for a bath and get ready for bed.

"It's a great surprise, Mat, that you came. Thank you." Johnathan placed another dish into the dishwasher. "Leo was happy to see you. It's great you come to visit every few months. You're the only one in our family he knows."

Matilda let out a sigh as she started to dry another wine glass with a dishtowel. "I can't make sense of them any better than you can. Listen, I'm sorry I didn't come after the bankruptcy."

Johnathan froze at the mention of the word with a dish in his hand.

"I should have come, Johnathan. I guess I was naive and too self-involved at the time to understand what you were going through. I just figured Mom and Dad would wire you some money after everything settled down, and you'd be fine. Perhaps humiliated and all, because of the failed business, but not depressed and in danger of, you know."

Johnathan stared out the window above the kitchen sink at the ocean waves. "Caroline told me."

"She didn't dare," breathed out Johnathan with his face flushing.

Matilda put a calming hand on his arm. "I'm the only one who knows. I told no one, okay? What I want to know is why you didn't call me? I didn't know Caroline had left you, and you were sleeping on a random guy's coach. Promise you'll call me before you consider throwing yourself into an ocean in the middle of winter again."

Johnathan dropped the plate, and it fell with a crash into the kitchen sink.

Matilda reached out and placed a hand on his arm. "I'm sorry, Johnathan. I won't talk about it ever again. I promise. I just, well, I wanted to tell you that I know what happened now and that I'm super, super sorry that I didn't fly here. I should have been the one helping you and not that crazy yoga teacher."

"He's not crazy."

"True. Mark's great. I didn't mean it like that. It's sweet what he did for you."

"Sweet? He saved my life, Mat. He took me in when I had nowhere else to go. He got me on a schedule; he got me a job working with him on a building site. He got me my job. More importantly, he helped me get my family back. I owe him everything."

"Wow. The way Mark talks is kind of out there, you know? All that 'be one with the universe,' 'the less you own, the more you possess,' and 'settle into the stillness of the present moment,' stuff he's always randomly saying." Matilda threw down the kitchen towel. "I love anyone who did all that for you. I'm trying to ask you to forgive me, Johnathan."

Johnathan turned to face his sister at last. Silent tears were trailing down her cheeks. He gathered her into his arms, resting his chin on the top of her head. "

You've changed a lot in the past year, too, Mat. What's going on? Why isn't Brad here?"

"They broke up," Caroline said as she walked into the kitchen. "It was a good decision, Mat. You don't want to be with a man who talks like that behind your back."

"What do you mean?" Johnathan hugged Mat closer.

Caroline placed a hand on Matilda's back. "Mat overheard Brad laughing and cracking jokes at her expense at a big party in New York."

Matilda pulled away to look up at Johnathan. "Some of it was harmless. You know, like how I'm more in love with my new handbag than him, and stories of me getting lost while we were traveling and not being able to figure out Google maps. But then some guy asked if we were going to get married or start having babies, and he said."

Mat buried her face back into Johnathan's chest.

"He said he was just with Mat for her money and that he wouldn't dare have a baby with a woman who would probably forget it at the park or worse because she's too preoccupied with herself. He said narcissists shouldn't have babies."

"Wow. That doesn't sound like Brad at all."

"I was in shock. It was like watching and listening to a stranger," said Matilda. "You don't think I'm a narcissist, do you?"

Johnathan decided to avoid the question delicately. "Brad seemed like such a good guy. I'm sorry, Mat. Is there anything we can do?"

Matilda leaned back, and biting her lip, looked first at Caroline and then at Johnathan. "I was wondering if I could stay for a while."

"Sure," he shrugged. "We have a guest room."

"Actually. I was thinking of buying the cottage down the street from you. If you don't think that would be crowding you."

Johnathan was startled with surprise. "You want to move here?"

"It was just an idea. I just realized I don't have any real friends after that incident, and Mom and Dad are so weird lately; I didn't have anywhere else I could think of I wanted to go."

"Come here," Johnathan pulled his sister back in for a bear hug and looked over her head at Caroline. Caroline nodded at him. "I'd love to have you move here, Mat. Leo will be thrilled to have his auntie living nearby. What are you going to do here, though?"

Matilda stood back and smiled as she wiped the tears from her cheeks. "I've sold a few of my paintings and have a few commissions. I can set up my studio in the new cottage overlooking the ocean."

"You're painting again? That's great, Matilda. Good for you."

"Okay. On that note. I am going to head back to the hotel for a bubble bath. I'll see you two when you get back from Paris."

"Well, you were right about paying more at check-in to sit in the emergency exit row. I'm not sure I could have fit my legs in one of those sardine cans behind us." Johnathan stood in the aisle examining his seat next to the window for a moment before sitting down.

Caroline sat down next to him and patted his arm. "Bit of a rocky landing to go from a life of sitting in first class to being in economy for you, isn't it?"

"The less we possess, the more we own," Johnathan broke into a grin.

"Yeah, you keep quoting Mark all you want. I know you're struggling with this today."

Johnathan shrugged and looked out the window. "I'm excited, babe. I'm on my way to Paris with my sweetheart. I can't help but be excited no matter where I'm seated."

Caroline rested her head on his shoulder and entwined her fingers with his. "By this time tomorrow, we will be admiring the Eiffel Tower."

Johnathan's phone began to buzz yet again. He took it out of his pocket and glanced at the screen. Johnathan had already received five texts from his Mom to call her and two texts from his Dad. Alison had tried to call him a few times, but he hadn't answered, and he wasn't planning to now. He watched the message of a new voice mail appear on his screen.

"Why don't you just talk to her?"

"The woman hasn't bothered to fly out to see me since months before the bankruptcy, not even to come and see her grandson. I called her. I didn't tell you. A few weeks before Leo's birthday, I called and practically begged for her to fly out and be there for his party."

"What if it's an emergency?"

"With my Mom, it's always some kind of an emergency. No. Not this time. We are going to Paris, and I am turning off my phone. Anna has your number in case she needs to reach you about Leo. It will be good for me to have a digital detox, just like I did on our honeymoon, remember?"

"Well, if you're sure," answered Caroline. "Then I have a surprise for you now that we're up in the air."

"What's that?"

Caroline smiled at him and got down her bag from the compartment overhead. She pulled out a scarf and unwrapped two glass champagne flutes and two mini bottles of champagne. "I thought I would pack a little first-class experience with me for you." She opened his bottle of champagne and handed him a flute before pulling out a gold-wrapped box of chocolates and a container of oil and herb-infused olives, prosciutto, crackers, and cheese.

"I even brought real plates. Look," she laughed, pulling out two tiny china plates.

Johnathan took a sip of his champagne and experienced a buoyancy that tingled along his spine and warmed his heart. "You are something else. You know that?"

"Something good?"

Johnathan softly kissed her lips and nodded.

# CHAPTER 16

Johnathan didn't get any sleep on the flight, but he had such a good time with Caroline that he didn't feel tired as the plane touched down in Paris. They hadn't had eight hours to be alone together and talk since their honeymoon. After talking for hours, they decided to watch a movie.

Johnathan didn't even mind sitting in economy once he realized the armrest between them could be lifted, and he could snuggle up closer to Caroline. Caroline turned on her phone as they awaited the doors to the cabin to be opened. One minute later, it began to ring.

"It's your Mom," announced Caroline. "Should I answer it?"

"No."

"But she's never called me before, Johnathan. It really could be an emergency."

"Don't answer it," Johnathan replied as he stood up to pull down their carry-ons from the overhead compartment. Caroline had already rinsed and replaced their champagne flutes and plates, but Johnathan stuffed in their books and Caroline's phone as well. Caroline snatched the phone back out of the bag and put it into her purse. As soon as the ringing stopped, it started again. Johnathan glared at Caroline, and Caroline put her phone on silent.

While they were waiting for the luggage, the phone began vibrating in her purse, and she took it out. "It's her. Again. Johnathan, please call the woman back. I won't be able to relax and have fun until I know that there isn't some emergency."

Johnathan didn't answer. He just grabbed her hand, and they walked outside to find a taxi.

On the way to the hotel, Johnathan pulled out his phone and called his mother back.

"Johnathan, thank god, where were you? Why didn't you call us back? I was so worried; you have no idea; I was tempted to call the police or something."

"Mom, I texted you that I was having a break from all technology for the next week."

"But that doesn't include your mother."

Johnathan smiled. Some things never changed. "What's up, Mom?"

"What's up? What's up? Have you not seen the news? You need to come back home immediately."

Johnathan held the phone away from his ear, the voice shrill and loud in his ear. His heart jumped into his throat. "Did someone die?" he managed to croak out. "Dad?"

"We're ruined, Johnathan. Ruined. We've lost everything. They're coming tomorrow to kick us out of the penthouse. Not that we will have anywhere to go. They're taking our place in the Hamptons, in Aspen, even that little studio I kept near Central Park out of nostalgia for my college days."

"Go to Daniel's," Johnathan soothed. "Or to Mat's place."

"Johnathan, don't you understand? They're taking everything Daniel and Matilda have as well. I think they've even frozen your assets, not that you have any. Everything. What on earth will we do?"

"Well, but Brad," began Johnathan, searching for a lifeline.

"He's being indicted too."

"Wait, what? What do you mean too?"

"Good heavens, Johnathan! Haven't you at least read the papers today? Your father, Daniel, and Brad are all indicted. I thank GOD on my knees that you signed yourself out of the company. Of course, everyone thinks you knew and just didn't want to turn in your own family. That's why your assets are frozen. I tried to tell them you don't have any, but they just said they'd make sure of that themselves."

Alison broke into tears. "We went to our friends, all of them. We begged. Begged! If they could just loan us the money to hire a proper attorney. They all refused. Can you believe they refused? They even told us not to contact them again because they don't want to be pulled into the mess. 'We don't want to look like we're complicit. You understand, don't you, Ali?' Can you believe it? What will we do, Johnathan? At least they're not in prison, just under house arrest until the court date. Thank God Mom and Dad aren't alive to be shamed by this fiasco. I don't understand what is going on. They must have it all wrong. Your father would never get involved in anything illegal. Come home, Johnathan. I need you. I have nowhere to go."

"Do you have a registry of all your jewelry, Mom? With the insurance?"

"Well, of course, I do."

"All of it?"

"Well, no. No, there's a bit I've inherited that I kept hidden away; your father doesn't even know about it. And I put some of your sister's jewelry in my box for safekeeping as well."

"Go get it all right now. Go sell it."

"I couldn't, Daniel. It's been in our family for three generations. It belongs to Matilda."

"Mom. I'm sure Mat will understand."

"Yes." Alison paused on the other end of the line. "Of course, you're right. There's nothing for it. Luckily I know just where to go to auction it off to get a high price. There is cash in the box as well. There's enough to find a place to stay."

"A low-cost place to stay, Mom. Like a flat, you can rent somewhere cheap."

"Cheap? Good heavens. Johnathan, I have to go. You're right. There isn't a moment to spare. The box is still under my maiden name, so if I hurry, I may be able to access the box before they take that too."

"Take care of yourself, Mom. Bye."

The taxi pulled to a stop in front of the hotel. Caroline jumped out and waited on the sidewalk. Johnathan sat in the car, numb and unable to move. At last, Caroline opened the door and tugged on his sleeve. Johnathan got out, collected their luggage, and stood motionless on the sidewalk, looking up at the five-star hotel.

Caroline walked into the hotel, and he followed at a distance. Caroline approached the counter to check them in. Johnathan didn't know how much time went by before Caroline returned to his side.

"That's funny. They insist your card has been declined. Shall we use another?"

Johnathan couldn't answer. He stood there like ice was crystallizing in his veins, slowly numbing him from the inside out. He just couldn't explain all of it here, standing in the middle of this hotel lobby.

"None of my cards will work."

Caroline grabbed the handle of her suitcase, linked her arm through his, and turned toward the doors.

"Come on. I need a coffee, and there's a romantic Parisian Confiserie just down the block with pastries in the window I spotted on the car ride here."

Caroline seated Johnathan outside at a table and went inside to look at the desserts. Johnathan's mouth had gone dry. He couldn't even swallow by the time she returned, carrying two glass bottles of sparkling water, a strawberry tart, and a five-layer chocolate mousse cake. Without a word, she disappeared and then returned with two coffees and sat back down. "No waiters here, isn't that funny? Self serve and yet they still serve the coffees in porcelain cups. How elegant are these coffee cup handles?"

Johnathan couldn't reply. His mind had stopped working. Caroline's voice came as if from far away, through a dull roaring vibrating around him.

"Johnathan. Johnathan drinks some water. Drink your coffee. Eat the cake. Then you can tell me what's going on. In the meantime, I will just go ahead and book us somewhere new to stay."

As if in slow motion, Johnathan saw his hand reach out for the water. He downed half the bottle in one go, spluttering a bit as the bubbles washed too quickly down his throat. He took a bite of cake but didn't taste the velvety chocolate texture in his mouth. He took a sip of his coffee, the hot liquid seeping down into his belly and warming his insides. Suddenly ravenous, he devoured his cake, then the strawberry tart. Caroline looked up in surprise but didn't protest. She just disappeared into the bakery and came out with another strawberry tart and two baguette sandwiches.

"Another coffee?" Johnathan murmured.

Caroline hurried back into the bakery and brought him out a steaming cup of café crème.

They ate in silence, Caroline examining him curiously, then shifting her attention to the people passing by on the street and the other guests at the three other tables next to theirs. Johnathan was grateful for her silence; she knew him well and showed her love by not asking any questions. Caroline knew he'd tell her when he'd processed whatever had happened in his own time first.

After they had finished their sandwiches and coffees, Caroline stood up as a taxi pulled up to the curb.

"Let's go, love. I've found us a new place to stay and paid for it upfront, so no complaints, yeah?"

Johnathan climbed out of the taxi and grabbed their bags,

still numb. He trudged up the narrow flight of stairs behind Caroline and the hostess, who at last opened the door to the flat with a flourish.

"And Voila, here we are. You will love it, just wait. You are in for a rare treat." The Parisian's eyes sparkled as she held the door open for both of them to walk inside.

Johnathan went instantly to the picture window, looking down at a lush private garden courtyard teeming with flowers around a small lawn. Next to a burbling fountain stood two red chairs and a little turquoise table. In the distance, there was a glimpse of Montmartre to be seen on the hill.

The flat was less spectacular than the charming private garden.

Johnathan wandered past the antique salon sofa with its mahogany rim and to the matching mahogany bookshelf that reached from floor to ceiling. Johnathan began to peruse the titles as Caroline chatted to the hostess.

Johnathan noticed that the apartment didn't look like a rental. It looked like the worn-in elegant home of an intellectual by the books on the shelves. There was everything from masterpieces of literature to works on political science, economics, art, design, medieval history, and philosophy. Johnathan barely registered Caroline asking if he would like to join them for a cup of tea in the garden. He shook his head absentmindedly and said thank you, no, praising the flat's library as he continued to peruse the books on the shelves.

Taking out a book by Peter Zumthor titled Thinking Architecture, he sat down in the wing-backed chair and began to read.

"Okay, love, I'll be back up in a bit. Are you sure you don't want to join us?" asked Caroline.

Johnathan looked up from the book, finding it difficult to bring his eyes into focus. "What was that?"

"Tea? In the garden? Do you want to join us? Madame Toussaint is going to tell me all about the best little shops, restaurants, and things to do in the area while we're here."

"Yes. I mean, no. Go ahead. Thank you, Madame. Your home is charming."

"Thank you," replied Madame Toussaint puffing up with pride. "Lots of love in this place. Plenty of joie de vivre." She looked around as if taking in the room with new eyes.

Johnathan looked at the woman properly for the first time, taking in her chique navy blue dress, red hair scarf tied up around her white hair, the pearls, the wrinkled face, and aged hands.

"Your books?" Johnathan gestured to the bookshelf.

"Alas, no. No, they were my husbands. He passed this past year. How he loved his books, my beloved Jacques." Madame Toussaint's eyes looked into the distance as if seeing a movie screen they couldn't. "We were married forty-nine years."

"I'm sorry for your loss," Caroline answered.

Johnathan nodded in agreement.

Madame Toussaint waved her hands. "Enough of that. Let's go down to the garden. I have such great tips to give you, and then I am off on the first plane to my daughter's holiday home in Ibiza."

Johnathan returned to his book as the women left out the door with their steaming cups of tea. It was as if his brain was grasping out for a lifeline. Johnathan wanted anything to distract him from the abyss of despair. He devoured the book page by page, barely noticing when Caroline opened the door and came to stand at his side.

"Hey," she crouched down. "Sorry that took so long. Are you ready to tell me what's going on?"

"How did you pay for this place?" Johnathan looked up at her with unfocused eyes.

"With my credit card. It won't be expensive. It's just that the refundable security deposit is high because it's her home. She doesn't want anything broken or stolen. It's lovely, isn't it? The flat? It will be like living like a real Parisian for a week. I'm happy we ended up not staying at that posh hotel."

"Good. It looks as if we may never be staying in one again."

"What's happened?"

"I don't want to talk about it. Tomorrow. Tomorrow."

Caroline placed her hands on his knees and stood up. "Fine. I promise I won't ask again tonight. But we're going out to dinner. Madame Toussaint recommended a hole-in-the-wall-looking restaurant just up the road with some of the best fresh-made pasta and whitefish in Paris. Let's go." She held out her hand.

Johnathan grabbed it and walked with her down the stairs and out onto the cobbled stone street below.

# CHAPTER 17

The following day Johnathan woke up bleary-eyed with a pounding head as if he had drunk one or two bottles of wine by himself. Wincing at the light glaring in through the bedroom window, he remembered draining a bottle of red with dinner the night before.

Caroline had kept her promise and hadn't inquired about what had happened on the phone with his mother, nor why none of his credit cards worked anymore. Instead, they had talked about their wedding, their honeymoon in Switzerland, and architecture.

Caroline had listened as Johnathan gave an impromptu introductory lesson on his favorite subject: design. There had been a moment of panic when Johnathan remembered that he couldn't pay for dinner. Placing a hand on his arm as he reached for the bill, Caroline silently slipped her credit card to the waiter, who quickly disappeared.

"Do you have money for this?"

Caroline laughed, her eyes twinkling at him. "I got along just fine before you showed up, you know. Anyway, this restaurant is incredibly reasonable. That's an advantage of being in a non-touristy neighborhood."

Johnathan realized all at once that he hadn't even thought to look at the prices on the menu. In the shock over his family's emergency, he had reverted to his pre-bankruptcy ways. How had that happened? He had just ordered whatever sounded delicious. Fortunately, Johnathan remembered Caroline ordering a carafe of the open wine by the glass for him before he could even look at the list.

Johnathan wandered into the gleaming all-white kitchen, noticing the vibrant dishes visible through the shelves' glass doors and the row of herbs in colorful pots along the windowsill. He didn't find Caroline in the living room, nor in the tiny bathroom with its claw-footed white bathtub. A glance out the window revealed Caroline down in the garden doing yoga on the lawn.

Johnathan let out a sigh of relief at the reprieve. He wasn't ready to talk yet. He didn't want to even think about it, and certainly not before coffee. In the kitchen, Johnathan tried to find a coffee machine but couldn't. At last, he realized Madame Toussaint must make her coffee in the French press each morning. It was too much work for Johnathan in his state of mind. He was used to pressing the button on his automatic coffee machine for a coffee creme or espresso, depending on his whim, and having the coffee pour aromatic and steaming into his cup.

Johnathan went back to the window, looking down at his wife, and experienced a wave of affection. Throwing open the door, he stumbled down the stairs to stand blinking in the sunlight.

"Can I join you?"

"Sure, love."

Johnathan padded over barefoot in his pajamas and began to flow through the poses with her. His breathing became deeper, slower, more even.

"Why are we stopping already?" he asked as Caroline sat down with crossed legs on the grass, closing her eyes.

Caroline peeped one eye open. "I've done an hour, and you've done forty minutes or so. It's enough, no? Meditate with me. Come," Caroline said, patting the lawn beside her.

Reluctant, Johnathan nonetheless sat down beside her and closed his eyes, repeating silently the mantra Om Sat Chit Ananda that he had learned from Mark. For a few minutes, it worked, but then the thoughts started exploding into his brain, forcing away any of his attempts to retain his focus.

What had his father done? Or had it been Daniel? How could Brad be involved in all of this? Why was he under suspicion? It must have something to do with their company or Brad's hedge fund. Why had his mother alluded to Johnathan's exit from the company as being the only reason he was still a free man? How could that be?

It wasn't illegal for his Dad to invest in some high-risk stocks. Or had his Dad lied? Or was all this as much a surprise for his Dad and Brad as it had been for him? Daniel always had had a taste for adrenaline and risk.

"Stop grinding your teeth, for goodness sake," Caroline admonished him.

Johnathan snapped his eyes open. Meditation this morning was futile. He leaped to his feet. The yoga had helped, he noted. His head's pounding had lessened, and his body felt more open and fluid.

"I'm going to go take a shower."

Caroline smiled without opening her eyes and nodded. Smiling, Johnathan knelt back down and kissed her cheek before bounding up the stairs. It was time to make a plan. He wanted to help his Mom, as he always had when she was in trouble. What about Mat? Was his sister in trouble too? Now they needed him more than they ever had, and he was ready to face the crisis.

"I brought coffee," Caroline called through the bathroom door. Johnathan tied a towel around his waist and headed straight for the kitchen. The dressing could wait. He needed the jolt of caffeine.

"I got you a latte with two shots of espresso." Caroline held out a cup of coffee, and Johnathan took it gratefully.

He took a sip and leaned against the counter top opposite Caroline. "All my assets are frozen."

"What? Why?"

"Mom told me yesterday that Daniel, Dad, and Brad were all taken into custody by the police. That's why my payment for the hotel didn't go through. All my assets have been frozen too." Johnathan held out his phone. "I can't bear to read about what the hell is going on. Can you read it out loud?"

Caroline reached out with a trembling hand for the phone and slid slowly down along the cabinet to sit on the floor with her knees pulled into her chest.

"Wall Street?"

Johnathan nodded, and Caroline began reading the news article.

"Daniel Arrozzini, Allen Arrozzini and Brad Laurent were all arrested yesterday. They have all been charged with fraud, money laundering, and embezzlement. According to investigators, Brad Laurent is charged with committing short-and-distort stock fraud and defrauding his investors by investing in worthless Chinese bonds and commodity markets, promising annual returns of between 21 or 42%. Thirty-two investors were swindled out of $67.9 million. Their money has disappeared without a trace. The cash in Brad Laurent's personal accounts has been frozen.

Laurent is thought to have diverted $15 million to his girlfriend's boyfriend, Daniel Arrozzini's company, a multi-million dollar real estate and architecture company.

At Arrozzini Architecture, they used internal transfers and false operating expenses to launder the money coming in from Brad over the past few months.

Daniel Arrozzini is also charged with using internal transfers and false operating expenses to embezzle money. Another $7 million was transferred under the guise of payment for consulting services to his father, Allen Arrozzini, just this past spring.

Allen and Daniel are charged with violating the Clean Diamond Trade Act for the importation of millions of dollars of rough diamonds from Sierra Leone, Liberia, Angola, and other unknown origins in Africa without Kimberley Process Certificates.

The Clean Diamond Trade Act was first enacted in 2003 by President Bush to protect against human rights abuses; the act prohibits the importation of diamonds mined from countries that use rough diamond sales to fuel war. The Clean Diamond Trade Act's intent is to impede belligerents' funds to fuel their continued civil unrest and death toll. According to experts, up to 3.7 million people have perished in Africa due to wars funded by conflict diamonds.

"These men are suspected of being involved in a highly intricate and professional global network of companies, arms dealers, miners, and diamond merchants that violate the trade and weapons bans," commented the federal bureau investigator.

The investigators have yet to find conclusive evidence that tens of millions of dollars of diamonds have already been sold throughout the United States, as they suspect.

"They covered their tracks well. We're asking for anyone who knows anything to do the right thing and come forward. The two men hired their team of highly skilled gemologists for the designing, marking, dividing, shaping, faceting, and polishing necessary to turn the rough diamonds into finished glittering jewels ready for sale. It was one of the senior gemologists who alerted the officials of her worries about potential fraud. Then the entire intricate story of fraud began to unravel after that."

Each defendant could face as many as 40 years in prison, millions of dollars in fines each, and other penalties.

Investigators are having trouble finding any trace of the money. Minimal amounts were found in Daniel, Brad, and Allen's personal bank accounts and investment portfolios. "It's like they knew we were coming for them and hid the money. Though where you can hide sums that big in this day and age without a trace, I don't know. We're asking anyone with any knowledge to step forward."

Matilda Arrozzini, who had recently, and allegedly, broken off her engagement with Brad Laurent and moved out to California to start a new life, returned to New York for questioning about her knowledge and involvement in her boyfriend and family's illegal activities. All her assets have been frozen, though she has not been charged with any crime. It is unclear if she has profited from her boyfriend and family's illegal operations or if she is hiding the money for them somehow.

According to more than one eyewitness, Matilda broke off her relationship publicly at a party in New York in which Brad was making jokes at his fiancee's expense.

"I mean; I don't think they could have staged that. Matilda was horrified. He said some terrible things when he thought she couldn't hear him, how he wouldn't put it past her to forget her own baby in the park. No, they don't have any kids. He was explaining why he wouldn't ever want to have any with her."

A few other people have anonymously admitted to our reporters that both Daniel and Brad have played fast and loose with rules and the law for years. They wouldn't give specifics. They deemed it unlikely that Matilda knew what was going on. "She's a pretty airhead. I don't think they would trust her not to let a secret that big slip."

Johnathan Arrozzini, brother of Daniel Arrozzini, is wanted for questioning as soon as he returns to the United States. All his assets have been frozen. Investigators have yet to find any connection between Johnathan and the fraud, embezzlement, and money laundering. But suspicions are high that he knew about his brother and father's illegal activities. It is unclear now if Johnathan jumped ship before being caught up in the criminal activities, if he was involved, or if he has somehow hidden some of the money for his family.

Johnathan Arrozzini resigned from his position as head of Arrozzini Architects a little over two years ago, walking away with nothing but the shirt on his back from the company. Anonymous insiders report that they saw Johnathan arguing violently with both his brother and father the day before stepping away from the company.

"They were arguing on the day of his wedding. Just before his wedding ceremony started."

Another anonymous eyewitness insisted that the fracturing began earlier in the week during a yoga retreat.

"I overheard and saw Johnathan arguing with his brother and parents more than once during the week. Maybe he was trying to talk them into stopping their illegal crimes. Who knows?"

Johnathan Arrozzini fled New York after the wedding for a quiet little town on the California coast. His unsuccessful attempt to start up a new architecture ended in bankruptcy for the new couple in less than one year. In the fall out of the bankruptcy, Johnathan's wife Caroline left him and filed for divorce. After losing everything, Johnathan eventually landed a job at Dream Lifestyle Realty, working as an assistant to Cindy Rhodes, where he still is employed.

Locals are polarized in how they perceive Johnathan Arrozzini. While some insist he is a devoted dad and warm persona, others think the bankruptcy and one hundred and eighty personality change suspicious.

"His parents were billionaires. So what was he doing sleeping on my yoga instructor's coach for months? I think he knew his parents were into shady shit and wanted no part of it. It's been good for the guy, though. He's a lot humbler and grateful then when he first rolled into town, that's for sure," an anonymous local told a local journalist.

"He's adorable with his son. I see them playing at the beach all the time. They come in here for an ice cream cone sometimes. He just seems like a normal guy," said another local.

"Worked with the man on the construction site for a couple of months. Picked it up real fast. Hard worker. Isn't that something that he was a billionaire and lost it all? You wouldn't have known it the way he kept his head down and never complained. He confided in me once about his son. He was upset about losing his family. He never said a word about losing all his money."

Johnathan is said to have reconciled and moved back in with his ex-wife. Federal investigators will be looking deeper into Johnathan's involvement, if any, with his family's criminal activities. For the moment, Johnathan will not be charged nor detained.

Caroline took a deep breath and let it out. Johnathan sat on the floor next to Caroline, his knees pulled into his chest and his forehead resting on his knees. His brain was buzzing, his ears ringing, the clock on the wall ticking abnormally loud. Caroline put a hand on his back.

"Johnathan?"

Johnathan raised his head to look at her. "Let's get out of here. Take the lunch cruise we booked down the Seine this afternoon. Kiss under the Eiffel tower. Drink a glass of red wine at one of those Parisian cafés and order appetizers. Come back and get dressed up and go out for a fancy dinner at a local restaurant around here."

Caroline looked at him for a moment. "Did you hear me read that article?"

"Yes."

"Yes, but did you hear it?"

"Caroline. We're in Paris. I don't know when I will be in Paris again with the love of my life. I had no idea what the hell my family and Mat's boyfriend were up to, but I wouldn't put it past them to pull me into it. If I'm going to land in prison, then I want a perfect day to remember. With you. Let's go."

He jumped to his feet and reached out a hand. "Aren't you and Mark always going on about; being in the present moment and all that shit? Well. Here I am. In Paris with you. Healthy and with some cash to spend. Or rather, you have some cash to spend. Let's go."

Caroline took his hand.

Johnathan pulled Caroline's chair closer to him on the seat for a kiss as they glided down the Seine river. Johnathan couldn't help but smile with the champagne glass in his hand and the sun warm on his face. Johnathan succeeded in releasing all thoughts of the fiasco awaiting him during the three-course lunch on the riverboat as they floated by the Louvre, Île de la Cite, and the Eiffel Tower.

They strolled along the river bank after the river tour and then wandered up a small street to a tiny Parisian café where they ordered a bottle of wine, some stuffed mushrooms, and a plate of grilled vegetables and marinated olives. As they sat watching the pedestrians walk by, awaiting the delivery of their wine and food, Johnathan couldn't keep his mind clear anymore; he plummeted headfirst into a cycle of endless questions.

How long had his brother been involved in illegal activities? Did it go back to when he was still a partner in the company? How could his Dad be engaged in any of this? How did they even get involved in the illegal diamond trade, and why? Was it even real? Why would they do all this? Was it even real? Could they be innocent? How could Brad, affable, good-natured, sweet Brad, have defrauded all his investors out of millions of dollars of money? Were they all going to end up in jail? Was he going to end up in prison with them? Was Leo going to grow up without a father?

"Can you bring me a pot of ginger or spiced tea, please?" Caroline asked the waiter.

"Why aren't you drinking your wine?" asked Johnathan.

Caroline looked up at him with big eyes and bit her lip as the waiter arrived with their appetizers.

"Caroline? Are you okay?"

Caroline took a fork and ate a stuffed mushroom while

returning her gaze to the people passing by the café. She looked back at him after a few minutes of silence.

"I'm pregnant."

Johnathan leaped to his feet and rushed over to kiss Caroline. When he looked at the expression on her face, his euphoria vanished as quickly as it had arrived.

"Did you know?"

He shook his head as he sat back down. "No."

"Johnathan, don't lie to me. Please. I can handle the truth. Did you know about your brother and Dad? Are you involved in any way?"

"No. I'm as shocked by all of this as you are."

Caroline nodded, her body visibly relaxing. "You looked shocked this morning."

Johnathan nodded. "I don't know how this is all going to play out. I don't know if they are guilty, first of all, and of what exactly. I'm also in the dark as to when all of this started. If they are guilty, then when did it start? Was it when I was still part of the company? Could I end up going to jail even though I had no idea any of this was happening?"

Caroline ate another mushroom, and they fell into silence. Suddenly Johnathan was ravenously hungry. He finished off the mushrooms before Caroline could eat more than one more. "Let's go back to the apartment and take a rest before we get ready for dinner."

"Are you sure? We could just get some takeaway. Or eat an early dinner here."

Johnathan shook his head. "I have something special booked for us. And who knows how long I could be eating horrible food in prison in the near future."

"That's not funny, John."

"You know I hate being called that."

Caroline crossed her arms over her chest. "I'm tired. How can you even still be hungry? We ate a three-course lunch and all these appetizers."

174

Johnathan shook his head. "All you need is a nap and a bath. We are going out, and we are going to enjoy ourselves. Don't worry, Caroline. The investigators will find out the truth soon enough and have nothing to do with any of this mess. I'm sure I'll have to go to New York City for a while, but I will be back in California in no time."

The waiter reappeared, and Caroline flagged him down to pay the bill. Hand in hand, they wandered over the cobblestoned streets past a bakery, a handbag shop, and a butchery. Caroline paused to look in the window of a toy shop, and Johnathan waited outside while Caroline went inside to buy something she spied for Leo.

"Maybe we shouldn't go home early," spoke up Caroline as she handed Johnathan the paper bag containing the wrapped gift to carry. "I mean, it won't change anything, will it? If you can keep it from driving you crazy with worry and fear about the future, then so can I. Who knows when we will ever be back in Paris together again?"

Johnathan slid his hand around Caroline's waist. "You're right, love. Let's stay. I'll fly straight from Paris to New York to face the fire at the end of our holiday."

"You'll miss Jolan and Astral's wedding."

"Ah, well, that is a price I will just have to pay," Johnathan chuckled.

"You still don't like him, do you?"

"It's hard to forgive a dude who put nude photos of my wife onto the Internet."

"I wasn't your wife then."

"Are you defending him?"

"Well, he did save Gram's house."

Johnathan gritted his teeth and said nothing. Caroline paused to look in the window of a book and card store with hand-painted cards held in rotating racks outside the front door. "I painted them all myself. If you would like something custom-made for you, I could do that as well," spoke up the owner, who was enjoying a cup of coffee at a table in the sun near the entrance.

Caroline agreed, and Johnathan wandered over to the used bookstore across the street as Caroline placed her order for a card for Anna and Annie. He was just thumbing through a used copy of architectural wonders of the world when Caroline appeared at his side.

"We need to come back tomorrow, and she'll have the card ready. Hey. I know you hate being indebted to Jolan. I'm close to having enough to pay him back. I just need another year or so. The last thing I need is to put myself into a cash flow problem. Lord knows my credit is no longer good enough to get a small business loan if I got into a pinch."

Johnathan grimaced, and Caroline wrapped both hands around his middle, pulling him to a stop. "I'm sorry. I didn't mean for it to come out like that. I know you feel terrible about the bankruptcy and the house and everything. You've apologized enough times. I don't mean to keep bringing it up."

"It's okay, Caroline. It's something we still have to deal with. I'll make it up to you. I promise."

"You already are," Caroline soothed and pulled on the front of his sweater, so his lips came down to meet hers for a kiss.

After a nap and a hot shower, Caroline came out of the bathroom looking refreshed and glowing. Johnathan let out a sigh of relief. He had prepaid for this dinner months ago.

"Okay. Here I am. Where are we going?"

"Just you wait. It's a surprise," declared Johnathan. "The car is waiting for us downstairs."

As the car approached the Eiffel Tower, Caroline punched Johnathan's arm. "If you think I'm climbing all those steps, you have another thing coming."

"No, I am taking you out to dinner at 58 Tour Eiffel at the top, and we can take the elevator, love."

Over the four-course dinner, Johnathan and Caroline watched the sunset, and the lights of Paris begin to twinkle in the twilight beneath them. As the night settled over the city, Caroline grew quiet, watching the city sparkling below.

The soft lighting of the restaurant was casting a soft glow on Caroline's features. Caroline picked up her teacup and took a sip with her eyes back on the dancing lights of Paris below them. As Johnathan watched her, a surge of joy and love flooded him, and he smiled so big his face began to hurt.

"I'm thrilled about the baby," Johnathan told her as the server brought a pistachio strawberry tart cake and a chocolate mouse with raspberry cookies. "How far along are you, lovely?"

"Almost four months." Caroline took a bite of her cake and then looked up at Johnathan. "You have to try this."

"What?"

"Listen, don't get mad at me, okay? I found out the week after you moved back in with us, and I needed some time to get my head around the news. It was a shock. And I wasn't sure how you were going to handle it."

Johnathan nodded, the smile fading away. "You needed time to find out if you wanted me to stick around."

Caroline looked up from her cake with enormous eyes; her fork paused halfway between her plate and her mouth.

Johnathan shook his head. "It's okay, Caroline. You admitted when I moved back in that you were worried I would go back to working crazy hours and not helping out around the house or with Leo."

Caroline replaced her fork on her plate. "That's not what I meant. But now that you say that, who knows? Maybe that's also why I took my time in telling you. The perfect one-eighty was almost too good to be true. You hadn't done so much as a load of laundry before we moved out. Now I am coming home to a clean house and a home-cooked dinner with Leo already bathed and in his pajamas each night. I don't see how you can keep this up. I may be waiting for the shoe to drop, so to say."

"Look, in my defense, I hadn't known how much you were doing on your own when we were married. I mean before the bankruptcy. I assumed you'd hired help to clean and cook and do the laundry and stuff."

Caroline nodded. "I guess it didn't occur to me. It wasn't ever an option I could afford before marrying you. I wasn't sure if it was something we could afford. You kept saying you needed to put everything into the new business."

Johnathan leaned back from the table, shaking his head. "Look, I thought you said you forgave me for all that? I'm not that man anymore. I guess the silver lining of the bankruptcy is that it forced me to learn how to clean, cook, and be a better father to Leo."

Caroline reached out her hand across the table. Johnathan placed his hand in hers. "Maybe that bankruptcy was a good thing."

"You know what?" Johnathan nodded. "I'm beginning to think it was, especially with the shake-out that's happening with my family and the feds."

"I am a bit nervous about how we are going to do this," answered Caroline.

"Excuse me?"

"We're having triplets, Johnathan."

Johnathan pressed his palms together and brought his fingers to his lips. He'd always wanted a big family. In one go, they would go from a family of three to a family of six. Johnathan leaped out of his chair, pulled Caroline up into his arms, and kissed her.

"I always wanted a big family," Johnathan declared as they sat back down.

"I wish we didn't have the awful news about your family hanging over our heads right now, and this would be the perfect moment," Caroline answered.

"Let's forget all that," replied Johnathan. "Just for this week."

The next day Caroline and Johnathan strolled back to pick up the hand-painted card for Anna. The smell of freshly baked croissants wafted out the front door of the bakery down the street. Caroline couldn't resist pulling Johnathan inside to buy two croissants still warm from the oven and two coffees to go. Sweet with a slight crunch on the outside, inside the buttery layers melted in the mouth. Johnathan and Caroline paused to savor the croissants while watching a street artist paint a canvas of the café across the cobbled stone street.

When the street artist offered to paint them into the picture, Caroline couldn't resist. They went across the street, settled into two chairs at a small table, and ordered two cappuccinos. Caroline laughed when Johnathan put down his coffee cup, and his entire lip was covered in milk foam. She reached out a napkin and wiped it off for him, then leaned across the table for a kiss.

They were just finishing their coffees when the artist appeared beside their table to show them the completed painting. Caroline couldn't resist purchasing the painting, which of course, was what the artist had intended.

They returned to the apartment to drop off the painting and the card and then set off for a day touring the art museums. While Johnathan could have spent many more hours at the Louvre, Caroline insisted she wanted to see the impressionist paintings at the Musée d'Orsay and only permitted him to grab two baguette sandwiches along the way instead of stopping for lunch. After hours of soaking in art, Johnathan was hungry and tired, but Caroline begged for just ten more minutes to admire a painting by Renoir.

After another five minutes, Johnathan's stomach began growling, and he pulled Caroline, still protesting, out of the exhibit hall and down the marble staircase.

Over dinner, in a small local restaurant, Caroline and Johnathan tried to figure out how to fit three cribs into the guest room or if they could sleep together in one crib when Caroline's phone rang. Caroline showed Johnathan the display to see it was his Mom. Johnathan held out his hand for the phone.

"Caroline?"

"Mom, it's me."

"Johnathan, you have to call back the investigators, or they are going to talk to the French authorities. Not turning up for questioning makes you look guilty, which I know you're not, but they don't. Johnathan?"

"I had my phone off for the week."

"This is happening, Johnathan, whether you like it or not, and hiding your head in the sand is only going to make things worse. I advise you to call back the investigator and get on the first plane to New York first thing in the morning to talk with them."

"You're right, Mom. How are you holding up? Where are you staying?"

"An Airbnb in Brooklyn. It's not too bad, considering it's just $51 a night since I paid for the entire month upfront. Of course, I scoured the bathrooms and kitchen with bleach, and I brought all my quality linens. The police didn't mind, isn't that nice? They let me take my time in the packing process. They said they couldn't sell sheets and towels anyway."

Johnathan shook his head. Only his Mom would prioritize packing up her luxurious sheets and towels in a crisis.

"Pity I had to give up all the furniture and all my lovely jewelry and shoes. Can you believe that, Daniel? I couldn't take all my shoes."

"Shoes are the least of our problems, Mom. I'll fly to New York tomorrow. I'll call you when I land."

"Wait! Johnathan?"

"Yes?"

"I'm sorry I didn't fly out to see Leo for his birthday. Give Caroline my best."

"Take care, Mom," Johnathan sighed. "Good-bye"

Johnathan handed the phone back over to Caroline and then finished his glass of wine in one go.

"It sounds like we are flying to New York tomorrow," commented Caroline.

Johnathan held up his hand. "Correction. I am flying to New York tomorrow. You are staying here and enjoying the rest of your time in Paris and then flying home to our son."

"I'm not staying in Paris without you."

"We already paid for the flat for the rest of the week. The plane ticket is non-refundable and can't be exchanged. It's going to cost us enough for me to book a new ticket to New York as it is. More importantly, I don't want you mixed up in any of this. We have triplets on the way. This will be your last chance in a long time to sleep in late every morning and do what pleases you all day long. Go wander the Parisian streets, eat as many pastries and croissants as you want, and sit as long as you want in front of paintings you enjoy."

Caroline's mouth twisted from side to side.

"I'm not taking no for an answer," insisted Johnathan. "Now, let's pay the bill and get out of here. I have one more evening with my wife in Paris. Let's go make the most of it."

# CHAPTER 18

"I find it suspicious that you decided just to walk away from your majority stake in the company you built, especially because you didn't accept any money in compensation. Why would anyone do that unless they knew there was something to run away from?"

"I've told you already. It was my brother's dream to be CEO of the company. On my wedding day, I decided I wanted a simpler life with my wife out in California. So I signed over my part of the company. That's all there is to it."

"It doesn't add up, Arrozzini."

The investigator paced around the table a few times without saying anything. Johnathan took another sip of his water. How long was the questioning going to take? He had been sitting there for more than an hour already, and the investigator kept asking the same questions over and over again.

"We have some eye-witnesses who were at your wedding who said you were angry with your brother at the wedding rehearsal. They saw you arguing just minutes before your bride walked down the aisle. If it was just a matter of wanting to walk away from everything for a new, simpler life, then why would you have been yelling at your brother? Why the anger?"

"Weddings can get emotional," shrugged Johnathan. "Listen, my brother can drive me crazy. He gave an inappropriate toast at the rehearsal dinner that humiliated my wife and me. I was furious with him because when Caroline jumped up from the table to run away, she fell hard on her belly. She was pregnant at the time, and we were both terrified. We spent the night before our wedding in the emergency room of the nearest hospital. The next day I was furious with my parents because they insisted that Caroline sign a prenuptial agreement. My brother kept making jokes about Caroline marrying me for my money and making it clear he didn't think much of her all the way up to the start of the wedding. Right before the ceremony, we were arguing about him needing to apologize to my wife if he wanted to stand by my side in the ceremony. My Mom just wanted me to forgive him and not cause a scene. My Dad didn't understand why Daniel couldn't apologize. My parents wanted us to make up and get over it, and I wasn't going to give in yet again. I refused and got a bit loud. That's all."

"That's quite a story," answered the investigator while smoothing his blonde beard. He pulled out the chair across from Johnathan and sat down.

"Tell me about this bankruptcy. Why didn't you accept money from your family when you lost everything? Or did they not offer?"

Johnathan paused. Should he say they hadn't offered him any money? Or had they already talked to his father, and he had said he had? Johnathan took another sip of water. It was best, he decided, to just stick to the truth.

"They offered. I refused. I didn't want money with strings."

"Let me get this straight. You preferred to sleep on the sofa of your friend Mark and accept a minimum wage job on a construction site rather than accept money from your parents?"

Johnathan nodded. "Yeah."

"Or could it be that you knew about their illegal activities from the start? Perhaps you were trying to get them to stop what they were doing your wedding weekend? They wouldn't, so you walked away from everything. When your startup failed, and you lost everything, you didn't want to risk taking money from people involved in illegal activities."

"I can't believe they did any of this," answered Johnathan, throwing out his arms. "The whole thing is crazy. Illegal diamond imports? How would they even get involved in something like that if they wanted to?"

The investigator scrutinized Johnathan's face in silence for a full two minutes. Johnathan looked back at him.

"I see here that your wife divorced you. Could that be because you didn't want to risk her being involved in all this? You knew what was coming and wanted to protect her?"

Johnathan let out a sigh. "I got into a dark place after the bankruptcy. A couple of months afterward, I went through severe depression and spent most of each day in bed. She couldn't take it anymore, took my son, and left. That's when Mark offered me his sofa. I had nowhere else to go. She filed for divorce. A few months later, we got back together, but she told me that she just couldn't be married to anyone ever again after going through bankruptcy. She has her own business. It's too backbreaking to build something up and then have someone else cause it all to be taken away."

Johnathan rubbed his eyes. It was torture talking about that dark time in his life. He hated that Caroline was no longer his wife, that she didn't trust him enough. On the other hand, he was relieved that her assets weren't frozen and she wasn't involved in all this, just as blonde beard had said.

"We will be going through all of your transactions and history with a fine comb Mr. Arrozzini."

Johnathan shrugged. "Sure. You're not going to find anything because I have nothing to hide."

"Well, that's what your sister told me, and now she has been charged with knowingly accepting fraudulent money from both her boyfriend and your parents. You do understand that helping them to hide any of their money or possessions is illegal?"

"Of course. And as I already explained, I haven't been back in New York for over a year. I've had little contact with my parents and none with my brother. I just voluntarily cut my baby-moon in Paris with Caroline short to fly here for questioning."

When Johnathan thought the questioning was finished, he was forced to sit there for another two hours answering questions. At last, the investigator went to the door and held it open. "You're free to go. Don't leave the country again. You can go back to California if you promise to come back to testify in the trial."

An hour later, Johnathan was walking through central park in an attempt to release some of the stressful days. His mother called and asked him to meet her, and he refused. His priority was getting on the next plane home to his son.

When he hung up, he wandered over to a park bench and sat down under the dappled light of a tree. He had been in too much shock before to think clearly. What if his Dad and brother were guilty? What if his mother and sister had known about what Brad, Daniel, and his Dad had been involved in the entire time? He couldn't risk hurting Caroline and his son for them. Johnathan resolved not to answer any more of their calls. He texted them that the entire situation was too shocking and overwhelming for him to handle and that he didn't want any contact with either of them until it was all over.

He called Caroline and asked her to book him a flight back home and a car to take him to the airport. He explained that the questioning was finished, for now, but his accounts were still frozen. It was surreal stepping into the plane a few hours later and walking past first-class to the very back of economy next to the window.

Johnathan barely fit his legs into the space in front of him. He let out a sigh of relief and loosened his tie when the seat beside him remained open as the plane took off. Johnathan looked out of the window at the skyscrapers jutting into the sky. He had never felt so relieved to leave New York.

Johnathan heard little feet running down the hall toward him when he opened the door.

"Daddy," yelled Leo and hurled himself into Johnathan's outstretched arms.

"I missed you, buddy. What are you doing still awake?"

"I couldn't sleep."

Caroline walked down the hall and circled her arms around both of them. "he was too excited to have his Daddy home. At last, I gave up and told him we could make some cinnamon popcorn and warm milk and wait up for you."

Johnathan closed his eyes, soaking up the feel of his son in his arms and Caroline's head nestled on his shoulder.

"Well, let me go wash my hands, and I will join you."

When Johnathan returned to the kitchen, Leo was dancing with his Mom in the kitchen and laughing. Johnathan leaned on the door frame and watched them. If he hadn't walked away from the company, the money, if he hadn't moved away from his family and New York when he had, he could have been in prison right now with them awaiting trial. If he hadn't gone through bankruptcy, he would never have learned to be the partner and father that he was now.

"Honey, you okay?" Caroline looked up in alarm.

The gratitude that rolled like a tsunami through him at that moment overwhelmed him. How was it that good could come out of bad? Johnathan told himself he would survive the uncertainty and the court trial in the next few months if he kept his focus on his blessings. He had Caroline, and in less than six months, their family would increase from three to six members.

Johnathan opened his arms, and Caroline wrapped her arms around his low back. He breathed in the smell of her strawberry shampoo and tears blurred his vision.

"I thought they might have gotten me mixed up in everything. Part of me thought I was going to prison with them," Johnathan murmured into Caroline's ear. "What if the police show up at my door with an arrest warrant still? Is my brother guilty? If so, then when did this all start? How did my Dad get involved, and Brad? How could Brad lose all those friends of the family their fortunes? I'm so grateful to be home. I don't understand any of what happened or how."

Caroline squeezed him tighter. "Just one moment at a time, Johnathan. Right now, you are home, with Leo, with me, and that's reason enough to be happy."

Johnathan nodded as Leo grabbed his leg and tugged on his shirt. Johnathan lifted him up, and Leo wrapped his little arms around his neck.

"Let's get you up to the bed, little man."

Leo yawned and then rested his head on Johnathan's shoulder. By the time Johnathan reached Leo's bedroom, he was fast asleep.

Johnathan rubbed his eyes and tried to focus on the menu board in the café. The triplets would be two months old in four days, and the time had flown by in a blur of feedings, diaper changes, and laundry. Johnathan knew that he had enough on his plate without harboring ideas about adding anything new into his life.

But that hadn't stopped him from getting up at five to finish his website and re-write his sales copy and email pitch for the twenty-second time before going to Mark's power yoga class.

Johnathan wanted to start a new business, and he needed financing. Fortunately, he had some new contacts that had expressed interest in backing him in a new venture.

The desire to get bigger, better, and farther in life had been eating at Johnathan for years. He'd dulled the voice with twelve-hour days and playing hard when he wasn't at his desk. Now Johnathan had a different desire that he couldn't shake; it was like a creative urge he'd thrived on in the best parts of his career as an architect.

The voice in his head wouldn't go away, especially when Mark insisted on a full ten minutes of meditation at the end of all his power yoga classes. Forced into enough stillness during the meditation that morning, Johnathan could hear the inner voice he'd been suppressing insist that it was time for Johnathan should go after a new dream.

Johnathan hadn't breathed a word of his new entrepreneurial dream to anyone; he didn't dare. He wanted to open a new business designing and manufacturing tiny homes of four hundred square feet or less. They could be built on wheels or optionally transited to a site and set on a foundation. He'd compared all the offerings, and the average price for a tiny home was on average over sixty thousand dollars. Johnathan had figured out that tiny houses weren't only in trend for those with too little money to buy something bigger.

Environmentalists, world travelers, and nature lovers had sizable incomes and could afford to pay more for their tiny home.

Johnathan had used his time at open houses, waiting for clients to show up, to look at tiny homes. While cooking dinner, he used the time to think, design, and plan. Johnathan knew he wanted to build tiny luxury homes, and he'd already decided how he would use some of his profits; he would build tiny houses for people who had gone bankrupt due to medical bills. Johnathan would never forget what it had been like to be bankrupt and homeless. What if Mark hadn't taken him in when he had?

Johnathan knew Caroline wouldn't have had him living on the street. Still, plenty of people were put in that exact position. Insane, Johnathan thought, how you could be financially stable, be diagnosed with cancer or another illness, and lose everything to medical care costs.

Johnathan shook his head. He didn't want to leave his job with Cindy. Opening a new business would be adding something on top of his existing workload, all while raising little kids. And what about the risk?

Johnathan was almost certain Caroline wouldn't want to

jeopardize the small amount of financial cushion they had built up, mainly because they would now be supporting his Mom. On his last call to New York, Alison had been stubborn but had relented to move out and live near them.

Johnathan's thoughts turned from the upcoming trial and back to the idea for the new startup.

Was bankruptcy not enough of a lesson? Did he need to subject his family and himself to that all over again? Idiocy and selfishness, the entire plan, Johnathan decided. He would table the whole thing and forget about it.

"Hello? Johnathan?"

"What? Sorry, Annie."

"Let me guess? A double shot vanilla latte," smiled Annie. "Tell you what. I'll throw in a donut for free. You look like you need something to make you smile."

"I'm happy. I've just never been this exhausted in my entire life. I don't know how I'm going to make it through the day. I feel like a walking zombie."

Annie nodded as she placed the donut on a plate. "Those triplets still not on the same schedule, huh? Caroline looks better than you do. I think you should call in sick and get some sleep."

Johnathan took a sip out of the mug and leaned against the counter.

"I can't. I'm walking clients through the new home I designed for them and handing over the keys."

"Wow, that went fast." Annie handed Johnathan his donut and watched as he took a big bite.

"We started a year ago. Thank you, Annie. Have a great day, and tell Dan I said hi."

"You too, Johnathan. See you tomorrow."

Johnathan rushed to his car and cruised to the new house built on the cliffs overlooking the ocean. He opened his car door and glanced at his watch when he saw his clients already waiting in the driveway.

"Sorry to keep you waiting," he said as he strode toward the couple. He reached out and gave the man with greying hair and tanned skin a firm handshake. "Good morning Patrick. Ellen, you're looking as radiant as ever."

"We're early. We have been looking forward to this moment," smiled the woman and tucked her curly brown hair behind her ear. "I was up before dawn."

"So was I," laughed Johnathan.

"How are your babies?" Ellen smiled. "You're looking tired, Johnathan. Don't worry. You blink twice, and they've all grown up and out busy with their own lives, and you miss it."

"There are advantages to the kids being grown, Ellen. Like our dream home to enjoy our retirement."

"I would prefer to be enjoying my grand babies, but I don't know that will ever happen," sighed Ellen.

"If you want some extra baby holding time, you just give me a call. Preferably at five in the morning so I can get some extra sleep," laughed Johnathan.

"You think you're kidding but if you need my help, give me a call," Ellen answered.

Johnathan unlocked the front door and held the door open for the couple to walk through. Ellen kicked off her shoes and immediately began to climb the smooth white spiral staircase upstairs, and Patrick followed. Johnathan found Ellen climbing clothed into her egg-shaped free-standing bathtub placed by the floor-to-ceiling window facing the ocean. Patrick took the remote control and turned on the fireplace opposite the bath.

"Can you believe this, Patrick? It will be like living at a spa." Ellen climbed back out of the tub as Patrick walked into the steam shower.

"So you figured out the ventilation problem?" asked Patrick.

Johnathan nodded. "The window automatically opens for two minutes when you turn the shower off."

Ellen walked into the corner of the bathroom and opened the door to the second shower. "Can I try it?"

"Go ahead," smiled Johnathan. Ellen flipped the switch, and a cascade of water fell from the ceiling like a waterfall in a sparkle of pink light. After a minute, the light turned to turquoise, then yellow, and the shower changed to soft rain. Ellen laughed and reached her hand out into the water.

Patrick shook his head. "The things they come up with now. Well, are you happy, Ellen? I don't see the fascination myself, but if you're pleased, that's what matters."

"What do you mean, Patrick? It'll be like showering under a rainbow." The light began to change to orange as Ellen turned the shower off.

Johnathan followed the couple through each room upstairs and then down to the main level, where the sunken living room faced floor-to-ceiling windows showcasing the view. Patrick ran his fingertips along the built-in bookcases lining the wall as Ellen walked through the kitchen door.

"I love it, Johnathan. See, I know it's all the trend to have an open floor plan, and that's what my daughter wanted me to do and everything. But my kitchen is my safe haven. I want to come in here and have a proper door to shut. Just look at that view." Ellen leaned against the white marble counter and looked out at the waves. "Are you bringing the kids over for a visit this weekend like you promised? We won't have the furniture moved in yet, but I thought we could go down and have a picnic on the beach. The weather forecast is sunny and mild."

"Caroline is looking forward to it, Ellen. She said to tell you we're bringing the dessert."

Johnathan smiled. Ellen and Patrick had become some of his favorite people in town and like surrogate grandparents to his kids. They had met on the beach while Caroline was still pregnant with the triplets and formed a tight bond. Since then, they had met at least once a month for a picnic or barbecue party. It was reassuring to have them to turn to in case of an emergency.

When Caroline's car had broken down on the way back from

the airport after the trip to Paris, she had tried calling Mark, but his phone had been off while teaching a yoga class. So she had dialed Patrick, and he had come to her aide.

Ellen walked over, slid open the door, and walked out onto the terrace wrapping around the entire house, and Johnathan followed her.

"What's this?"

Johnathan pulled the cover off a round outdoor beach sofa made of weather-resistant poly rattan and covered with soft white pillows. He pulled up the adjustable wind and sunroof and stepped aside. "This is a present from me for you, Ellen. You were worried about being constantly in the wind up here on the cliffs. Just snuggle in here, and you are protected from the wind and can enjoy the view and fresh air."

"Wow, I love it, Johnathan. Thank you." Ellen climbed onto the sofa and leaned back against the pillows.

A few minutes later, Patrick joined them and smiled over at this wife. "What's this?"

"A home warming gift from Johnathan. Come over here," Ellen patted the sofa next to her.

Patrick was just climbing up next to his wife onto the sofa when they heard the doorbell chime.

"Who can that be?" laughed Ellen.

"Maybe it's the neighbors welcoming us to the neighborhood. I'll go get it," declared Allen.

Johnathan stayed on the terrace with Ellen while she started to update him on her two children's lives.

"It's for your Johnathan."

"For me?"

Johnathan followed Allen back through the southern beach modern kitchen and into the circular entryway.

"Johnathan Arrozzini?" asked the man standing at the door in shorts and a t-shirt.

"Yes?"

The man held out a manila envelope, and Johnathan took it. "You've been served. Have a nice day, sir."

Johnathan took a deep breath and blew it out, his cheeks bulging out like a puffer fish. He looked over at Patrick and shook his head. "Sorry about that, Patrick. Cindy must have told him where I was; I'm sure she didn't know who he was."

"No need to explain," Patrick held up his hands. "We didn't say anything, but we've been following the trial every day. Neither Ellie nor I believe you had anything to do with any of it."

Johnathan didn't know what to say. Johnathan hadn't had the nerves to read about the trial. He had avoided the Internet at all costs the past few months, which hadn't been hard, given that he was juggling taking care of Leo and the triplets while work continued to increase.

"Patrick? Who was at the door?" Ellen came into the entryway and looked from one man to the other.

"Did someone die?"

"Nothing like that, Ellie. Johnathan here just got served."

"Served what, dear?"

Patrick smiled and put his arm around his wife. "With papers Ellie."

"I'm so sorry to interrupt your big day Ellen," Johnathan smiled. "I will give you each your keys and be on my way."

"Nonsense. You come back out onto the terrace with me. I brought a thermos of coffee from Annie's café and some treats to celebrate. I won't take no for an answer."

"I'll go get the bag out of the car," Patrick said, "and you two go enjoy our view."

Ellen was just pouring Johnathan a cup of coffee when his phone rang. Johnathan excused himself, and he walked around the corner of the house to take the call.

"Johnathan Arrozzini?"

"Yes?"

"This is Adam McMillan from the U.S. Attorney's Office for

the Southern District of New York. I'm sure you are aware that the trial against your brother and father began a few weeks ago."

Johnathan tried to swallow, but his mouth had gone dry. "Yes."

"You were just handed the subpoena. You need to come to New York to testify in two cases. As you are aware, both your father and brother were charged with fraud, money laundering, illegal diamond trade and sale, and embezzlement. We will pay your transportation and lodging."

"I don't know anything. How can I be of any use in the court case?"

"You are summoned to appear in New York federal court in twenty-eight days," continued Adam. "The papers contain all the necessary information on how to arrange travel and lodging for the trial. I wish you a good day."

Johnathan starred at the phone in his hand. He had forgotten to ask how long he would be obligated to stay in New York. How could he leave his kids, job, life, and travel across the country for three weeks?

Johnathan took a sip of his coffee as he returned to Ellen and Patrick.

"Well, if neither of you has any questions, then the big moment has come to hand over the keys to your new home." Johnathan held out two pairs of keys, and the couple took them. "I'll show myself out. You two just relax and enjoy your new home."

Ellen sat up straighter. "Who was that? Who served you papers, dear?"

"You don't need to answer, Johnathan," spoke up Patrick. "My wife gets too curious for her good."

"I'll give you strawberries and a donut," offered Ellen.

Johnathan tilted his head to the side. He had already had a donut but shrugged. If any day was a two-donut day, it was now. He reached out and grabbed the donut Ellen offered and took a seat on the steps leading down the cliff to the beach.

"I've been served a subpoena to testify in the court case

against my father, brother, and my sister's ex-boyfriend in about a month."

"Oh dear," Ellen said. "I am sorry, Johnathan."

"Good that you didn't get involved in all of that mess yourself, Johnathan."

Johnathan ate his donut in silence for a moment. He finished his coffee, and Ellie offered him a refill. With a steaming cup of coffee in his hands, he looked out at the waves and his mouth twisted to one side, then the other.

"I still can't believe they did any of it. Why? I keep coming back to that same question. Why would they do it? They all had plenty of money. What happened? What didn't I see? When did it even start? Was I still in New York with them when it started and oblivious? Or did it start after I moved out here?"

Johnathan shook his head and took another drink of his coffee.

"Stop beating yourself up about it all, son. You'll drive yourself crazy if you get pulled in by those thoughts. I recommend you keep your focus on the babies, Leo, and your lovely Caroline," said Patrick.

"And we're here if you ever need our help," added Ellen.

Johnathan changed the subject to the upcoming festival in town and the local political debates. After a few more minutes, Johnathan left his friends in their new home and headed back to the real estate office.

Johnathan hadn't seen either his father or brother since their arrest. What would it be like to see them again in court, to look down at them sitting at them as he answered the lawyers' questions? What if somehow he got pulled into the mess and ended up behind bars himself?

# CHAPTER 19

Johnathan walked into Caroline's office on his way back to his own.

"Hey, honey. How did dropping the triplets and Leo off at Anna's go? They were all crying at the same time when I left this morning."

"They settled down as soon as they were all in the car. Anna is like a baby whisperer. I don't know how she handles all three babies and Leo alone."

Caroline laughed. "She doesn't, Johnathan. Her best friend Ellie comes over and helps out from nine to three every day."

"Who is Ellie? Do you trust her?"

"Are you serious? You don't trust Ellen?" answered Caroline.

"Wait, do you mean Ellen Brown? Wait, she's best friends with Anna? How do I not know all this?"

Caroline laughed again. "I've told you that multiple times. You need to get some sleep, babe. Tonight you are off baby duty. I've booked you a room at the bed and breakfast near your office. You need to sleep through the night, and you'll feel better."

Johnathan instantly began shaking his head. "No way. I am not leaving you alone with four little kids."

"Yes, you are."

"I said no, Caroline," roared Johnathan.

Caroline pushed back from her desk and stared at Johnathan. "You're yelling? Now you definitely sound like you need to get some sleep, babe."

Johnathan slumped down into the chair across the desk from her and threw the manila envelope on the table. "I was served this morning. I need to go to New York to testify in twenty-eight days."

"Damn, well, we knew that was coming. Four will be a handful without you, not to mention that I have some big clients I need to deliver Badass Branding packages in a couple weeks. What was the due date?" Caroline sat up on the edge of her seat and began typing on her keyboard with her eyes glued to the screen and began muttering to herself. "Maybe Mat will be able to come to stay with me and if I ask Ellen to step in on Saturdays."

"Caroline."

"Yeah?" Caroline paused while typing and looked up at him.

"I was subpoenaed today to testify against my brother and father."

Caroline collapsed back in her chair and began massaging the sides of her jaw. "So, epic fail there. I was instantly thinking about me and how I was going to handle you being gone. I can't even fathom what you must be going through right now. I'm so sorry."

Caroline got up and went over to Johnathan and slid onto his lap, wrapping her arms around his neck and kissing his forehead.

After a moment, Johnathan leaned back to look at Caroline. "You know how I've been saying that good things come out of bad when I returned from New York after questioning?"

Caroline nodded.

"I don't see any good that can come out of this."

Caroline took a deep breath, biting her lip. "I want to be optimistic here, but I don't see it either."

The bells on the door jingled as Matilda stormed into the

office. "I've been subpoenaed. Can you believe it? I've already spent hours being questioned. They know I knew nothing, and I didn't know that someone opened a bank account in my name in the Bahamas. I thought everything was sorted and behind me. Now, this!" Matilda waved the manila envelope in the air. "You do know that the investigators were given an anonymous tip that there was a storage space rented in Daniel's name? When they opened the storage space, it was filled with raw diamonds."

Matilda fell into a chair beside them and hung her head. "I can't believe I'm being forced to testify against our entire family."

"You mean Dad and Daniel."

Matilda looked up. "You're kidding, right? You didn't know? Mom's been in prison for three days.

"What?" Johnathan jumped up out of his chair. "How did I not know that? Why? How? This just keeps getting worse and worse."

Caroline stood up and went over to Matilda, who was visibly shaking and began to massage her shoulders.

"Why am I beginning to worry that you and I won't be coming back from New York for a long time, Mat?" asked Johnathan.

Johnathan straightened his tie for the seventh time and smoothed his suit jacket. He looked up at the judge and over at the jury. Matilda had been doing an excellent job of remaining calm under fire. It was torture showing up every day and not knowing when it would be his turn up on the stand. His thoughts began to drift to his kids and Caroline.

How was Cindy doing his job and hers right now? He needed to call and check in with her once again. He had been able to keep up with his design work for the renovations from New York for the past week, but it was difficult to concentrate and have time to interface with the homeowners.

Johnathan wondered how Caroline was going to juggle the

kids over the weekend all by herself. Ellen and Patrick had been planning their thirty-five-year wedding vacation for years, and Anna wasn't up to watching the kids on her own all week and stepping up to help on the weekends as well. He would have to call Mark and Jenny and see if they could go over. Caroline had insisted she could manage the babies and Leo for one weekend on her own, but Johnathan wasn't sure; the triplets had been teething, and Caroline hadn't gotten much sleep all week.

"Johnathan Arrozzini, please come forward."

Johnathan blinked and looked up, his blurred eyes refocusing on the courtroom.

"Johnathan Arrozzini?"

"Yes," Johnathan sprung to his feet, his heart hammering in his chest.

The lawyer took his time asking Johnathan innocuous questions for so long that Johnathan's heart slowed, and he began to get bored. Out of nowhere, the lawyer asked Johnathan why he had altered the books to reflect his architecture firm's higher-earnings. Johnathan sat up straighter in his chair and answered that he had done nothing of the sort, ever.

"I didn't have anything to do with the financials other than to aid in pricing projects for clients. I was primarily responsible for the design work and project management of the buildings I designed for clients. Daniel was in charge of managing the running of the company as CEO."

Over two hours later, the judge announced the lunch break, but Johnathan remained sitting in the box, too stunned and worn out to stand up. The lawyer had made it sound certain that Daniel had been doctoring their company's books and embezzling money for years. But why would Daniel do that? Hadn't their company been doing well? He had thought that they had made higher profits with each passing year. Was that all a lie?

Johnathan wished that he could just get his parents and Daniel into a room and find out the truth, no matter what it was. The lawyer was getting in his head. He didn't want to inadvertently incriminate his brother, mostly because he didn't know that Daniel was guilty. Was he? If the lawyer was convincing Johnathan of his brother's guilt, that didn't bode well for the jury's verdict; unlike the jury, Johnathan desperately wanted his brother to be innocent and kept trying to keep an open mind.

At last, the judge announced lunch. Johnathan stood up and wandered dazed out into the hall. Someone put a sandwich in his hand and a soda in the other. Johnathan looked down at the soda and couldn't remember the last time he had drunk one. With Caroline, it was always green smoothies, teas, or sparkling mineral water. All too soon, it was time to return to the courtroom. Johnathan didn't know how it could get any worse until it did.

The lawyer submitted a document to the court showing Johnathan's signature to open a bank account in the Bahamas.

"Is this your signature Mr. Arrozzini?"

"It looks like my signature, but no, it is a forgery."

"So you have no hidden bank account in the Bahamas?"

"No."

"Then why is there a bank account in your name?"

Johnathan shook his head, holding up his hands. "I have no idea. Identity fraud?"

"Do you think your brother, father, or mother could have opened up this account to hide some of their money under your name?"

Johnathan shrugged. "I can't believe they would do that to me."

"Is it possible?"

Johnathan shook his head. "I honestly don't know. What do you need to do to open a bank account in the Bahamas? Is it even possible for someone to open an account under someone else's name?"

"If you didn't open the account, and they didn't open the

account, then who opened the account?"

"Are you sure there is an account?" Johnathan wiped his hands on his trousers and sat up straighter in his chair.

"Permission to approach the bench," said the lawyer.

"Granted," answered the judge.

The lawyer handed a piece of paper to the judge, who passed it to Johnathan. The paper was a copy of the bank account, with his name on it, containing seven point three million dollars.

"I repeat. If you didn't open the account, and they didn't open the account, then who opened the account?"

Johnathan still starred down at the document in his hands. "I don't know."

"Do you see the date the account was opened?"

Johnathan searched the paper, and his stomach hollowed out, his hands began to shake. The date was right after his filing for bankruptcy.

"You do understand that hiding money in a bankruptcy is illegal?"

"I don't understand," Johnathan's mind began to rev back up, the adrenaline coursing through his veins, making his brain focus. "You must know that this money didn't come from any of my personal accounts in California. Where was the money transferred from? I mean, do you know from whom this money came from?"

"You tell us. Where did the money come from?"

Johnathan shook his head. "I have no idea. I filed for bankruptcy because I had nothing. I couldn't pay my creditors. We lost our house."

"But you're still living in that house, is that correct?"

"First of all, it's a cottage, not a house," said Johnathan. He glanced over at the jury. The last thing Johnathan wanted is for the jury to think he was living a lavish lifestyle.

"Does it have an ocean view? Are your steps away from the ocean?"

"Well, yes, but it's tiny.?"

"So how were you lucky enough to stay living in your luxury beach side home despite your bankruptcy?

"Luxury? It's a cottage," replied Johnathan. "It's Caroline's Gram's cottage."

"And where is this grandmother?"

"She's dead. Caroline was raised in that house. Also, I don't know what you're trying to get at here, but Caroline divorced me. Jolan bought the house to save it from being taken from Caroline, and we rent it now from him. We're saving up to repurchase it someday. And anyway, after the bankruptcy, I had nothing, and I spent a few months sleeping on a friend's sofa."

"But now you are back together living in the house? Are you aware that it is not legal for someone filing for bankruptcy to transfer any valuable asset, in this instance a house, to a friend or family member before filing for bankruptcy so you can keep the asset?"

"I didn't do that. The cottage was foreclosed on when we couldn't make the payments. Caroline's best friend bought it from the bank so she wouldn't lose her grandmother's home. Like I said, Jolan owns the cottage, and we pay rent every month. I've brought all of the legal documents of Jolan's ownership of the property from the bank and our rental payments to Jolan to live in his property."

"Why did you sleep on a friend's sofa when you had millions of dollars in an account in the Bahamas?"

"Because I didn't have millions in an account in the Bahamas." Johnathan crossed his arms over his chest and let out a big breath of frustration.

"Mr. Arrozzini, do you know that it is illegal to submit falsified evidence and documents to the court?"

"Yes."

"Do you think I am submitting false documents to the court?"

Johnathan paused, pressed his lips together, and smoothed his sweaty palms down his trouser legs again. "I'm not sure, honestly, sir. All I know is that I never put any money into

202

an account anywhere in the Bahamas in my entire life. I don't understand who put that money in my name or why."

"Do you believe your father, brother, or mother could have put that money in the account in your name to help you out after the bankruptcy?"

Johnathan looked over at his brother and father at the defendants' table for the first time since taking a seat in the box and then shook his head. "No. I explicitly told them I didn't want their money."

"Why did you prefer to sleep on a friend's sofa instead of accepting money from your family?"

Tears stung the back of Johnathan's eyes, and he blinked as he swallowed the lump in his throat. His eyes were glued to the floor. He couldn't chance to look at his family.

"Mr. Arrozzini?"

"Look, I was sliding into a dark place fast when I realized that my business was failing and I would need to declare bankruptcy. I called my brother, my Dad, Mom. I told them I needed help, not money, help. I needed them to fly out and be with me." Johnathan paused. "They all said it wasn't a good time, they couldn't get away from New York, and anyway, they would just wire me some money."

"So they did wire money into the account in the Bahamas?"

"No. It's not easy asking for help. I was clinically depressed, and I needed them to come to be with me, not their money. I was spirally downward. When they insisted they couldn't, well, I told them I didn't want their money and to never contact me again."

"Did you mean that? Did they believe you?"

"I don't know. I didn't hear from them. There were some dark months after the bankruptcy. My wife left me, filed for divorce, I didn't see my son."

Jonathan rubbed his fingers over his eyes and looked down at his shoes.

"I was suicidal. A friend helped me get my head back on

straight, get a job, and start building my life back up again. I had no contact with my family during that time. When my former wife and I reunited, she talked me into calling them and asking them to come to visit for Leo's birthday. They refused. Well, my sister came. The next time I talked to my Mom was when she called me in Paris to inform me about the indictment of Daniel and my father and that I was wanted for questioning."

Johnathan could feel his body start to shake. He tried to take deeper, smoother breaths, but it didn't help. His entire body was shaking, triggered by dredging up the worst months of his life, his anguish at his family's refusal to come to help him, and his growing fear that he would be the next one in the family to land in jail.

"Could it be that your brother, father, or mother transferred the money into an account in your name, without your knowledge, in an attempt to protect assets should they become indicted for their crimes?"

"No. No, I don't think they would do that to me," answered Johnathan.

"Do you know how your brother and dad imported the illegal rough diamonds into the United States?" Johnathan's body continued to tremble, and he was horrified that everyone in the courtroom may be able to see it.

"Mr. Arrozzini? Can you please answer the question?"

"Sorry. What was the question?"

"Do you know how your brother and dad imported the illegal rough diamonds into the United States?"

"No idea. I don't believe they did it at all." Johnathan paused and looked directly over at the jury. "How would you even get an idea like that? How would you know who to contact to do something like that?"

"Have you ever witnessed or heard about your father or brother doing anything illegal?"

"No," Johnathan instantly fired back.

"Were you aware that your father lost almost eighty percent

of he and your mother's fortune investing with your sister's boyfriend and into risky startups?"

"He did tell me he lost some money. Are you sure it was almost eighty percent? That can't be right. Why would he take such a risk? I don't understand," stammered Johnathan.

"Were you aware that your brother had five multi-million-dollar homes on three different continents as well as three different wives and six children?"

Johnathan's jaw dropped, and his eyes snapped to his brother's face. Daniel starred stonily ahead, not meeting Johnathan's eyes.

"No way. That can't be possible. I know for a fact that can't be possible because-"Johnathan didn't finish his sentence as Daniel caught his eye and shook his head. Johnathan had wanted to say that Daniel couldn't have a bunch of wives because he was gay. Clearly, Daniel didn't want this information to be released in court.

"The wives have come forward with their stories to the investigators. Do you know any of these women?"

"No. And I can't believe this is true. I mean, isn't it illegal to marry more than one wife? How is that even possible?"

"So you didn't know about the wives, each unaware of the others, each living in luxury on a different continent?"

"No. That can't be true. I mean, I was living and working in New York with Daniel until I got married. He had an apartment in the same building. How would he acquire all these houses and wives? He went on a few holidays and did some traveling for work, but I was often with him. I would have known about wives, let alone his kids. Daniel wouldn't keep news of his having children secret from me."

"Are you sure of that? The wives and luxury houses pre-date your marriage and move to the west coast. It is looking like your brother kept you in the dark about a lot."

"No. I keep telling you. No. I can't believe any of this is even true."

Johnathan kept staring at his brother, but Daniel didn't meet his gaze. The lawyer continued to ask questions, and Johnathan kept shaking his head and answering no.

At last, the lawyer announced, "no more questions, your honor."

As Johnathan walked past the defendant's table and out the door, Daniel looked up and into Johnathan's eyes. Tears were running down his cheeks. Johnathan had never seen his brother cry in public before.

# CHAPTER 20

Johnathan starred out of the airplane window, his sunglasses still on his face to hide his swollen teary eyes. He kept telling himself it was over, he should be relieved that he was a free man and was on his way home to his family, but it wasn't helping. Daniel's tear-streaked face was haunting him. Johnathan was so confused and dumbfounded as to how his family could have gotten themselves into such a mess.

Three wives? How many kids had the lawyer said Daniel had? How could Daniel keep that a secret? Was it even true?

The only solace Johnathan found was that his mother wasn't seeing any of the trial taking place. Being in prison was at least preventing her from sitting in the audience. She would have her court trial, and then Johnathan, he had been informed, would need to fly out to testify yet again.

At some point, Johnathan fell asleep, his head resting against the window frame. It wasn't until the plane touched down that he jolted awake and looked out at the sunrise.

Caroline was waiting for him at the airport. Silently he scooped her into his arms and breathed in the familiar scent of her strawberry shampoo.

"Where are the kids?"

"Anna and Ellen are watching them for the day. I've booked us for a day-long yoga retreat. You need some stress reduction after what you've been through."

Johnathan shook his head, still holding her tight. "No, babe. I just want to chill, be with my kids, have a beer."

"No beer. I already paid. We both need this. Come on. I packed your clothes for you."

Johnathan wasn't in a state to argue with her. She grabbed his hand, and they walked to the car. The entire way to the yoga studio, they were both quiet. Johnathan was relieved that Caroline resisted the urge to bombard him with questions about what had happened in New York.

As they pulled into their tiny coastal town, Johnathan let out a sigh of relief. Home. It felt like coming home. Caroline parked near the yoga studio and grabbed two yoga mats from the truck. He followed her out to the beach, where a group was already rolling out their mats. Mark jogged up and gave Johnathan a fierce hug, slapping him hard on the back.

"Good to have you back, brother."

Johnathan nodded and settled down on his yoga mat into a child's pose next to Caroline. Ninety minutes of power yoga later, Johnathan was sweaty, exhausted, and felt better than he had in weeks laying in the final relaxation pose on his back. After the class, most of the people ran out towards the ocean to jump into the water. Johnathan sat on his mat, watching them. Caroline came up behind him and tried pushing him to his feet. Johnathan gave in and stood up. Hand in hand, they went running into the waves.

Johnathan picked Caroline up in his arms, kissed her, then, with a grin, dropped her into the water. Caroline came up, spluttering, and tackled him, knocking him off his feet. His head submerged under the cold water, and he came up laughing. He chased Caroline, but she scampered away back up the beach to the shower to rinse off. He followed her and took his turn rinsing off the salty water.

Caroline threw Johnathan a towel as he returned to her; he roped it around his neck, looking out at the ocean. Mark was just laying out trays of oatmeal, green smoothies, and bowls of nuts and dried fruit. Caroline took one look at Johnathan and tugged on his hand. She scooped up two bowls of oatmeal, and he grabbed their green smoothies. They sat back down on their yoga mats to eat. When they were done with the oatmeal, Caroline smiled at Johnathan.

"Come on. I know what you want."

Johnathan followed Caroline up the street to Annie's café. Caroline ordered two lattes to go as Johnathan chatted with Dan. When they walked out of the café, two previous clients stopped Johnathan and said hello. AS they walked outside sipping their coffees, Caroline handed Johnathan a bag with a donut inside.

"I know there is only so much healthy food you can take," she grinned.

"Believe it or not, I missed your healthy stuff. I never want to drink another sugar soda or eat another sandwich on white bread again for lunch. But donuts, well donuts I could eat every day."

"You're lucky you can eat them and get away with it," laughed Caroline.

"Have a bite, babe," said Johnathan, holding out his treat. "Go on."

Caroline took a bite and let out a sigh. "So good. Why does Dan have to make such amazing donuts?"

When they returned to the beach, Mark called for everyone to join him for a walk along the beach. Johnathan and Caroline decided to stay behind and drink their coffees slowly instead.

"I promise I wasn't snooping, but I found the file on your new business idea. Tiny houses? I love it, especially the part about donating tiny homes to cancer survivors who have gone through bankruptcy. Why haven't you said anything about any of it to me?"

Johnathan shook his head. "No way, I'm not risking what we have by attempting a new startup. I was just playing around, is all."

"Designing tiny houses for fun, I would believe, but you created business plans and full cost analyses. You even contacted suppliers for price quotes and have sales pitch copy done. I wouldn't be surprised if you built a website already."

Johnathan didn't answer. He looked straight out at the seagulls circling over the waves.

"So there is a website. I say go for it. I looked at the business plan. If you keep your job with Cindy."

"Of course, I'm keeping my job with Cindy. I enjoy it, and it's consistent income."

"Well, then the risk is manageable. I say go for it."

Johnathan shook his head. "Just drop it, okay? I just got back from testifying in court. I missed you and the kids. I have a mountain of work waiting for me in the office. The last thing I'm going to do is even think about a new business venture."

Caroline looped her arms around Johnathan and squeezed. "I love you. My lips are sealed. Just know that if you change your mind, you have my support. Only this time, make sure you create an LLC as I did instead of a sole proprietorship, okay? Let's keep your business assets and liabilities separate from your personal assets and liabilities the next time around."

Johnathan cringed, and Caroline gave him a big hug. "It's in the past handsome. I love you. We're moving forward and building a beautiful life."

Johnathan nodded and leaned his head against Caroline's.

When Mark returned, he insisted everyone join him for the qi gong class. Johnathan complied and found himself entering a trance-like state. After the class, Mark asked everyone to meet him upstairs in the studio in fifteen minutes for the meditation session. Johnathan looked over at Caroline, and she shook her head.

He grinned, knowing she had read his mind that he was ready

to bail and go home.

"You are doing the meditation with me," said Caroline. "Let's go."

The last thing Johnathan wanted was to sit still and face the thoughts fighting in his head for attention. When he sat down for the meditation, it wasn't Mark, but Caroline, who started speaking next to him. Caroline guided them into breath work. After ten minutes, she then explained the meditation before opening up the silence and space for the group to do deeper on their own.

Johnathan expected thoughts to torture him while sitting still with no distractions, but that didn't happen. Instead, one emotion after another rolled through him. Profound sadness, despair, hurt, anger, vengefulness, and then once again sadness. At some point, the sadness softened, space growing around the emotion, and he felt nothing but the energy vibrating in him. When Caroline announced the end of the meditation, he folded forward like everyone else and rubbed his arms and legs before laying down on his back to rest. Johnathan felt Caroline pulling a blanket over him, and then he instantly fell asleep.

Johnathan woke up with a start on the floor of the studio. Everyone was gone. Johnathan yawned and stretched. Sitting up, he began to fold up the blanket. Johnathan wandered back down the stairs. Out on the beach, he could see Caroline, her head thrown back, laughing next to Mark and Cindy. He wandered out to the beach blanket and sat down next to Mark.

"Sleeping beauty joins us at last. I saved you a spinach salad and a sandwich," Mark said as he opened the cooler next to him.

"Thanks, Mark. Good to see you, Cindy. Thanks again for covering for me while I was gone, Cindy. I'm sure you had some long days on my account." Johnathan shaded his eyes to look over at Cindy. Caroline fished in her purse and handed Johnathan his sunglasses.

"You're welcome. I'm not going to lie. It wasn't easy without you. I'm glad you're home again. This morning was a godsend. Just want I needed to burn off the stress," said Cindy.

Johnathan was about to take a big bite of his sandwich but paused. "What happened this morning?" Johnathan looked around at the amused faces around him.

"You didn't see me this morning, did you, Johnathan?" asked Cindy as she reached out a slapped his knee. "I thought it was weird that you didn't say hello back. I thought you were trying to be all Zen or something, so I let you be."

Johnathan looked from Caroline to Mark, then back at Cindy. "I didn't hear you say hello. I didn't see you."

"Yeah, you were kind of out of it this morning, man. Caroline had your number. You needed this," answered Mark and slapped Johnathan hard on the back.

Johnathan nodded. "Yeah. Yeah, You're right. I didn't realize just how in my head I was. It's been a lot. And unfortunately, Cindy, it's not over. I have to go back to testify in my dad's trial and then my mother's trial. It's so messed up. I'm not sure when."

"We'll figure it out, Johnathan," soothed Cindy. "Just buckle down and work like a maniac in the meantime."

Mark playfully pushed Cindy, knocking her over into the sand. "Hey, don't undo my good work by stressing him out."

"I'm increasing demand for your services, love," laughed Cindy as she sat back up. "Why would anyone come to yoga if they weren't stressed out?"

"To reach a state of enlightenment beautiful. I keep telling you. Yoga is not a mere antidote to stress," shot back Mark.

"You're my antidote to stress," answered Cindy as she placed her hands on Mark's knees and leaned in to kiss him. Mark wrapped his arms around Cindy and fell backward onto the sand, pulling Cindy on top of him.

Johnathan's jaw dropped open. "What's happening? Caroline?"

"Jenny broke up with Mark. She told me she couldn't take

him telling her to, 'just be in the present moment, love,' one more time. That and she fell in love with a guy who was down here for a weekend who recently made millions selling his tech startup. She's already moved to San Francisco to be with him."

"Wait, what?"

Mark and Cindy sat back up, and Mark slid his arm around Cindy and kissed her cheek. "I have to admit that I've been drawn to Cindy's energy for a while."

Johnathan laughed. "Her energy, Mark? I think it's rather you have a thing for beautiful woman with legs for days."

"And here I thought he was after my money," laughed Cindy. "You all know I've had my eye on Mark for a long time. I have a thing for men with washboard abs and kind hearts," Cindy said and pushed her long hair over her shoulder.

"I am not after your money," spluttered Mark.

"Of course not, love," soothed Cindy. "You're spiritual and deep—all into energy and enlightenment. I one hundred percent support yoga as long as it keeps you looking hot. I don't even care if you make much money, love. I can afford a trophy, husband."

"Cindy," laughed Caroline.

"Let her talk her rubbish" Mark nodded. "She's scared at how deep she's falling in love with me and so making a joke out of it. I have your number, lady."

Cindy nestled her head onto Mark's shoulder and held his hand. Johnathan knew that Cindy wasn't falling in love with Mark. She had been in love with him for as long as he Johnathan had known her. Every morning they went to Mark's power yoga class together before work, which hadn't stopped Cindy from going back every Thursday for restorative yoga and the social hour afterward.

"It's time to get ready for the hike," announced Mark half an hour later.

"Hike? Caroline, I'm going to pass. I want to see my kids."

"Please, Johnathan? It's the last part of the retreat. Anna

and Ellen will meet us out at the campground afterward with the kids, and Patrick said he would barbecue. Leo's looking forward to roasting his first marshmallow. After all that time in a courtroom, you could do with some more time out in nature."

Johnathan's head rolled back, and he looked up at the clear blue sky. He looked at Caroline, and she wrapped her arms around him with a pleading look on her face. "How long is this hike?"

Over two hours later, Johnathan was the first to walk into the campground and see Patrick roasting sausages and vegetables over a fire. Leo spotted him and came running full-throttle toward Johnathan. Johnathan held out his arms and bent down to catch his son. Johnathan stood up, holding Leo tight, and kissed his cheek.

"Man did I miss you," he said.

"I'm not a man. I'm a boy."

Johnathan laughed and carried Leo over to a picnic table and sat down, hugging Leo in his arms. Leo struggled to get down, and Johnathan placed him on his feet. Johnathan kissed Ellen and Anna hello and then turned his attention to the triplets.

"Hi there, Ayden Archer, Austin. How are my beautiful babies?" Johnathan didn't know who to pick up first. How did other parents with triplets decide? Did they always pick up a different baby first to make it fair? Ayden began to cry, so Johnathan picked him up first. Ellen handed Johnathan a bottle, and he settled onto a lawn chair to feed Ayden.

"They're beautiful babies. They look more like their mama than you, though," commented Ellen as she sat down next to Johnathan. "Unlike Leo. Leo looks more like you every day."

"I missed this," Johnathan smiled. He bent down and kissed Ayden's forehead and breathed in his baby smell.

Johnathan didn't tell anyone about his time in New York. He wanted to forget, to flee from all of it. Johnathan wasn't ready to face what he'd been through and how close he'd been to landing in prison himself. As he held his son and stared into the campfire, he couldn't help wondering who had placed the millions into the bank account under his name in the Bahamas and why. One question set a dozen swirling back into his head. How had his brother kept all these wives and kids a secret? Could it even all be true? The illegal diamonds, the fraud, and the embezzling had all rolled together somehow, but how? How had it all started?

Another baby began to cry. Anna brought over Austin and a bottle, and Ellen took Ayden. Johnathan shook his head and let out a gush of air. At some point, he might find out the truth, but it wouldn't help agonizing over what had happened and why. Johnathan concentrated on the feel of his baby in his arms, the smell of the fresh cool seeping out of the woods into their clearing overlooking the ocean.

Johnathan savored the sound of Caroline's laughter as she ate tortilla chips and Ellen's famous homemade salsa with their friends. Johnathan resolved not to think about his brother, father, and mother's fate. It was too painful. He would just have to be patient and wait for the outcome of the trials. As Johnathan lifted his baby onto his shoulder to burp him, he wondered how long he would need to wait to find out the truth about the mess his family was caught up in and the trials.

Little did Johnathan know it would take years before the truth would be uncovered.

# CHAPTER 21

## FOUR YEARS LATER

Johnathan entered the room and sat down at the table. "Hello, Dad."

"Johnathan. You came." Allen jumped up and reached out a hand. Johnathan started to shake it, changed his mind, and wrapped his arms around his Dad. They both sat down on either side of a table.

Johnathan swallowed. "So, how are you?"

Allen leaned forward, placing his elbows on the table. "I've been worse." Allen smiled, but it didn't reach his eyes. "How are your, kids? Caroline?"

Johnathan cleared his throat. "Leo started first-grade last week. He's busy. Piano lessons, swimming lessons, soccer. The triplets started pre-school but refused to play with any other kids and just stick to themselves. Ayden's already started learning to read with Caroline. He sits there for hours looking through books. Austin flat out refuses to learn even the alphabet. All he wants to do is paint. Archer can't sit still long enough for me to tie his shoes, let alone focus on learning or painting. He's always outside in the garden, playing with sticks or building in the sandcastle. I guess I thought they would be more the same, being identical triplets."

"I've never heard of identical triplets."

Johnathan smiled and ran a hand through his hair, remembering when the triplets were born.

"It's rare for sure. We were calling them our miracle babies, but Leo got upset and wanted to know why he wasn't a miracle baby too. So we dropped it. Yeah, so things are great. It's what I always wanted."

"You always wanted triplets?"

Johnathan shook his head. "I always wanted a big family. Caroline would have liked a little girl. So who knows. Maybe we'll give it one more try. Caroline's worried we could end up with three more instead of one more, but the doctor told her that is highly unlikely to happen again."

"I never knew you wanted so many kids."

Johnathan paused, looked at his Dad, and smiled, shaking his head. He ran a hand through his hair, making it stand up straight. "I guess there's a lot we didn't know was going on with each other."

Allen nodded but didn't say anything.

"I still don't understand, Dad, even all these years later. What the hell happened? Why would you get involved in all this? I mean, I can't even figure out how it could all start."

Allen crossed his arms over his chest and leaned back in his chair. Johnathan just waited. He had waited a long time to hear the truth. Was this the visit when his Dad would give him the truth about what had happened at last?

Allen glanced at the guards and around at the other people in the visiting room. He leaned forward again, placing his forearms on the table. Johnathan bent forward over the table as his Dad began to talk in a low murmur.

"What a Dad won't do for his kid, am I right?"

"You did all this for Daniel?"

Allen nodded, looked up to the ceiling, lost in thought. Johnathan waited patiently.

"Daniel got himself into trouble. He had been taking some extra money from the company to enjoy himself. It got out of hand. I had no idea at the time about the wives and kids or any of that. He came to me desperate because he was worried

217

someone would uncover that he had been embezzling money. And well," Allen didn't continue for a moment. He rubbed his forehead with his fingertips.

"I thought I could invest in some promising start-ups and with a sure-deal in China via Mat's boyfriend and make a high enough return on the investment to give him the money he needed to make things right."

"And the diamonds?"

Allen let out a big rush of air and shook his head, looking down at the table. "Honestly, son, your guess on that one is as good as mine. I don't know how that happened. You'd have to ask your brother. All I know is he showed up at my office one day and told me I didn't need to worry about my investments tanking, he had made some good investments of his own, and he would wire me money. I didn't ask too many questions. I was too relieved that I didn't need to go home and tell your mother that I had lost the majority of everything we owned."

"So Daniel got himself into trouble, you tried to bail him out and got yourself into a mess, then he did even worse things to try to fix things for both of you?"

Allen nodded. "That's the simplified version."

"Oh man," answered Johnathan. "He always was an arrogant, greedy bastard."

"Johnathan. That's your brother you're talking about."

"Seriously? Are you going to defend him? When you're in here for the next fifteen years because of him?"

"He's still your brother."

Johnathan couldn't keep his head from continuing to shake in disbelief. He felt like a damn bobble head doll.

"Look, at least when you found out, you walked away. I raised one son with a good head on his shoulders."

"No, Dad. I had no idea about any of this. Daniel was an ass; it's like he wanted to drive me away. And then I also walked away because I didn't want the lifestyle, the drama, the twelve-hour days in the office. It was always more with Daniel. He wanted more growth, more projects, bigger projects, a bigger company. I was exhausted to the point of burnout. I just couldn't do it anymore. Then there was the way Daniel treated my wife in that speech at our rehearsal dinner. It was the last straw. I wanted to get as far away from that bastard as I could after that. I had no idea about any of the rest of it."

"He loves you—your brother. I'm not defending him," Allen held up his hands, "but he's experiencing intense shame at everything he did and how he hurt everyone. He wrote me that he's tried reaching out to you many times. He's written you countless letters."

"There's nothing he can write that I want to read."

"So you haven't read his letters?"

Johnathan shook his head. "I could have gone down with him, Dad. Don't you understand? Instead of raising my beautiful family, building sandcastles with my boys on the beach, having barbecues with friends, designing people their dream homes, snuggling with Caroline, and watching the sunset over the ocean on the porch, I would have been in jail. I would have been in jail for something I didn't know about or do."

Allen pressed his fingertips into his eyes as he hunched even more over the table.

"Dad. Listen, Dad, I didn't want to upset you," said Johnathan.

Allen nodded, took a deep breath, and sat back up in his chair. "I'm so happy for you that you have all that out in California. You don't know what those photos you send to me every month mean to me. And those pictures the kids color for me. I have them hanging up."

Johnathan closed his eyes, swallowed, took a deep breath himself. "Look, Dad, I love you. When you get out of here, you're coming to live with me. Okay? You'll be living in a house filled with teenage boys at that point, but there it is. The offer is on the table."

Allen tried to close his eyes, but it was too late. The tears dripped down his cheeks. He smiled and reached a hand out as the guard announced that the visiting hour was almost over.

Johnathan squeezed his Dad's hand.

"How's your mother?"

Johnathan smiled. "She opened an art gallery with Matilda. She lives in a little one-room studio with a balcony and a view of the ocean. It's all been a lot to process. The trial, the two years in jail, the transition to living out in the world again, only with no money. She's making her way."

Allen nodded. "Good. Yes. Well, if you can, give her my love."

Johnathan smiled. "She told me to tell you the same thing. And that she's not going anywhere. She just needs time."

Allen's shoulder slumped, and then he grinned. "I've always said she's my everything."

"Well, the good news is, when you get out of here and find her, you can start over."

"In another ten to fifteen years."

The guard announced the end of visiting hours. Johnathan hugged his Dad. "I love you, son. I'm sorry."

"I love you too," Johnathan replied. "Hang in there."

Johnathan waited a week after his trip to go to the box he'd stuffed into his desk drawer at work. He called Caroline, asked her if she could manage to put the kids to bed without him so he could work late. Johnathan could hear music playing in the background and his mother's voice singing along. Caroline told him there was no hurry. Alison was over making dinner, and Matilda was out in the garden playing with the kids.

Johnathan put down his phone and sat staring at the box for a few minutes. At last, he lifted the lid and pulled out one of the letters from the bottom of the pile.

*Dear Johnathan*

*Hey man, I just wanted to drop you a note to see how you are. What's been going on in that little town in Cali? So, I've started meditating. There's this chill old dude who comes to the prison on Thursday mornings and teaches meditation. You maybe remember my resistance to it, but what else do I have to do in this place? I figured it would be worth a try. I've been going all year.*

*I'm sorry. Sorry for everything. I hope you can forgive me.*

*Live it up for me out there.*
*Daniel*

Johnathan opened another letter and another. Soon his desk was littered with paper and torn open envelopes. Was he closer to knowing the whole truth of what had happened to land his brother in jail and why? No. Johnathan had learned more from his trip to visit his father than all of the letters Daniel had written to him combined. Johnathan stared out of the window at the trees blowing in the breeze and let his mind clear.

Johnathan didn't hear the knock at the door. Cindy peaked her head inside his office and took in Johnathan's hair sticking up in all different directions, his kicked-off shoes under the desk, and the pile of letters on his desk.

"You okay? I was working late myself and thought I would head downstairs for a beer. You want to come?"

"We don't drink during the week," Johnathan reflexively replied.

Cindy leaned against the door frame. "We don't, or you don't? Cause honey, you look like you sure as hell could use a drink to me. Forget the yogi stuff for a night. I won't tell Caroline if you don't tell Mark. God love them both, but sometimes you just need to kick back and drink a couple of beers to enjoy this life and think things over."

Johnathan wiped a hand over his forehead and then looked back up at Cindy. "A cold beer does sound pretty good about now."

Cindy motioned for Johnathan to follow her. They went to the bar beach side down the street. Cindy ordered two hefeweizen beers with fresh lemons. Cindy handed Johnathan a beer and told him to follow her. She kicked off her heels and walked out into the sand toward the waves. She stood sipping her beer, looking out at the sun setting over the ocean as the waves washed over her feet. Johnathan kicked off his leather loafers and wandered out to the water's edge.

"Come on in—nothing better than a cold beer and standing in the ocean to up-level your vibration. Oh shit, Johnathan, now Mark has me talking like him too. Slap me the next time I say something like that, yeah?"

"Here," Johnathan handed Cindy his beer to hold and bent down to roll his pantsuit legs up.

Johnathan laughed as he stepped into the cold water. He took a sip of his beer and watched the setting sun turning the ocean a soft shade of peach, pink, and blue.

"You want to talk about it?" asked Cindy, still looking out at the sunset and ocean.

Johnathan continued to look ahead as well. "You go first."

"Mark asked me to marry him," Cindy said so softly that Johnathan almost didn't hear him. "I told him no."

"Wait, what?" Johnathan turned to look at Cindy. "I thought you were crazy in love with him."

Cindy's head fell back, and she let out a moan. "I know. I am. I don't know why I said no."

"You're an idiot."

Johnathan didn't say anything more; he took a sip of beer and waited. Johnathan had always been comfortable with silence. He had no problem withstanding next to Cindy, drinking beers together, taking in the sunset together in the quiet. The strange thing was that if you didn't ask any questions, people tended to tell you all sorts of things.

"I've been on my own since sixteen. Did you know that? My parents are good people, but honestly, can you see me fitting into an Amish community?"

"Whoa, what? You've never mentioned you're Amish."
Johnathan looked at Cindy's designer sleeveless red suit dress, her long blonde hair, manicured nails, and the luxury handbag on her arm. He grinned at the thought of Cindy sashaying into an Amish community. No, having a yogi as a boyfriend was a big enough stretch. Cindy was unabashedly materialistic and felt no shame discussing with Johnathan her ambitions for more abundance, luxury holidays in five-star resorts, and living one day in a multi-million dollar home.

Cindy splashed her feet in the water and took another big drink of her beer. "I'm not. That's the point. At sixteen, they give you the chance to have a try at living in the 'outside' world, and most go back after a few years to get baptized and stay living in the community for the rest of their life. I didn't."

"So you were shunned by your parents?"

Cindy shook her head. "No, that's if you choose to be baptized, and I didn't. My parents treat me as the one that got away. They tell me they're still praying I will see the light and run back into the open arms of the church, where I belong."

Cindy walked back across the beach and settled into a lounge chair with her feet in the sand. She looked up at the stars beginning to appear above them.

"Look, Johnathan, I love beautiful things, getting into high thread count sheets at night, putting on expensive makeup and shoes. Sure, it's been hard. I spent more years than I care to count surviving on noodles and hunting through second-hand stores for clothes. I got sick once, and I thought about going home. I couldn't. It didn't matter how lonely I got, or how desperate; I couldn't go back to a place that saw personal growth, individual accomplishment, and my Dolce & Gabbana heels as wrong."

"You do love your shoes."

Johnathan finished his beer, and Cindy told him to wait for her. She sprang to her feet and slipped back into her heels. Five minutes later, she came back with two more beers, and a waiter followed her with a plate of nachos.

"I'm not going to be submissive to my husband," Cindy said as she crunched on a big bite of nachos. "I refuse."

Johnathan ate a couple of bites of nachos before answering. "I can't remember the last time I ate nachos. These are so good; with Caroline, it's always healthy food. Which don't get me wrong, I love it, and I'll cook it, but man did I miss this. So," Mark took a sip of his beer. "Do you think Mark is expecting you, of all people, to play the role of a submissive wife?"

Cindy shook her head. "It would be so easy to fall into that role. I watched my Mom be that way my whole life; I love my mama, and she's the most loving person I know. It would be hard not to unconsciously model her if I had kids."

"Well, that's a deal-breaker there. If you don't want kids, then you can't marry Mark. He wants a houseful, just like me."

Cindy smoothed out her dress. "I know. And I don't want to stay home and raise a house full of kids. That's why I told him no."

Johnathan laughed. "I think you would have a hard time fighting Mark out of being the one to stay home with the kids when they're little. He's pretty set on being a full-time Dad and teaching a few yoga classes in the early morning on the side."

Cindy rolled her eyes. "Sure, he says that, but he doesn't mean it."

Mark shook his head and leaned forward, stealing the plate away from Cindy and placing it in his lap. "That, my dear, is where you are wrong. I lived with the man in a small space for months. He didn't want to talk about his past. He did, however, spend plenty of time bemoaning the fact that there was no chance he would find a woman who would be happy with him not being the primary breadwinner. That man wants kids and to be home with them; that's what he wants. The dude loves homemaking more than anyone I know. What other bachelor's studio looks like his? What other guy do you know loves cooking and baking like Mark does?"

"Enough about me. What were all those letters on your desk?" asked Cindy.

Johnathan's smile disappeared from his face. He set his beer down on the table, interlaced his hands behind his head, and leaned back in his beach lounge chair, stretching his legs out farther in front of him. "Letters from my brother?"

"They guy in prison? You write him letters?"

Johnathan shook his head. "I've never written back."

"And he just keeps writing you letters anyway?"

Johnathan nodded. "For years now. I've never read any of them until tonight."

Cindy whistled and settled back in her lounge chair deeper too. She dug her perfectly French manicured toes into the sand. "Are you going to do it? Write him back, I mean."

"Yeah. I think I will." Johnathan was startled at the words coming out of his mouth. He wasn't furious anymore. He was thinking about his family, the trial, and the near-miss he'd had with landing in prison with them. And there it was, after years of inner turmoil, sudden attacks of anxiety, and hostility toward his brother and father. He was at peace.

"What was that?" Johnathan blinked over at Cindy.

"I asked what your brother wrote in all those letters."

"Random stuff. Over and over again for forgiveness," said Johnathan.

Caroline stood over Cindy and Johnathan, her hand on her hips, her eyes flashing. "Johnathan! What are you doing? Why weren't you answering your phone?"

"I forgot it up in the office. I just came down for a quick after-dinner drink with Cindy to celebrate. Mark proposed."

Cindy reached over and punched Johnathan hard on the arm. "Hey idiot, I wanted to tell her."

Johnathan picked up his full beer glass and smiled up at his wife.

"You two make such a gorgeous couple. I'm so thrilled for you Cindy," Caroline bent over and hugged Cindy and kissed her multiple times on the cheek. When she stood up again, she pulled over a chair, kicked off her shoes, grabbed the full beer glass out of Johnathan's hands, and took a big drink.

"Caroline. You don't drink during the week, or like, ever."

"Don't you go telling me what I do and don't do too, or I'll lose it," snapped Caroline.

Cindy raised her eyebrows, and Johnathan, whose eyes had widened at watching his Buddha-bowl-eating, mantra-chanting, matcha-tea-drinking, wellness-fanatic, yogi wife, chug down half of the beer in one go.

Caroline wiped her mouth with the back of her hand. "Johnathan, I swear to you, I am thrilled you have had this amazing reunion with your sister and your Mom, but you have to talk to them. We need some more private family time, just you, me, and the kids. They can't just drop in whenever the hell they feel like it and start bossing me around in my own home. I'm going to lose it."

"You should meditate more," answered Cindy with a straight face. "To release your stress and raise your vibration. Isn't that what you've told me every time I'm hyperventilating overwork? Rise sister, rise? When a house has been on the mark too long, or a client has viewed a house more than twenty times and still can't commit? Aren't you supposed to be a chill yoga teacher? But you can't even handle your mother-in-law without resorting to chugging alcohol?"

Caroline set down the beer with a thud on the table and snatched up one of Cindy's heels. "For that, this is going in the ocean." Caroline stood up and started running toward the ocean.

"No," yelled Cindy. "Not my shoes! Anything but my shoes! They're brand new." Cindy jumped to her feet and flew after Caroline kicking up sand as she went. Johnathan watched as Cindy tackled Caroline around the waist, and they fell into the sand laughing.

"New idea. I'm confiscating these heels. They're gorgeous,"

giggled Caroline as Johnathan wandered over to stand above the two women struggling in the sand.

"You're a yoga teacher. You're not supposed to be materialistic. And you don't wear heels, remember? They're bad for your body alignment?"

"To hell with that. I'll be a yoga teacher in great sling back designer shoes," answered Caroline, pinning Cindy to the floor. "Release ownership of the shoes, and I will let you up."

"Don't yogis commit to nonviolence? You're hurting me, Caroline."

Caroline's eyes widened. "Oh no, I'm so sorry, Cindy," began Caroline.

Cindy pushed Caroline off balance and onto her back and sat on her. "Take that, you crazy yogi. Now give me back my shoe," laughed Cindy.

Caroline held out the shoe, and both women started to struggle to their feet. Johnathan was nearly bent double laughing, but he held out his hands to help pull the ladies to their feet. He pointed to the bar behind them, where all the people were watching.

"What the hell is going on with you two today?" asked Johnathan.

He laughed so hard his stomach began to hurt. Cindy and Caroline smoothed their clothes and their hair.

"Come on, babe. I'll buy another round of beers," said Cindy

"I told your Mom and sister I would be right back," protested Caroline.

"Give me your phone, love," said Johnathan.

Johnathan called his Mom and told her he would have a drink with Caroline before they came home. Alison declared it a fantastic idea and told them not to hurry home.

"I don't want a beer. I want a pink martini," declared Caroline as Johnathan handed back her phone.

"That goes for me too," declared Cindy.

"Hell, I can go for a pink martini myself," came a voice behind them.

"Mark," Cindy turned with big eyes.

Johnathan gave Mark a quick bear hug and headed inside to the bar. "Five pink martinis, please." "What the hell is a pink martini?" asked the man behind the bar.

"I don't know. She just wants it to be strong and pink," shrugged Johnathan.

When he came back out, followed by the bartender balancing a tray with five pink martinis, Mark was just pulling Cindy into his arms. Johnathan watched him lean Cindy backward and kiss her.

"I knew you would come to your senses and say yes," said Mark.

When Johnathan walked back to join the group, Caroline had just burst into laughter, throwing her head back, and Johnathan admired how beautiful she looked in the moonlight. The bartender set the drinks down on the table as Mark pulled Cindy back to her feet.

"Johnathan, I want you to be my best man," declared Mark. "We're getting married."

Johnathan passed out the drinks, and they toasted the engagement.

As he sat back down next to his wife, she took his hand. He noticed a flash on her finger.

"You're wearing your wedding rings," he murmured as Cindy pulled Mark in for yet another kiss.

Caroline nodded and leaned her head on his shoulder. "I have been wearing them for weeks. You just noticed?"

"Yeah."

Johnathan hated every day that Caroline was no longer his wife. He knew he wouldn't ever speak up about it, though. Caroline had been adamant that he should never bring the subject of their divorce up again. It would feel good to talk about Caroline as 'his wife,' to people, to know that they were committed for life. Sometimes a little voice would terrorize him that Caroline was only with him for the kids. When they grew up and left, then so would she.

"Hey," Caroline reached up with her fingertips and brought Johnathan's eyes to look into hers. "I'm yours forever, love. Just because we don't have the paper doesn't mean I'm not fully in this. I'm not going anywhere. I fall in love with you a little bit more every day. Okay, not when you disappear and leave me with your Mom for hours alone," she laughed.

"Sometimes," Johnathan took a deep breath and looked over at Mark and Cindy, who were whispering together. "I worry you are just sticking around for the kids."

Caroline grabbed Johnathan by the shirt collar and pulled him in for a kiss. "No possible way," she answered when she pulled away. "We'll be drinking pink martinis on the beach when we're ninety."

"Not matcha green tea?"

Caroline shrugged. "I found out it can contain a lot of lead."

Johnathan grinned and pulled Caroline to her feet. "Let's go home, love."

They hugged Cindy and Mark and set off up the boardwalk toward home.

"Do you ever miss it? All the money and power and whatnot that you had before?"

Johnathan nodded his head as their cottage came into view. "I'd be lying if I didn't say sometimes. It's fun being able to order anything you want for dinner at a restaurant, to fly on a private jet to enjoy your private beach, to slide behind the wheel of a car that is beauty on wheels."

"If you could get it all back again, and I mean this time have us in your life too, would you?" asked Caroline.

Johnathan considered the question. "I love our life and the rhythm and pace of our days. There's more time now, more space, to sit out on the beach and just breathe, to sit on the floor and play with the kids and savor the smells coming from my cooking in the kitchen. I love to leave the office at five-thirty most nights and have time to stroll to pick up the kids."

Caroline smiled and took his hand in his own. They walked in silence the rest of the way home. When they arrived on the front doorstep, Johnathan pulled Caroline into his arms and held her close. The smell of the roses climbing up the porch railing mixed with the salty smell of the ocean. Johnathan soaked in the warmth of Caroline's body pulled close to his. He considered telling her that he had read Daniel's letters, that he had sent him one back, and that he had forgiven his brother.

Before Johnathan could decide, Caroline gave him a quick kiss and pulled away, yawning. She opened the front door, and Johnathan could hear laughter filtering out of the living room down the hall.

Johnathan followed Caroline down the hall. Matilda was getting to her feet as he entered the room. Johnathan insisted on walking his Mom home to her studio a few blocks away.

Matilda hugged them quickly on the sidewalk, wished her Mom good luck for the next day, and headed in the opposite direction to her cottage a few steps down the street.

"What do you need good luck for?" asked Johnathan.

"I'm starting a new job tomorrow at the downtown hotel."

"What? Why? I thought you were working in the gallery with Mat?"

"Oh, I'll still help out there too. I was lamenting the fact that I have no cleaning lady and no money for designer handbags anymore. You do know how much I loved my handbags and champagne, for that matter. Anyway, she suggested I apply at the hotel where her Gram used to work. You'll find me at the front desk tomorrow from six in the morning until two."

"I can give you money, Mom."

Alison shook her head, "No, don't be silly. Caroline offered the same thing. The point I was making to her is I want some money of my own that I earn myself for a change. I'm nervous but in a good way. It feels like taking charge of myself, of my life, for the first time in, well, I don't know."

Johnathan nodded. "I understand. Good for you, Mom. I'm proud of you."

They walked a few steps in silence, and the ocean waves sound was the only sound save their footsteps.

"Okay, what is it?" Alison asked. "There's no need to be walking me home; it's right down the street."

"I know what you did, Mom."

Alison pulled her sweater tighter around her against the evening chill. The breeze blew her white hair in wisps around her face. Had her hair gone white in prison, or had she stopped dying her hair without access to her stylist? In either case, she hadn't started up coloring her hair again. Johnathan liked how his Mom looked with white hair; he decided it softened her features and made her blue eyes look even bluer.

"Okay, okay. It was just a little ice cream in a waffle cone. Honestly, Johnathan, sugar is not evil. I don't care what your lovely wife and health nuts think. We need to enjoy life. And yes, I put on sprinkles too."

Johnathan took his Mom's arm and threaded it around his. They walked arm and arm down the street a few paces in silence. Johnathan kept looking straight ahead as he said, "I know you didn't wire that money into the account under my name in the Bahamas to hide away money."

Alison stopped in mid-step.

"How do you know? Did you wire that money? Wait, don't answer that. It doesn't matter."

"No, of course not. Where would I have gotten over seven million dollars?"

"I knew you didn't. Call it a mother's intuition that you were innocent. Sorry I doubted you, John." Alison patted Johnathan's arm with her free hand. "You see the trouble your brother managed to get himself into, right? He managed to come up with millions from various sources. I could hardly believe my ears when I found out."

"So wait, it was Daniel who opened the account under my

name in the Bahamas?"

Alison started walking again, tugging Johnathan forward. "No. No, I have no proof, of course, but I'm certain it was Brad."

"Brad? How would he be able to open an account?"

"You know we treated him like one of the family. He had access to all our files; he could have stepped into the office when we weren't around. We've always had some files with social security numbers, copies of identification, tax records. They weren't out in the open, mind you; they were hidden away. We should have had them in a safe. I'm sure he found them."

"Why did you admit to doing it then, Mom? I can't understand. A little over two years in prison for something you didn't do? Why?"

Alison stopped and looped her arm through Johnathan's.

It's easy. The investigators told me you were going to go away to prison for a long time. I couldn't have that. You have four little boys who need you at home. So I confessed it was me."

"I don't know how to thank you," Johnathan said as he wrapped his arms around his Mom; Alison gave a chuckle of surprise at the hug. After a moment, she lay her arms gently around Johnathan and patted his back in return.

His mother had always been loving but never physically affectionate. She'd always given them quick kisses on the cheek. Had she ever hugged him as a kid? Johnathan couldn't remember a time. He remembered her soft, cool hand smoothing over his hair as he fell asleep and when he was ill. Every night she tucked the blankets in tight around him before saying good night and gave him a quick air kiss.

Johnathan pulled slowly away and started to speak, but Alison shook her head and gave him a gentle shove in the direction of home. She plastered on a bright smile.

"Off you go then. I need to get to bed. It's my first day tomorrow."

Johnathan didn't walk straight home. Instead, he made his way down to the beach and looked out at the dark black of the ocean under the star-studded sky. How swift an illusion can swirl and dissolve, he thought. There are so many facets to a person, their story, each intention, and action they take. For years he had been carrying the heavy burden like two buckets of granite hung around his neck, of feeling the victim, the least favorite child, the luckless idiot prey to the whims of fate and failure.

Johnathan had misinterpreted his mother's coolness and lack of physical affection as a lack of interest or love in her children, in him.

Johnathan could now see with clarity.

He needed a fresh start. It was time to let the past and all the anger squeezing his heart in a vise, constricting his lungs, pummeling his stomach, weighing his body down, go.

It was time to let it all go.

Something opened in Johnathan at that moment. A surge of creativity and fearlessness he had never known before. It was time to reprint his desperate swim in the ocean when he'd almost gave up this life.

Johnathan tore his shirt off, his pants landing in the sand next to his phone and watch. He ran into the cold of the ocean and dove into the dark waves. Johnathan swam with great strokes out into the waves. He paused, treading water to look up at the moon. Joy coursing through his veins like adrenaline, he glided back, stroke after smooth stroke, back to shore. Alone and naked on the beach, he lifted his arms up into the air in exhilaration.

Johnathan grabbed his clothes and walked back up to the cottage, and slipped through the door. With bare feet, he climbed the stairs and slipped into a hot shower, the warmth relaxing every muscle. Wrapped in a towel, he padded to the cracked door of Leo's room. He looked inside and paused, watching Leo sleeping. Next, he peeked into the triplets' room. All three were curled up in one of the three beds together. Johnathan smiled. Every night they started out in their own beds. Every morning Johnathan found them cuddled together in one.

He tiptoed down the stairs and opened his computer, and stared at his tiny home designs.

Caroline opened the door and blinked at him sleepily. "Everything okay, honey? Why haven't you come to bed yet?"

"I was thinking about doing it?"

"It?"

"Building the tiny luxury homes to create smaller footprints, tighter-knit communities, less urban sprawl, and more green space for children, and all of us, to feel the vibration and seasonal rhythms of the earth."

"Maybe you've spent too much time with Mark."

Johnathan nodded. "You're right. It's too risky."

"That's not what I said." Caroline wrapped her silk robe tighter around her and came to sit on Johnathan's lap. "What does your higher-self, your intuition tell you?"

Johnathan rolled his eyes.

Caroline laughed and said, "here, place a hand on your heart. Close your eyes. Ask, is this new business the right choice for me?"

Johnathan peeked an eye open. "And then?"

Caroline whispered. "Listen for a yes. Do you hear a yes?"

"Yes, but I feel mega anxious," said Johnathan, snapping his eyes open.

"Courage Johnathan," smiled Caroline.

Johnathan clicked through and submitted his LLC documents, then went to push the publish button. His website was live. He opened the email draft with the sales pitch he had worked on for weeks and didn't hesitate. He pressed send.

"Hell yes. Here we go. Heaven knows you deserve a change in fortune," said Caroline.

"From where I'm sitting, I'm feeling pretty damn lucky."

# CHAPTER 22

Johnathan settled into his chair and looked at the heap of letters on his desk. Absentmindedly he picked the first letter Daniel had ever sent him up from the desk. Every note had such a weird PS at the end of it.

The first letter Daniel had sent said, "PS. Ever notice that the last sentence is always most important? I couldn't bear you not knowing how much I love you, so I'm writing you these letters so you can understand everything."

Johnathan picked up another letter and read, "PS. Remember when we landed the biggest project we had ever won in China? They were slimy, those guys. You did good work, but I wish we had never gotten involved with that project." Another read, "PS. You always had this crazy idea I was the favorite, but it was always you. It wasn't just the parents; you are all our favorite."

Johnathan let the letters fall out of his hands and stared down at the letters. All of a sudden, a flash of insight hit him. He began arranging the letters in chronological order. He read the postscript statements in order and out loud into his voice note app on his phone. When he was done, he played the voice memo of all the post scripts combined.

Ever notice that the last sentence is always most important? I couldn't bear you not knowing how much I love you so I'm writing you these letters so you can understand everything.

You've always been the most important person in my life.

Remember when we landed the biggest project we had ever won in China? They were slimy, those guys. You did good work, but I wish we had never gotten involved with that project.

You never knew that the China project fell through, and they never paid us. I just thought you should understand the complete picture of that project.

I loved that trip we had in Bali and the day we spent trekking to the different waterfalls. I can still close my eyes and hear the water and the family's laughter. For one day, we were a perfectly normal, happy family. Wasn't that beautiful?

You worked so hard as an architect and all those twelve to fourteen-hour days you put in. Imagine, you could have lost everything because of me.

You always had this crazy idea I was the favorite, but it was always you. It wasn't just the parents; you were – you are all our favorite.

We worked so hard building up our business. I couldn't stand the thought of us failing yet again. Isn't it ironic that you ended up going bankrupt anyway?

Sometimes you can have the best of intentions but just

dig yourself into a bigger mess.

I see now that I should have been honest with you from the beginning.

Remember how it was when I was a kid? Whenever I messed up big time, I tried my best to hide it from everyone, especially you.

You deserve a beautiful life with your lovely family. I always liked Caroline.

I was a jerk at your wedding because I wanted to drive you away.
Scrambling to get out of a CHINA-sized mess is how you can get yourself into an even worse one. You know how when you step on a slide, there's no way to stop? That's what happened.

Poor Mat. She was bamboozled by a real con man. I didn't see that one coming, did you?

I do not miss all those business trips I did; not even being in here makes me miss those stomach-acid-churning, panic-attack-inducing, cold-sweat-trips I did for Dad.

I'm sure you never noticed that, unlike you, I always did everything, everything that Dad has asked me to do. Always.

Every time I came home from a trip, I counted the days down until the next one with raw, cold fear. It was awful. I'm glad you never saw the Dad beneath the mask.

You know I would never keep a secret like having kids

away from you. Wives, sure. But kids? Never. You can choose to believe me or not; it doesn't matter. Just know I love you.

Mom brought me a photo of your new babies. Triplets! Wow, man, that's amazing. I don't think you will be sleeping much for a while. Speaking of which, I don't know how Dad sleeps at night.

It just takes making one wrong choice, becoming beholden to one gangster, for everything to spiral out of control to the point of no return.

Haven't you ever noticed how I have ALWAYS been able to push your buttons and manipulate you to get you to do what I want? That was a beautiful wedding in Bali, wasn't it? I don't regret the rehearsal speech. It served its purpose, (well almost). Though I didn't know she was pregnant. So happy the baby was okay.

Dad would have taken you down if I'd let him.

Man, you can be too forgiving and Zen for your good, brother. I thought the rehearsal speech would cause you to cut ties with the company, and I was correct.

Interesting that there is nothing Mom hates more than a scene, but she let me shout around in front of all the guests at your wedding before the ceremony started. Why did she do that?

You know Mom is super clever but can't see Dad for who he really is.

Do you feel free, John? Are you happy?

Don't visit Dad anymore.

Sorry, not sorry. I did what I did. You get what you get. You deserve all you have, but Dad. Stay away from him, Johnathan.

I love you. That's what it all comes down to; I'm your big brother, I've always felt the need to protect you, and I love you. It was stupid, the choice I made. But they were done for better reasons than you thought. Better me than you. Stay away from Dad.

Johnathan picked up the last letter from Daniel and read it through one more time.

We lived in his house of lies
all our young lives
you didn't know
at least you got away
Be free now
Go and fly away
Live it up, my friend,
laugh and play
I'll be locked away
But we'll reunite someday
If you forgive me
For the lies I told
For the hurt I sowed
It's not too late
For me to say
I love you, little bro.

Stay away from Dad. I beg you. And please forgive me.
Daniel

Johnathan sat back in his chair and let out a sigh. It didn't make much sense to him. Why was Daniel telling him to stay away from their father when Daniel was the cause of the mess? Was his brother trying to blame the mess he'd created on their Dad now? Johnathan decided Daniel must not know that Allen had, at last, admitted the entire story to him about what had happened.

Johnathan realized it didn't matter. All the unanswered questions, who he could trust, and not trust, who was lying or telling the truth, it didn't matter to him anymore. He didn't need to know more to let go.

Regardless of who had led whom into the illegal activity, Johnathan's heart had shifted into a new place.

Johnathan tapped the pen against his mouth. He pulled out a card with a photo of himself, Caroline, and the kids on the front and picked up a pen.

**Dear Daniel, you arrogant, stupid bastard, I forgive you. Yes, I mean it. I forgive you. Be at peace. You have my love. Yes, we'll reunite someday.**

**Yours, Johnathan**

Johnathan slid the card into its envelope, addressed it, added some stamps, and left the office. He wandered down the street, hesitated a fraction of a second, grasping the envelope, part of him still reluctant to let go. Courage Johnathan, he told himself.

Taking a deep breath, Johnathan let it out and whispered, "I forgive you."
He let the letter fall from his fingers into the post box.

"Johnathan?"
Johnathan looked up and saw Caroline down on the beach

with the triplets and Leo building a massive sandcastle.

"Daddy," yelled out Leo. "Come help us build."

Johnathan slipped out of his leather shoes and pulled off his socks. He loosened his tie as he walked through the sand toward his family. All at once, a lump formed in his throat, and his eyes blurred.

All of the bends, shifts, and almost could-have-happened, and he was here, a free man, looking down on his kids happily digging, at his beautiful wife in her favorite red swimsuit, her legs and arms covered in sand, her hair wind tasseled, and her teeth flashing white as she smiled up at him from ear to ear.

Jonathan reached down, pulled Caroline to her feet, smoothed the hair out of her face, and kissed her.

"Wow. What's gotten into you? What are you doing here? You told me you had a pile of paperwork and a late afternoon house showing."

"I read through all Daniel's letters. I just came down to post the letter I wrote to Daniel. I told him I forgive him."

Caroline looked taken aback. "Wow. Why now?"

Johnathan shook his head and kissed Caroline again.

"I wouldn't trade you for a billion dollars. You know that?"

"What about a trillion dollars Daddy?" asked Archer.

"A gazillion dollars," shouted out Austin.

"Not for a gazillion dollars," answered Johnathan with a grin. "You can't put a price on soul mate."

"You say that all the time," said Leo.

"Doesn't he?" asked Caroline. "But he never asks me if I'd trade him for a billion dollars."

"Would you, Mom?" asked Leo.

"Well," said Caroline while tilting her head in thought. "Let me think. A billion dollars sure is a lot of money."

"Is that so?" Johnathan scooped Caroline up in his arms and carried her to the ocean.

"You don't scare me," said Caroline. "You wouldn't dare go in the ocean with your fancy suit on."

"Well, the joke is on you, love, because this isn't one of those designer suits. It is an off-the-rack, cheap as hell suit."

Caroline's eyes widened as Johnathan waded into the ocean.

"Don't drop me, Johnathan. It's cold today."

"Do it, Dad," yelled Leo, jumping up and down on the beach, and the triplets joined in the shouting.

Johnathan dropped Caroline into the water, and she came up, spluttering and pushing her wet hair out of her face. Johnathan took a step backward as Caroline's eyes flashed.

"That's it."

Johnathan ran backward as Caroline hurtled toward him, almost catching his arm before he exited the water. Once on dry land, Caroline continued to chase Johnathan with a surprising speed. Johnathan looked back over his shoulder, tripped on a sand bucket, and fell hard onto the sand. He rolled over, and Caroline lay down on top of him, her cold swimsuit drenching his suit and her wet hair dripping down his face and along the back of his neck.

Caroline gave Johnathan a quick kiss and jumped to her feet, her hair dripping down her back. Johnathan stood up and looked down at his soaked shirt and the water all down his suit trousers.

The boys began to laugh. "You look like you peed yourself, Dad," laughed Leo.

"I have an appointment in half an hour," exclaimed Johnathan. I don't have time to go home and change. "

"Maybe you'll air dry by then?" asked Caroline. "Next time, you should think of that before you go throwing people into the ocean."

"But you wouldn't take the bazillion dollars, right mom? Right?" asked Archer while jumping around them. "You'd choose Daddy."

"Yes, sweetheart, because of the type of man he is, and choses to be, no matter what happens."

Johnathan's focus rushed like a wave into his body. Yes, that was what it was, that was what he'd been struggling against, the never enough, never enough, never enough. Whenever he framed his reference back into who he wanted to be, the man he wanted to be, for Caroline, for his children, for himself, despite being a billionaire, bankrupt, broke, defamed, respectable, loved, despised, lied to, hurt, maligned, praised, criticized, celebrated, ignored, cherished, adored, challenged, tempted, forgotten, loved.

Courage in being the man he wanted to be, despite where he may be, the highs and lows, the money or lack of, the job or lack of, the support or the lies. Courage to be a man of integrity, loyalty, resilience, grit, creativity, adventure, playfulness, kindness, forgiveness, strength, love. Courage in being the man Caroline and his kids deserved.

Courage in being.

COMING SOON.....

# COURAGE

## HEATHER NADINE LENZ

# MATILDA

# More Books by Heather Nadine Lenz

# GIFTS FOR YOU

Get Your Free Meditation, Moon Manifestation Journal, Free 10 Minutes a day 30-Day Yoga Challenge and more at:

https://www.ignitewellnessopentojoy.com/energize-elevate

## ABOUT THE AUTHOR

I'm passionate about yoga, wellness, and finding joy in daily life. I love the smell of rain and my first sip of espresso in the morning.

I love that feeling after yoga asana and meditation when I fall into bliss and feel grounded to the earth, so good in my body, and elevated into lovefulness all at the same time.

Joy for me is the rush of jumping into an alpine lake on a hot summer day with my three kids, the taste of champagne bubbles on my tongue, seeing dew sparkling on flowers in the morning, and scooping the ones I love in for a bear hug.

What brings you joy?

My work as a wellness coach, author, and yoga instructor all aim to increase your well-being so you can thrive and open up to more moments of joy, grace, and profound peace in your daily life. You may be shocked at how tiny incremental changes to your daily habits can result in dramatic changes in how well you feel. If you're ready to transform your health and wellness reach out to me at:

https://www.ignitewellnessopentojoy.com/energize-elevate

heather.n.lenz@gmail.com    or on Instagram: https://www. instagram.com/yogawithheathernadine/

Wishing you radiant health, happiness & serenity – Heather